I'm Just a Teenage Punchbag

JACKIE CLUNE

CORONET

First published in Great Britain in 2020 by Coronet
An Imprint of Hodder & Stoughton
An Hachette UK company

This paperback edition published in 2021

1

A CIP catalogue record for this title is available from the British Library

Paperback ISBN 9781529382457
eBook ISBN 9781529382433

Typeset in Celeste by Hewer Text UK Ltd, Edinburgh
Printed and bound in Great Britain by Clays Ltd, Elocraf S.p.A.

Hodder & Stoughton policy is to use papers that are natural, renewable
and recyclable products and made from wood grown in sustainable
forests. The logging and manufacturing processes are expected to
conform to the environmental regulations of the country of origin.

Hodder & Stoughton Ltd
Carmelite House
50 Victoria Embankment
London EC4Y 0DZ

www.hodder.co.uk

For my lovely teenagers Saoirse, Thady, Frank and Orla – for providing me with the laughs, the tears, the anecdotes which pop up in this book, and for the generous proof-reading.

For Richard who is more of a parent than me, allowing me to fanny about writing while he does pretty much everything else.

For Robert Caskie who has been so patient, kind and loving as I found what it was I wanted to say, and for pairing me with Hannah Black at Hodder, who has been such a fantastic editor and co-conspirator. Thank you.

For the Bunga Bunga women who have been there since the beginning of this parenting journey, and without whom I would be madder than I am now. Thanks especially to Caroline Dalyfor her help and support.

For my sister Maggie, and my brothers Ray and Adrian – we knew what it was to be loved by Dad and Mammy.

For my dad Don Clune.

For my mum Teresa Clune.

Jackie Clune, December 2019

Part One

Part One

Chapter One

'Mum – if you tell ANYONE that I like Kayle Harvey, I will stab you in the vagina.'

'That's OK – I'm not using it much these days anyway.'

I love our cosy mum-and-daughter chats. Amelie has confessed to a feeling that isn't boredom for the first time in eighteen months and is now regretting the power she feels it gives me. Who would I tell? Why would I care? Does she think I have nothing better to do than talk about her all day?

'Seriously, Mum. You always do that. You think my life is funny – it's not funny. You're embarrassing.'

'I'll add it to the list.'

'What do you mean? What "list"? Don't make this about you!'

'I wouldn't dare. Heaven forbid something is not about you for five minutes.'

'And you haven't got a list.'

'Yes, I have. I take all the helpful feedback you give me very seriously. There's a very long and arse-clenchingly awful list of my shortcomings that I've committed to memory in the hope that I'll avoid them in future: the way I laugh; the way I laugh twice sometimes at the same joke; the way I laugh when I say hello to people on the street – for no reason!; the way I talk, do my eyebrows, miss bits when I shave my legs, dance, sing out loud in Tesco, watch depressing TV, have no taste in clothes, repeat stories three times. The way I breathe.'

'You breathe SO LOUDLY!'

'I know. I'm a terrible person. It won't happen again.'

'Good.'

Without my actual consent, I have been sucked into the quick-sand of teen parenting. I thought the hard bit was over. They can wash themselves (and occasionally they do), they can feed themselves (Coco Pops) and they can be left alone without burning the house down (so far) – and that's the tricky bit, right? Getting them to sleep, eat, walk, talk? No. Turns out that wasn't the tricky bit. The tricky bit gets trickier every day as I attempt to get them to wake up, stop eating everything, sit down and shut the fuck up. I can't get anything done without someone needing me to do something for them.

Which is why I'm writing a blog this year. I'm going mad. I've stopped answering to 'Mum' now, because nothing good ever follows that word. They've taken to calling me by my first name in a bid to get my attention. 'Ciara!' they scream, upstairs, down-stairs, in public, in the car. 'Ciara! Have you topped up my lunch money? Ciara, where are my socks? Ciara, I TOLD you I had to hand that form in! Where is it? Ciara? Ciara!!!!'

I'm not well.

I wince at every slammed door, raised voice and sudden loud noise. I jump like a shell-shock victim from the trenches. I have Present Traumatic Stress Disorder. I need to get this all into some sort of perspective before they cart me off to the home for burnt-out carers. Or before they kill me.

Or I kill them.

So instead of murder, I'm going to write. I always planned to. My degree in English Literature is going to waste here, not to mention my ten years in a small publishing firm. It was going to be my day job – then Martin turned up, caught me off balance after one too many bastards and here I am holed up in suburbia, a married mum of three. I don't work. I don't have to because Martin earns good money and he hates housework. Useless at it. Strategically useless. Burns everything – food, ironing, children – but likes things just so. I did think about going back to work but childcare was so expensive and Martin wasn't keen – he thought I'd regret leaving the kids so young. Ha! Little did we know that that was my small window of opportunity to slip back into the work force. Blown it now. Obsolete and in charge of three teenagers who don't care if I'm here or not. Even Asda didn't want me. 'Too qualified' and I won't do weekends.

Life is a far cry from what my university-self thought it would be – marching, protesting, sit-ins about abortion rights, gay rights, civil rights. That was how I spent my free time back then. I thought I'd leave uni, live in a commune, write a novel about a feminist utopia and hang around festivals forever. I thought I'd have seen the world by now, not just endless damp campsites in Normandy. The last thing I wanted was a life that resembled my poor mum's – stuck at home with a twin tub and a head full of dreams. So I'm going to write this blog and if it's any good then maybe I'll even publish it. It's the modern mum's weapon of choice, isn't it? Blog the pain away. Laugh and the world laughs with you. Weep and you weep alone. I'll use my blog to paint a relatable but poignant modern portrait of a hardly functioning family that resonates with, empathises with, women like me. I'll spin it. I'll gag it up. Make it pithy, fun, life-enhancing. It will be called something like . . .

KILL ME NOW!!!

Or . . .

Slummy Mummies Rule!!!

Or maybe . . .

Yummy Mummy Scrummy Funny Honey!!!

And it's going to be great because it's going to help other women who, like me, sometimes think 'Is this it? Is this what I am now – a used dishcloth of a woman with grey roots, nasolabial folds and no appetite for life?'

So here it is. My first instalment. I've even bought the domain. Yes! I have my own domain, finally! Project Self-Esteem starts here.

BLOG 1 – This Is Pants

This morning's drama comes courtesy of the daughter – 15, tall, dark and gobby, steals all my things, occasionally vegan (only when it's inconvenient) and chronicler of my failures – who is whining at my door that she has been ill during the night.

'I even farted and a little bit of poo came out!' she whinges, somehow making it sound like my fault. 'I don't think I should go to school – can you get me some water?'

I stagger into the bathroom for a pee, where I'm confronted by a pair of my new posh knickers bearing the shadow of the poo fart now discarded in the bin. How's that for a metaphor for motherhood?

Who am I kidding?

I can't write about that. No one wants to hear about teenagers nearly pooing themselves, do they? About women sliding down the bathroom door and crying silently into an old Disney fleece? They want to read about cute toddlers and mummies in rivalry over bake sales/school sports day/the biggest part in the Nativity play. They want disingenuous faux desperation, not your actual stomach-churning existential crisis.

If I write a blog . . . then *no one but me will ever read it.*

It's just for me.

I'll write it for fun.

I'll write it to stave off dementia.

I'll write it so that I don't go batshit crazy.

If a woman blogs in the forest but no one gets to read it . . . can she have a KitKat and a massive lie-down?

I wouldn't write things like . . . I really hate my life sometimes. Most of the time. I'm fifty and fucked. My husband barely registers my existence. My kids find my breathing annoying and the last time a man looked at me with any kind of desire was 1989 and Madonna's 'Like a Prayer' was number one. Too fucking right, Madge, life really is a mystery.

So there's no way I can ever actually *publish* my blog. It'll be like therapy – but cheaper. I tried real therapy. I went to the lovely German doctor about two years ago and started crying. I said I thought I must be menopausal and she asked me why I thought that.

'Because I want to kill my family,' I sobbed.

'OK . . . *und* how do you stop yourself from doing zat?' she asked, tapping at her keyboard.

'Wine,' I said, not even ashamed that I sounded not only like a psycho but also an alcoholic.

'Have you tried yoga?' she asked, still tapping away.

Oh fuck off. I've never met a yoga teacher who isn't an absolute bastard. Flex Nazis in sports bras.

So I sat there crying and sweating while the doctor asked me about self-harm and suicidal thoughts and told me about deep breathing. So embarrassing. She wanted me to take antidepressants because she thought I might be in the perimenopause.

'Sounds like a lounge singer – Perry Menopause!' I quipped

between sobs. I refused the pills. She said they would even out my mood, numb the feelings a bit. I said I couldn't be much more numb.

So she suggested therapy.

I spent eight months paying someone called Angela £60 a week to tell me I had low self-esteem.

No shit.

I tried everything to get me out the other side of the menopause meltdown. I went to herbalists, acupuncturists, I even went to a bloody shaman because Jude, my only remaining friend from school, told me that despite my pathological mistrust of anything remotely hippy, it was worth a go to save on bedlinen, anger management courses and divorce lawyers. She said that, for her, a combination of howling at the moon in a Devon field and drinking tequila slammers made a massive difference to her menopause.

Jude said she is now so empowered by Red Clover, St John's Wort and Black Snakeroot – her gut must resemble a wild meadow – that she is even more productive than she was in her twenties when she left us all behind and moved to Singapore to virtually run a bank. She's back now, living in the arse-end of nowhere in a mill by a river and growing rare orchids in a greenhouse. She still likes her husband and they never had kids so she wins. I see her once or twice a year if I'm lucky.

The last time was Mum's funeral, where she cried almost as much as I did and we reminisced about Mum's late-night toasties after we'd been out on the piss underage. It was good to have her there. I haven't seen her since, of course, because I always have the ironing to do and the kids need me to butter their toast in the mornings. And Martin is useless. If I were to go away for one night he'd panic and make everyone use paper plates in case he blew up the dishwasher.

So now Jude and me mainly text each other. She tells me funny stories about the villagers where she lives, and how they post videos of local youths destroying flowerbeds, and I send her London knife-crime statistics and stories about how the German doctor can't pronounce 'v' so asks me if my 'wagina' is still dry.

I swear if men had the menopause like we do it would be all bells and whistles at the pharmacy – none of these 'one size fits all' cancer-inducing patches and sick-making pills. They wouldn't write irritating articles about living their best life because of fucking green tea and deep breathing. Why does it always feel like, whatever we go through – PMS, post-natal depression, menopause meltdown – someone is saying it's actually our own fault? That we are simply not trying hard enough to be well?

BLOG 1 DRAFT 2 – A Foggy Day

It's one of Mother Nature's cruellest jokes that our daughters become ripe, plump and luscious just as we turn into shrivelled, nasty husks. Every day she gets perkier, shinier and more desirable, and every day I get saggier, duller and more invisible. I'm a fog. A dense, grey foggy morning in February. She is dawn on a Spring bank holiday – primroses, larks, the smell of cut grass—

No. What am I saying – that I am sexually competing with my daughter? Creepy.

But I need to claim something back. For me. My space. My thoughts. Not her agenda, her needs, my things in her room. I will win. The pen is mightier than the open-pored.

I'll keep this blog as a diary. No one will ever know. It will be my private land, my personal province, my offline empire in the sad, lonely kingdom of self.

Yay.

I can hear the boys twatting each other and shouting 'PENIS' repeatedly. I should go.

BLOG 1 DRAFT 3 – How To Win Breakfast: The boys. Where to begin?

Perhaps this morning's conversation might best paint the picture. After the character-assassination attempt from the daughter, I find myself in need of some affirmation and turn instead to my thirteen-year-old identical twin boys. P – lanky, irritating, bumfluff moustache and virtually albino eyelashes, and L – almost the same but a bit chunkier and altogether nicer, but still a bit of an arse.

'What's the most important lesson I've ever taught you?' I enquire, coquettishly scraping dried cat food into the bin.

Both boys are sitting bleary-eyed at the counter eating what can only be described as a vat of Coco Pops. They consider my question gravely for a few beats, chewing like a pair of pensive calves. P eyeballs me, deadpan. 'Go to the toilet if you think you're going to shit yourself.'

What is it with my kids and shit?

L pipes up. 'Don't bite people if you're angry.'

'Well, they're both invaluable tips but I was hoping for something a bit more meaningful.'

The daughter – A – has entered the kitchen with moments to spare before she misses the bus, and is busy putting cherries into a tiny Tupperware box for her lunch ('No one eats actual lunch any more, Mum – BASIC!').

'You've taught me that no matter how hard things are I should just do my best because that's all we can do in life,' she says. She doesn't even do her sarcastic voice. I feel a surge of pride. At least one of my kids listens to me, takes in my wisdom and my belief in effort without undue pressure. She's a chip off the old block.

Then she asks me for twenty quid. It's someone else's birthday at school, which means she has to buy balloons, cards, gifts and ice creams. All paid for by me. She couldn't possibly use her own money – she needs that for expensive eyebrow make-up and ludicrously priced T-shirts and lacy 'bralets' from dark shops you have to queue to get in to. She knows she has to suck up to me because last night I confiscated her phone (apparently in direct contravention of her 'actual human rights') and she knows I won't give it up without a fight. It's the one thing I have that gives me any purchase in this house.

I've heard of households where all devices are placed on the kitchen table until homework is done/piano is practised/school uniform is hung up and chores are ticked off the efficient-yet-tasteful chalkboard. These families are sickening, so let's discount them straight away. I mean really – who has a family where that works?

Homework done? My boys will delight in spending three hours on a worksheet about pasta shapes – a pointless torture that a six-year-old could do in five minutes – just because they know it will wind me up if they are slow.

Piano practised? All children detest piano lessons and we only make them learn to assuage some mid-life sense of angst that we have not achieved all we should have achieved and time is running out. Piano practice in my family happens five minutes before the lesson, which helps no one. I might as well let them sleep in on a Saturday morning and burn twenty-pound notes over the hob while listening to Graham Norton on the radio.

School uniform hung up? Ha ha ha ha ha ha ha ha.

Wait.

Ha ha ha ha ha ha ha.

It gets washed, ironed and hung up – by me. Then it gets thrown in a pile (with the pants still inside the trousers) every night. I have asked, begged, pleaded and threatened but it makes no difference. I've resigned myself to five more years of pulling blazer sleeves back out the right way.

Chores? I can't stand the arguing. I'd rather empty the dishwasher myself than listen to the Treaty of Versailles being re-enacted in my own kitchen. They are superb at dodging the merest hint of a menial task.

'Can I have my phone, please, Mummy?' she smiles.

'Have you had breakfast?' I ask, mock-innocently. Ha. Another gauntlet thrown down.

Teenagers have two settings when it comes to food:

1. Eat everything in the fridge within minutes of it being restocked. Eat any combination of meals in any order, with random bowls of cereal as hourly punctuation.
2. Refuse all food with a sneer of disgust.

My kids used to eat pretty much everything, but now it's hard to keep track of who hates mayonnaise, who will not touch tomatoes, who despises chilli and who won't eat anything but white food. I make them a packed lunch every day (we tried school dinners but they just ate doughnuts) and it's become a half-hour I dread. From 7.15–7.45 you will find me slumped against the chopping board staring balefully at twenty different sandwich fillings that have all been spurned as 'disgusting'. The girl is the worst, having fallen prey to the Kardashian/Instagram obsession of 'clean eating' – which, in her teenage brain, means drinking green juice and only eating pizza three times a week. I don't handle it well, this food faddiness. I offer you three transcripts below: BAD MUM (what actually happens), GOOD MUM (how the daughter would like it to go) and BEST PRACTICE PARENTING (how it should go).

BAD MUM SCRIPT:

ME: (shouting up the stairs) Do you want a chicken sandwich for lunch?
GIRL: (deep into 45-minute eyebrow application session) What?
ME: Do you want roast chicken sandwich for lunch?
GIRL: No.
ME: Ham?
GIRL: No.
ME: Pasta pesto?
GIRL: What??
ME: PASTA PESTO?
GIRL: No.
ME: Well, what do you want?
GIRL: Nothing.
ME: You can't have nothing!
GIRL: I'll just have crisps.
ME: That's not healthy.
GIRL: I'm not hungry at lunch, Mum. I hate lunch.
(20 minutes later when she finally comes downstairs)
ME: What are you going to take? You shouldn't just eat junk!
GIRL: (putting crisps and chocolate back in the cupboard) OK. Bye.

ME: Wait – what are you going to eat? You haven't had breakfast either!

GIRL: MY BUS IS IN THREE MINUTES, MUM??!!

ME: THAT'S NOT MY FAULT, IS IT? YOU'VE BEEN UP THERE FOR 45 MINUTES DOING MAKE-UP!

GIRL: (rolling eyes) I'M INSECURE, OK?!!!

(Door slams. Soul sinks. Give up.)

GOOD MUM SCRIPT (TEEN VERSION):

ME: (going up to her room rather than shouting up the stairs) What would you like for lunch today?

GIRL: I don't really eat lunch.

ME: You don't really eat lunch? (letting her know I've heard her)

GIRL: No, I don't like it.

ME: OK . . . you don't like lunch . . . got it. Sorry. So can I get you a healthy and filling breakfast? A superfood smoothie like the Kardashians have?

GIRL: I haven't got time. I have to paint slugs on my eyebrows.

ME: OK, darling. You know best.

GIRL: Mum, can I have some money for McDonalds after school?

ME: Take whatever you want out of my purse, sweetheart.

GIRL: OK. Now leave.

BEST PRACTICE PARENTING SCRIPT:

ME: (waiting until she appears) I've packed you some fruit, a yogurt and there's some leftover pasta salad if you want it. Help yourself.

GIRL: (reluctantly grabbing lunch bag) Bye.

ME: You're welcome.

I know I shouldn't fret so much about it. Some would go so far as to say that providing her with fruit and yogurt was too interfering and mollycoddling. Some might say you should leave them to go hungry. But I was raised by an Irish mammy (aka The Feeder) so I don't feel comfortable providing nothing. I thought I had cracked this situation, but yesterday morning she came downstairs before anyone else and sat down on the floor in front of me with tears in her eyes.

'What's wrong?' I said.

'I don't know.'

'What's going on with you and food? Are you trying to lose weight or something? Because starving yourself is not the way to do it.'

'It's just that sometimes I eat so much junk then I feel really bad and the next day I try not to eat too much.'

Oh God. I thought she was more sorted than this. I thought we had done positive body image. But it looks like the years of my own negative body carping and yo-yo dieting has rubbed off on her. I thought I'd been careful not to do too much self-loathing in front of her, but little eyes and ears see everything.

'It's just every time I look in the mirror I think I'm really fat and ugly.'

'But you're not fat – you're slim and you're beautiful!'

'IT DOESN'T HELP ME WHEN YOU SAY THAT!'

It kills me to watch my own daughter, however annoying she might be, hating on herself so much. All I can do is try to counter the endless stream of social-media pressure to be a certain way, look a certain way, eat certain things, obsess about the size of your bum/nose/boobs, the colour of your pasty legs, the width between your thighs, the bumpiness of your complexion, the yellowness of your teeth. How come she takes all this in and is so hard on herself when the boys barely function and DON'T CARE about any of this stuff?!

Before I had kids I was a vehement opponent of the sexist trope that a child's biological sex accounts for a large degree of their psychology and behaviour – that clichéd gender behaviour (boys are aggressive, girls just want to please, etc.) is in some way innate and not learnt. Nature v Nurture. And to a large extent I still feel that gender behaviour is copied and intuited from our gender-prescriptive sexist culture.

Everyone says boys are no trouble, that it's teenage girls that are the nightmare. I disagree. I can cope with the eyebrow obsession, the eye-rolling and the door-slamming. I can cope with the sarcasm that drips from every pore. I can even cope with the mountain of wet towels, ridiculous friendship-group politics and sudden demands for vegan-only packed lunches. But boys . . . whilst I adore mine . . . are just . . . so much like badly house-trained puppies that I have to resist the urge to put collars on them and make them beg for food.

They smell. They are almost phobic about showers. They can't see the point in doing anything apart from gaming and/or watch-ing other boys gaming online. Left to their own devices they would stay in their bedrooms all day (apart from short, irritating-but-necessary breaks for Coco Pops), fighting in virtual wars with other boys they've never met, shouting obscenities into their headsets.

They can't follow simple instructions. For example, the other day I had to leave them to get ready for football themselves. I packed their stuff, left it out for them, gave them £10 for food after, told them to make sure to take a key because I wouldn't be home until after them.

When I arrived back later the front window was wide open

and the house was dark. As I opened the door the dog was
whimpering from somewhere but I couldn't find her in the house.
I ran outside and found her cowering on the window ledge,
trapped behind the bins after the exciting adventure afforded to
her by the open window. Turns out they had not taken a key
('You didn't tell us to') so had pushed the sash window open, had
a fight about someone touching someone else's bum, forgotten
to close the window, thus releasing the dog into the night. When
I shouted at them they stared blankly at me then said, 'We're
hungry.'

'Why didn't you eat at the football club?'

'We didn't have any money.'

'I gave you £10 for food!'

'We lost it.'

Utter fuckwits, the pair of them.

They are not remotely ashamed, disturbed or chastened by
the fuck-ups they make on a daily basis. Which means they are
either psychopaths or natural-born politicians. They should be in
the Tory cabinet.

The girl, on the other hand, is usually super-organised,
fragrant, self-sorting and highly motivated. If she were to make
just one of the stupid mistakes the boys make she would be
mortified.

How do men end up running the world?

That's a bit better. I like the veiled despair. It's a thing, isn't it, in
Mummy Blogs? 'Ha ha ha my life is shit ha ha ha!' Not going to
press 'Publish' though. Jesus. I want a fag.

I'll take the dog for a walk. 'Sadie! Sadie!' I shout from the
back door. Sadie, an extremely haughty French Bulldog the kids
had to have four years ago, who they absolutely *promised* to

walk every day, is sitting out on the patio staring into the nothingness. She doesn't really like me either, even though I'm the only poor sod who feeds her, cleans up her poos and makes sure she gets out every day. I try to talk to her sometimes but she stares impassively, snorts a bit then collapses on her side as though I've just bored her to death.

Sadie deigns to turn to look at me when I call, but then trots down the steps to the back of the garden to bark at some invisible assailants. 'Sod you, then,' I mutter. Vincent, our skinny black rescue cat strolls in, eyes me disdainfully then does some cursory purring in order to procure a sachet of slimy jelly. We got him when the kids were little to teach them about caring for something and being kind. We didn't know that he was a vicious bastard street fighter who stays out all hours then comes home at dawn demanding to be fed, before collapsing on the bed all day like some drunk abusive partner.

Sometimes I feel Sadie and Vincent gang up on me. They sit by the back door almost sneering at my attempts to befriend them as if to say 'Look at us – we're supposed to hate each other, but even we prefer each other's company to yours!'

Or maybe I'm tired and paranoid.

Time to talk to Mum. It was always at moments like this – when I felt bored and ignored even by the animals in my life – I'd give her a call. She'd never have her hearing aids in so it would inevitably be a frustrating first five minutes of me repeating 'Have you taken your tablets this morning?' over and over again. At least now that she's in an urn she can't keep insisting I'm mumbling, or that my phone is shit. I'll get her down from the shelf.

Hi, Mum. I wanted to call you today. But then I remembered. I didn't pick up the phone or anything. OK, my hand might have twitched involuntarily towards my pocket, where my phone was, but I didn't call. I don't do that any more. The people who bought the house inherited the number so it started to get a bit awkward ... me ringing 'home' and trying to engage the new owners in a chat about how the garden is doing just so that I could picture the house again, picture you in it, sat in your chair with a mug of tea. So then I thought why not just ... talk to you anyway? Is that mad? I know you can't talk back but I can imagine what you'd say ... if you weren't reduced to five pounds of dove-grey grit, poured into what I have to say is a deeply unattractive maroon plastic tub.

So, how are you, Mum? I don't know if you are in heaven, if there is a heaven, or if you're floating about somewhere in a shimmery sort of vapour, but I know that you are around somehow. I can feel you tutting every time I hang the washing out badly, or when my cakes don't rise. You were so much better at all this than me. I know you could be grumpy and you nagged us a lot when we were lazy, selfish teenagers, but mostly you loved us so much. You always said we were the best thing you ever did. I've been thinking about that a lot lately. How you used to say 'You are my biggest achievement' with such a smile on your face. How you would belittle yourself in front of women who worked because you felt they expected you to, but how actually you felt sorry for *them* that they didn't have *your* life.

I wish I felt like that. I wish I felt so sure in my choices and happy with their outcome. You seemed to thrive in our company, you feasted on me and Aidan like we were hot buttered rolls. You couldn't get enough of us. Even until right before you died you'd hug us tight and tell us how you'd lie awake at night, steroids playing havoc with your sleep, hoping that we were tucked up in our beds safely.

I remember when Amelie was born. Seventeen hours of labour with no pain relief, only to be told they'd have to do a C-section anyway because she was too big. Then they gave her to me and left me on my own with her for the night and I couldn't get up to her because of the cut, and she started crying and I started crying because I was out of it and in pain and I felt helpless and scared, and there was blood all over the sheets and no one came to help me, so both of us, me and Amelie, just lay there crying until dawn. Then a nurse finally came and handed her to me and I felt . . . nothing. Just so tired and numb and kind of horrified by the mess of it all. You visited with Dad later that day. I remember you picked her up and cradled her so naturally. You were overjoyed.

I remember staring blankly at you and saying 'I don't love her yet' and without missing a beat you replied, '*I* do!'

And I could see it was true.

I remember when I was pregnant you asked if I had a layette set. I didn't know what you were talking about. You explained it was a baby package for newborns – knitted blankets, cardigan, hat, bootees. You said you would knit one for me. I remember laughing at you and saying 'Mum, it's not the 1960s – I'll just put the baby in a onesie.'

You tried hard to mask the hurt you must have felt and I was irritated by your old-fashionedness, your insistence that the old ways were the best, your inability to move with the times.

How I wish I could take that cruel laugh back. How I wish I had let you knit me blankets, shawls and bootees and all the other things you couldn't understand I didn't want. Because you would have liked it. And now you're gone and you will never knit anything ever again. And I don't have those things to hold and cherish, made with your nimble fingers, your cool pastry-making hands, your brow-stroking, bleach-roughened thumbs.

Sorry, Mum. Went a bit maudlin there. I know you hated it when I got sad. 'Keep on keeping on,' you said. So I will. For now.

Chapter Two

'Dinner time!' I yell from the foot of the stairs. I've spent the best part of a day trying to make moussaka. Years ago we went to a Greek restaurant and the kids liked it, so now and again I make it 'as a treat'. A treat for everyone except me, because it's really annoying to make. It takes about twelve hours and involves several fiddly and potentially hazardous processes – salting the aubergine (don't want it to taste bitter), frying off the beef (but not letting it dry out), par-boiling the potatoes (but not too much), then making the bloody cheese sauce for the topping which always ends up looking like lumpy custard. It's sitting on a place mat now in the middle of the dining table ('dining'? What family 'dines' these days?) bubbling away, the steam rising from the crust. I admire my handiwork. This is a good one. Just the right amount of cinnamon.

This is what life should be like. If you give up your career to raise your children, and your husband Martin goes out to work all day, and you live in a nice semi-detached suburban house with bland but practical Ikea furnishings, and you hoover the stair carpet regularly because it's new, and your pathway has lavender growing all the way along it even if the geraniums in the window boxes always die – if you have achieved all this, despite the sleepless nights and the hard times and the boredom and the self-sacrifice, then at around 7 p.m. each night the rewards are great. Your loving family will, one by one, come clattering down the stairs to sit in convivial bonhomie and share the triumphs and disappointments of their day while passing each other plates of delicious home-cooked food. There will be laughter, gentle teasing, fond smiles and, for once, at least at dinner time, it will all be worth it. A passer-by, on looking into your dining-room window, would be charmed by the domestic idyll they spy, and filled with warmth and a nostalgia for their own childhood meal times.

Ten minutes goes by. No one has come downstairs.

'DINNER!!!' I shout again.

'One minute!' shouts Lorcan.

No one else responds. I continue to stand at the foot of the stairs weighing up the irritation I feel at having to shout, versus how out of breath and cross I'll be if I have to go all the way upstairs to drag them out of their rooms. There's nothing for it – they are probably wired up to devices and can't hear me anyway. I heave my tired limbs up the stairs, cursing the discarded school bags and shoes that vie to trip me up and break my ankles on the way.

I knock on the boys' door. No response. I go in and find Paddy's asleep in his school uniform and coat, his massive feet still encased in his dirty school shoes. I shake him gently.

'WHAT?!' he says, waking with a start.

'It's dinner time!'

'I'm not really hungry,' he says, turning over. Out of the corner of his pocket a family-sized chocolate bar wrapper flicks me the Vees.

'What are you doing eating all that chocolate before dinner? No wonder you're not hungry! Now get up and come downstairs!'

'All right, all right,' he says, rolling off the bed and onto the floor. His sandy hair is sticking up in all directions. He'd look appealingly childlike if it weren't for his massive arms and gangly legs. He's turning into a mini Martin. Lorcan deigns to take off his headphones if only so he can reach his brother for a swift kick.

I knock on Amelie's door. No response. I go in. She wheels round accusingly, on red alert for violence in case it's one of her brothers. There is zero tolerance of either of them anywhere near her room.

'What?' she asks hotly.

'Dinner. I've been shouting for ten minutes!'

'WELL, I DIDN'T HEAR YOU!' she yells, never one for quietly acquiescing. 'What is it?'

'Moussaka.'

'Disgusting.' She gets up, making a performance of how revolted she is by my pathetic offering yet how gracious in consenting to sit at the table.

'Boys! Dinner!'

'I'm coming, Mum. I was just finishing a game. I got ten kills and my squad—'

'Yes, I'm not interested, Lorcan,' I say, going back down the stairs.

Martin comes in from work just as I'm heading back into the kitchen.

'Hello, love. Just in time for dinner. If any of the bastards actually come down.'

'That's not very nice, Mother dearest,' says Lorcan, wrapping his arms around my neck.

'Smells good. What is it?' asks Martin, kicking off his shoes and leaving them where they fall in the middle of the hallway. I pick them up and place them in the shoe rack.

'Moussaka.'

'Not for me, thanks,' says Martin.

'What? Why not?'

'You know I never eat before football.'

Ah yes. Bloody football night.

'I'll have some after.'

He disappears into his 'study' – a boxroom where I keep the clothes airer and the hoover, with a tiny desk and computer in the corner. God knows what he gets up to in there.

Finally all three kids arrive to sit down at the table. A row erupts over who sits next to who. It's very similar to the fox, the chicken and the bag of grain – if Lorcan sits next to Paddy they will punch each other. If Paddy sits next to Amelie he will deliberately slurp his food to annoy her. If Amelie sits opposite Lorcan he will kick her under the table and say it was Sadie, who is parked in her usual position under the table, where she will no doubt receive half the food I have cooked when the kids unsubtly pass it down to her to avoid having to eat it themselves. The bastard cat Vincent stares vindictively from the worktop, waiting to lash out at anyone who passes.

'Just please sit down, shut up and eat!' I say.

I dish out the food and they start to pick at it.

'I hate aubergine. It's so slimy,' moans Paddy.

'Just leave it on the side of your plate, then,' I say.

'Amelie, stop turning it over like you're looking for worms and eat, please.'

'I'm on a diet.'

'What? Why?'

'Because literally everyone at school has an eating disorder, Mum, and you keep making this really fattening stuff!'

'Its called FOOD, Amelie, and it's not that fattening. I used spray oil! Have some salad with it,' I say, pushing the bowl towards her. She picks at a few leaves sulkily.

'Mum, Paddy thinks he's really cool at school. He's always taking the piss out of me in front of his friends,' says Lorcan. He's the quieter of the two, and is often a convenient punchbag for Paddy's insecure posturing.

'Don't be mean to each other. There are enough people in the world who will bring you down – don't do it to your own family.'

'I could bring him down any time,' says Paddy.

'No, you couldn't,' says Lorcan.

'Yes, I could, FAT MAN!'

'Please stop! Paddy there is literally a couple of pounds' difference in your weight so why you call him Fat Man I do not know!'

'Because he's FAT!' laughs Paddy. Even if it is just a few pounds it's something to have over his brother. Lorcan lets his mask slip for a brief moment and looks hurt.

'Are you going to cry to Mummy now?' taunts Paddy.

'Nothing wrong with crying. That's called toxic masculinity, isn't it, Mum? Laughing at boys crying?'

'Yes, it is. Now eat your dinner.'

Amelie takes the opportunity to push her chair back noisily and scrape the contents of her plate quickly into the bin.

'Where are you going?' I ask.

'Upstairs?' she says, as if explaining to a simpleton.

Paddy follows suit, racing her up the stairs for no reason other than to provoke a fight.

Lorcan stares at me balefully. His plate is still full.

'At least you're going to sit with your old mum and eat your dinner, aren't you, Lorcan?'

'No, because she's not OLD,' he smiles. 'But I'm not really hungry.'

'You as well! Don't tell me you ate a whole family bar of chocolate too?'

'No. It's just . . . I hate moussaka. It's kind of disgusting.' And with that he strolls out of the kitchen, swiping a packet of Hula Hoops from the cupboard on the way. I clear the plates into the dog's bowl and start to load the dishwasher. So much for the family meal. Vincent waits until my back is turned then leaps onto the table. When I go to wipe it down he is licking greedily at the cheese crust of the remaining moussaka.

I'll give that bit to Martin.

'Ciara, have you seen my football shorts?'

Martin is shouting from upstairs. I don't know if that's what he actually said but it's an educated guess. Apparently I can hear through doors, ceilings, entire floors of the house and be able to locate all items within a five-mile radius at a moment's notice.

I go to the foot of the stairs and crane upwards. Martin is standing in his saggy pants, his hairy belly nudging the banister. He's not bad-looking for a slightly overweight man of fifty-one with bog-standard male pattern baldness and facial psoriasis, but he's a far cry from the trim, athletic man of thirty I married. Let's just say his hair product shelf is pretty empty and his underwear drawer is larger than it was. Mind you, he could say the same about me, and sometimes does. 'Little pickers wear bigger knickers!' he occasionally warns as he catches me staring into the open fridge. What does he see when he looks down at me, I wonder. Does he make the same physical inventory that I find myself, unkindly, making from time to time? Does he look down at me from the top of the stairs and think, 'Who is that short, slightly dumpy middle-aged woman with the dark frizzy bob and grey roots, and why is she wearing those old jogging bottoms? I can tell by her drooping jaw, her bingo wings and her spare tyre that she hasn't been jogging much lately, so I can only deduce that this is my poorly-dressed rather disappointing wife, who is now a far cry from the socially awkward, shy but at least svelte woman I once married.' Does he? If only he paid enough attention to me to have noticed. Martin only comments on my appearance to express disapproval if I change anything. I once tried highlights and he said I looked 'desperate'. I suppose I was, but not in the way he meant.

'Muuuuuum!' screams Lorcan from behind his bedroom door. 'Where are my new boots?'

Here we go. I think this would make a good blog actually . . .

BLOG 2 – Milking It!

It's Monday night. That means it's football night. For the past two months the boys have been going with M to play 5-a-side football on an indoor pitch. They've waited years for this – M has been huffing and puffing around in his old baggy shorts every Monday for the last four years, but it's only now he has deemed the boys mature enough to be allowed into the hallowed male kingdom of astroturf, asthma pumps and ill-advised victory knee-slides.

Initially they were thrilled. Going out at 9 p.m. on a school night, getting special boots, being with Dad in the car and maybe getting a Lucozade from the machine after. Now the novelty has rather worn off and they moan as if they are being asked to lay the bloody pitch rather than just run around on it pretending to be Sergio Aguero with acne.

I hate Monday nights because if the kids are still up after 10 p.m. I see it as a direct theft of my time. I can't relax, sit down and enjoy anything on TV if they are milling about after football because I have to be on hand to sort out any of the numerous hostilities that will inevitably break out. I also have to guard the

milk supply in case of a fridge attack. These happen in between
the hostilities, and can be just as disturbing, watching three
teenagers chugging PINTS of milk like big spotty babies in
leisure wear. All those nights I sat up trying to coax one single
ounce of formula down the twins, only to have them sick it all up
on me moments later with a warm, yogurty belch. Now the
bastards are paying me back by drinking so much milk they are
turning into calcium-rich triffids. They are huge, already taller
than me and able to neck vast quantities of the stuff without so
much as swallowing. I don't like them drinking so much milk
because

a) there's none left for my tea in the morning and I have to drive
   to the corner shop to buy some with my big coat covering my
   pyjamas and my 'these aren't really slippers' slippers on
b) they never eat what I cook for them, then come drifting down
   an hour later to fill up on dairy
c) I feel they are being deliberately provocative about how shit
   they used to be about drinking it when I really needed them
   to

Still, with the house to ourselves, me and the girl have the
opportunity to bond.

Who am I trying to kid? Bond?! Why do I feel I have to present
the acceptable face of teen parenting when it's just me reading
this blog? There's no one else to impress.

Well, when I say 'bond' what I mean is, with just me and the girl
in the house we have ample opportunity to replay the same
conversation we've been having for the past six months in which

I attempt to 'chat' while she smirks and scrolls through her phone.

I tap on her door as soon as M and the boys have gone. She doesn't hear it because apparently it's very important to listen to loud music about gangstas and hoes when you are trying to do homework. I knock again. The music snaps off.

'What?!' she says, not even attempting to disguise her irritation.

'You OK?' I ask, peering round the door.

'Yes,' she sighs. The room is a mess. There are clothes, books, shoes, coats everywhere. She is oblivious, lying on her front across the bed fiddling with her phone.

I survey the wreckage for a moment then edge my way in towards the bed. She lets out a very audible groan as I clear a space to sit down.

'How's the homework going? Don't know how you can concentrate with that loud music on.'

'Oh God, you sound like such a cliché, Madre,' she says, going back to her phone.

'Well? How's it going?'

'Good. I came top in the maths test today.'

'Well done. The tutor is paying off then.'

'Yes.'

We sit in silence, her eyes flicking up and down over the screen in her hand. I lean over to see what she is looking at, and she slams the screen face down onto the bed.

'What?!' she says accusingly.

'Nothing! I was just looking to see what was so fascinating!'

'Nothing! Is there something you want from me because I'm kind of busy?'

'OK. No. That was it. Just to see how you are, that's all.'

I slope back downstairs. I don't know what to do with myself in the evenings. I spend all day waiting for them to come home and then when they do they don't want to be anywhere near me. What is the point of having teenage children? Surely they should be sent off to some kind of camp from the ages of twelve to seventeen? They would come back as nice people, able and willing to talk, help out around the house and keep track of their basic possessions. We, in the meantime, would retrain, go to college, drink a fuck of a lot of Martinis and recuperate after the heavy primary-school years.

Not bad. I do feel a bit better. There were many evenings I'd have killed just to have half an hour, ten minutes even, to myself, but nowadays, if I'm honest, it feels kind of lonely once they are all ensconced in their teen cells. I knock around the kitchen pretending to tidy up, pretending I've got stuff to do. But I haven't. I did it all when they were at school. I'm about to scroll through the channels for a TV programme to watch on catch-up that of course I've forgotten the name of, when my phone rings.

My phone never rings.

Probably a cold caller primed to ask me loads of personal questions before offering me a great deal on my energy supply – if only it was for MY energy supply.

I look at the phone and my heart sinks. It's Debbie. Debbie from up the road. Debbie who only has one child, a drippy daughter called Meredith who is the apple of her eye. I mean, who calls their child 'Meredith' ? That's a name for a Victorian parlour maid. Meredith and my boys have been in the same class since nursery and whenever they have one of their regular little spats Debbie is right on it, expressing her 'concern', giving her 'opinion', offering advice on how I can 'manage the boys better'.

Debbie is a real downer. Everyone calls her Debbie Downer in this house. Not to her face, obviously. To her face I am the epitome of diplomacy, acquiescence and two-faced nodding and smiling. She has a permanently worried expression on her little grey face, and she dresses almost entirely in beige. She scuttles around the streets like a tiny field mouse with general anxiety disorder. She's been a single parent ever since her husband Stephen left three years ago. I think she bored him out of the door. I should feel sorry for her really but it's impossible because she's such a pain in the arse.

'Hi, Deb, how's it going?' I say, settling myself in for a long and depressing monologue.

She sighs.

'Hi, Ciara . . . I hope I'm not interrupting anything?'

'Well, I've just got George Clooney in the shower but I'm sure he'll be a while towelling himself off so . . .'

'Sorry?'

Christ, she's dull.

'Never mind. How are things?'

'Well, I just wanted to have a quick word about—'

'The boys?'

'Oh, have they spoken to you already?'

'No, it was just instinct.'

Here we go.

'It's just that Meredith came home from school very upset today because Lorcan and Paddy told her you said they shouldn't speak to her.'

'What?!'

'Yes, they told her that you said something not very nice about her and Meredith is devastated. You know how much she likes you, Ciara, and she can't believe—'

32

'Wait a minute – what am I supposed to have said?'

'Well, I don't really want to repeat it . . .'

'No, come on, I really want to know. I'll kill them – it's a load of rubbish! They're just trying to cause trouble.'

'Well, they said that you called her . . . hang on, I've written it down somewhere . . . oh here it is, hang on, I'll just get my glasses . . . right, yes, so you said, "Don't tell that girl anything because she's a manipulative little shit!"'

There is a long silence.

Of course I didn't say that. Did I? Was it a moment of weakness when I couldn't stand another bloody drama in the playground? If Meredith gets any hint of a chink in our family defences she sticks her little nose right in it and makes as much trouble as possible. Maybe it's because she's an only child but she is massively attracted to trouble. She loves a drama – especially if she is the perceived victim.

'Well, that's just ridiculous, Debs – as if I'd say anything like that! Meredith has probably got the wrong end of the stick! Don't forget, she is prone to these little fibs when she's annoyed with the boys . . . I'm not saying she makes up tall stories but her nickname at school is J. K. Rowling . . .'

Good one.

'Well, this is the thing . . . Paddy recorded you saying it and put it on their class WhatsApp. The whole class heard it . . .'

'What? Why?!' Weirdo.

I'll kill them. I'll fucking kill them.

'Debs it was nothing personal – they're all manipulative little shits at times, aren't they?'

'Meredith may be many things but she is never manipulative.'

Like you would know, I think.

33

BLOG 3 – Hell Is Other People's Children

I mean, who really likes anyone else's children? I can barely muster feelings of warmth towards my own. Mostly other people's children are either a shining, all-singing, all-dancing, trumpet-playing reminder of just how dumb, talentless and lazy your own kids are, or they are so annoying and rude you have to sit on your hands so that you don't accidentally slap them round the chops every time they come over for a play date.

My daughter's friends are generally OK now, give or take the odd bitchy teen cabal. When they were younger, though – OMG, as they would say. Horrible tantrums, nasty playground sanctions on any girl with the wrong shoes, rigidly policed embargoes on lunchtime seating arrangements for girls who were too fat/ boring/smelly to be in with the in-crowd. The perpetrators of the ritual cruelties were a shifting cast of swishy ponytailed pre-teens in long white socks. I'm sure my own daughter took her turn to be Imelda Marcos when it came, so I'm not claiming neutral privilege here. It just made me see them all in a rather nasty light, and I find it hard to forget that the nice young woman sitting in my kitchen chatting about her GCSE choices once reduced my daughter to tears by repeatedly singing the Peppa Pig theme tune every time she walked into class. Mums don't forget shit like that.

The boys though. The boys. The things they say to each other! The casual violence. The vile Freudian micro-aggressions about what they'd like to do to each other's mums! I sometimes steal their phones and scroll through the 'chats'. The hostile, threatening tone of what they refer to as 'banter' is horrifying.

In my day if you really wanted to upset someone you called them a spaz. Here is a recent charming exchange I

found on P's Instagram chat, with the equally charming socio-
path Jake, a boy in their class with bad teeth and an even
worse attitude.

P: You're a dick, bro.

J: You are. Retrad.

P: I think you mean retard. You retard. Can't even spell it.

J: Fuck off.

P: Cripple.

J: Who's a cripple?

P: Your mum.

J: No she aint.

P: She will be when I've finished fucking her.

J: Don't chat shit about my mum. Watch, man. Watch tomorrow.
   Man's gonna shank you. Watch.

Maybe I should be looking at Amelie's phone more? I kind of
trust that she doesn't get involved in such nastiness, but why did
she hide the phone when she caught me looking? What is she
trying to keep from me?

Upstairs I hear the shower go on. Here's my chance. She
leaves her phone in the bedroom when she has a shower ever
since the time she dropped it onto the tiled floor and the screen
smashed into a million impossible-to-hoover pieces, prompting
Amelie to come running downstairs ashen-faced and dripping
wet, looking as if she had just witnessed a multiple-fatality pile-
up of cars laden with babies and kittens.

Should I?

Before I even decide, I'm upstairs creeping past the bathroom
and pushing her door open. The books, clothes and random bits
of paper have been shoved under the bed, and on her pillow lies

her shiny slab of heaven, her one-stop world, her everything –
her iPhone.

I know the passcode. Of course I do. It's her birthdate. She's a
narcissistic teen who believes that – forget about the ice age, the
discovery of penicillin, man landing on the moon – *the day she
was born* was the year dot and the *actual* start of world events.

I tap on her Snapchat icon and scroll through a conversation
with someone who has no name but is identifying themselves
with a string of aubergine emojis where the name should be. I
half close my eyes, squinting at the screen, daring myself to look
and at the same time feeling shame-faced about what I'm doing.
Is this spying? Is it even legal? It must be – I pay her phone bill,
so I'm allowed, right?

It's a pretty banal chat about who saw who first, referencing
other people on the school bus. It's clear that it's a boy she is
talking to. There are pages and pages of emojis, impenetrable
abbreviations and silly teasing. Then there is a link to an article
headlined 'Sperm is the Perfect Face Pack!'

I gulp. Yuk. Some hairy-arsed youth is sending my lovely little
girl pseudo-scientific erotica! Underneath the link, aubergine
boy has pasted a row of water-splash emojis – what does *that*
mean?! Surely he can't be alluding to ejaculations? After the
emojis he has typed 'Just sayin . . .' with a winking emoji and
half a dozen laughing faces. Obviously he's joking-not-joking.

I hear the shower switch off – how come she's been so quick?
She normally stays in there for a good half-hour. I click the
screen off and pretend to be tidying her clothes away when she
comes in wrapped in towels and eyes me suspiciously.

'You really must try to hang your blazer up at least . . .' I fuss.
She grunts and grabs at her phone.

'Have you been on my Snapchat?' she demands.

'What?'

'Because I've got a message here saying I've been typing a long time and no message?'

Shit. Busted. What should I do? Fess up and confront her about this boy? Or plead ignorance even though she absolutely knows the truth?

BLOG 4 – One Person's Spying Is Another Person's Necessary Intel

Teenagers seem to think that adults have no right to know anything about their lives. When my kids were little they were absolutely shit at keeping secrets. At Christmas they would cajole the husband into giving them money to buy me some rubbish or other which they then wrapped badly ready for the Big Day. They would then literally itch to tell me exactly what it was they had bought. They would follow me around the house saying 'Mummy, I'm not saying it's a soap but I know you like soaps and this one was £3.99!'

Nowadays I feel like Claire Danes in *Homeland* every time I ask a simple question.

'What did you have for lunch?' 'WHY?????'

'Who was that at the door?' 'Oh God!'

'Have you brushed your teeth?' 'STOP INTERROGATING ME!!!'

Is it any wonder I've had to resort to espionage to make sure that nothing dodgy is going on? How do I know they are not dealing drugs/offering sexual favours in exchange for homework/ planning to get a bit stabby in the playground?

I don't buy this idea that teenagers automatically deserve privacy. They don't get it without earning trust first. And if they are trustworthy, they have nothing to fear from the odd spot check, so what's the problem?

I ponder the twisted parental logic of this as Amelie glares at me, waiting for my answer.

'Yes,' I say finally, 'I did look at your phone.'

'JESUS!!!'

'I'm sorry, I was worried, you've been a bit moody lately and I was concerned you were being bullied or . . . or I don't know, getting involved in something unhealthy, or . . . or . . . being groomed by a paedophile!' I splutter, not even convincing myself.

'You weren't worried, you were just being nosy! For God's sake, Mum! I feel – VIOLATED!'

'I do worry about you, and I think actually it is part of my job to make sure that—'

'Part of your job to be a snooping, nosy, interfering saddo?'

'Yes,' I mumble.

'Why don't you just ask me if you want to know something?'

'OK. Have you got a boyfriend?'

'Oh God! I can't believe you're asking me this!'

'Well, who is this boy?'

'Are you assuming I'm heterosexual? Maybe it's not a boy!'

'OK. Is it a boy?'

'Yes. But he's not my boyfriend – I'm just talking to him.'

'What does that mean?'

'I'm just talking to him! That's it.'

'Right. So . . . do you, like, hold hands?'

'Oh for God's sake, don't be so disgusting.'

OK, so holding hands is disgusting but talking about the beauty benefits of semen is fine? Got it.

I need my mum. I slink out of Amelie's room, leaving her to continue her sophisticated courtship online, and get Mum out of the cupboard.

Hi, Mum.

You wouldn't have put up with any of this. I was a slow starter sexually, mostly because the nearest our family got to discussing sex was when I was reading out the inscription on a fifty-pence coin and everyone blushed when I said 'Regina'.

I went on the pill when I was eighteen but you found the packet, carefully hidden in my underwear drawer. You sat me down and gravely told me how men were only after one thing. I was mortified. I had no real idea about sex. I'd had a boyfriend for a year but we only did what the swimming pool described as 'petting' because I was a good Catholic girl. What would you say now if you knew that your beautiful granddaughter, the girl you doted on and adored from day one, is the casual receiver of sexual suggestions from a boy she is 'talking to'? You'd go ballistic. Things are very different now, Mum. My kids seem to know so much. I walked into the bathroom last week and found Paddy shaving around his testicles! Why?!

I can't believe I just said 'testicles' to you, Mum, sorry. Maybe it was me that was the prude. Maybe I internalised your Irish Catholic modesty as shame. Maybe you were OK with it all really and just wanted to protect me. At the time I thought you were an embarrassing throwback, a Nun in mums' clothing. Now I feel exactly as you must have felt when you discovered my pills – sick to the stomach that your lovely young daughter was probably about to be groped by some breathless, handsy youth.

I look up from my mutterings and Amelie is standing at her bedroom door staring across at me.

'What are you doing?' she asks.

'Nothing. Just . . . talking to Grandma.'

'You're weird,' she says, shutting the door behind her.

The clatter of boots in the hallway signals the return of the Football Three. I put Mum back in the wardrobe and head downstairs to wrangle the boys into a quick shower.

'You're shit! You let in three goals!'

'No, I didn't. I nutmegged you!'

'Boys boys boys, just take your boots off and get in the shower, please,' says Martin. He's sweaty and red-faced, his baggy shorts sticking to his legs as he stands trying to kick his boots off without bending over.

'My bloody back,' he grimaces. 'I'm getting too old for this.'

'Well, stop then. You could always stay in with me!'

He huffs, like that's the most ludicrous idea in the world. I mean, what would we talk about? Would we sit with an M&S Meal For Two over candlelight while he tells me about his day at the hard coalface of insurance? Would he regale me with dramatic stories of how the IT department are having trouble blocking social media platforms for the junior staff? Would I make him laugh about how I thought we'd run out of dishwasher tablets but then found one down the back of the bin? Would we sit on the sofa while he watched recordings he'd made of *World at War* while I sat there wondering what had become of the dreams we once had of travelling, seeing the world and finding adventure? Ludicrous.

Chapter Three

The boys have come home with their mid-year reports. Oh God. Another catalogue of failures. I can hardly bear to open them, such is my dread. Now I'll have to DO SOMETHING with them, because heaven forbid they should be allowed to be *average*. I'll be expected to get them tutors. I'll be asked to monitor their homework and buy them cue cards for revision. Timetables and interventions will be scheduled. I'll be required to tell them they are *exceptional* but *not doing their best*! If they don't get level 9s it will be because I didn't do enough.

BLOG 5 – Because You're Not Worth It

There was a time when the only vital function of bringing up children was keeping them alive until they were big enough to bring in the harvest. These days that, apparently, is not good enough. These days we have to do other things like support their study, encourage them to express opinions and boost their self-esteem. You must never say that anything they produce – that crappy art coursework, a half-arsed essay, a really terrible school performance – is anything less than genius. You must never tell them they aren't very good at something. You must never berate them for not coming first, not winning. You must always tell them that the important thing is that they tried their best and that as far as you're concerned they ARE ALWAYS the best – not because it's kind and loving, but because this is the way to SUCCESS.

41

Children these days are seen as failures if they don't get As. And by association, so are the parents. My sons are not on message. I have tried to sit with them while they fart and giggle their way through homework, I have given in and done it for them, I have let them fail in the hope that they will buck their ideas up – but nothing works. They just don't care. I have taken to trying to shame them into caring. These days, if they don't do as well as their friends in exams or competitions I tell them it's because the kids who won deserved it more because they worked harder or were naturally better than them. They try to argue for a minute or two, they try to feel sorry for themselves but they usually end up admitting I'm right. It's heresy these days to say that to your kids but I hope they'll thank me for it one day. There's a fine line between encouraging them and duping them into a false sense of security. Keep 'em on their toes, I say, so they go into adult-hood understanding the rules of the game. What's the point of high self-esteem if it's predicated on a total lack of self-awareness? They need to know when they are crap, because life sure lets you know it.

I'll admit I cross the line sometimes. The other day, in the spirit of honesty, I ended up depressing P. In a fit of niceness I bought some Pop Tarts for the kids and toasted three at break-fast time. Two of them broke into pieces in the toaster so I gave those to A and L, knowing that P, being the mardy high-maintenance one, would kick off if his was broken. He sat at the table enjoying his Pop Tart while the other two went to brush their teeth and let out a contented sigh.

'That was lucky, Mum – I'm the only one who got a Pop Tart that wasn't broken!' he crowed.

'It wasn't luck, mate. The first two broke and I thought "I'd better give them to the other two because P will have a massive meltdown if he gets a broken Pop Tart. So no, it wasn't luck – it was me trying to manage your bad moods.'

He went silent. I imagined the sweet sticky goo turning sour in his mouth. I felt the harshness of my words ringing in the air so I went over to him to check if he was OK. His head was bowed, and he almost whispered, 'Well, that doesn't make me feel very good about myself . . .'

I can be such a bitch. But is it bitchy if it's true?

Chapter Four

'Mum . . . can I talk to you?'

Oh blimey, there must be something wrong. I'm trying to tidy the endless piles of washing away, surely one of the most pointless tasks in my day; no sooner is everything hung up in the relevant cupboards than it's all over the floor again covered in chocolate and mud.

Amelie is standing outside the boys' door. She hovers uncertainly watching me stuff pants into already overflowing drawers before coming in and sitting on the bed.

BLOG 6 – Let's Talk About Sex

Why do I feel repulsed by the idea of my daughter's burgeoning sexuality? I wish I was one of those cool parents, one of those middle-class hippies who lets boyfriends sleep over, throws condoms around the bathroom and makes lewd jokes at breakfast. But I'm not. I feel physically sick every time I think of her in bed with some boy. I want to scratch my eyes out at the very thought of it. And now the worst thing has happened.

She has a boyfriend.

She denied it at first. Teenagers are pedants about terminology, about what you name things. Semantics are everything. You can be 'liking' a boy, 'talking to' a boy, sending videos of yourself twerking and possibly even giving birth to his children before you'll give him the tag 'boyfriend' these days. Hence, when I first got an inkling there was a lanky lad in expensive leisure footwear sniffing about and I hacked into her phone, she hotly denied any boyfriend and did a good job of making me feel like a controlling dowager aunt from 1862. Today, though, she has come clean.

Oh God, I can't even type the word 'come' now without wincing. She has a boyfriend. His name is Rodney. She has no knowledge of *Only Fools and Horses* so jokes about Del Boy and Grandad are a waste of time – time that could be spent nailing planks across her bedroom door. I had heard of this boy – she has been stalking him since September, and I have to hand it to her, when she knows what she wants she goes for it. She has screen shots of all his Instagram pictures, her favourite being one of him in a swimming pool. She likes this one because he has 'amazing abs'.

She's fifteen. When I was fifteen I didn't know what 'abs' were. I remember admiring a boy who worked on a market stall because he wore Mod badges of The Jam, but I never gave his body a second thought. Why am I shocked that times are so different?

Anyway, Rodney has finally asked her out. This is how she tells me:

A: Mum . . . you know that boy I've been talking to?
ME: Yes. The one with the abs.
A: Yeah. Well, he asked me to be his girlfriend.
ME: (internally weeping) OK. What does that mean?
A: It doesn't mean anything.
ME: OK . . .
A: The thing is . . . you know I've liked him since the summer?
ME: Yes. I remember the summer of stalking.

A: Well . . . the problem is . . . now that I've actually got to know
   him . . . he's kind of . . . really quiet . . . and he says he likes the
   Tories.

ME: (internally cartwheeling) Oh dear – that's a bit of a
   deal-breaker.

A: I know, right? But now I have to go out with him.

ME: Why?

A: Because I stalked him, and if I turn him down now everyone
   will call me a sket.

ME: What's a sket?

A: A ho. A prostitute. A slag.

ME: What? That doesn't make any sense! How can you be a
   prostitute because you say no to a boy?!

A: You don't get it, Mum! Everyone knows I liked him, and now
   he's asked me out, if I say no I look bad, like I led him on.

Ah. In my day this was called a prick tease. I don't say this
though – I'm not saying 'prick' to her. It might give her ideas.
Confused though I am about the complex and contradictory
sexual politics of my daughter's social group, I cannot help but
feel a bit pleased that she has learnt a salutary lesson – Be
Careful What You Wish For.

ME: Well, that's a good thing to have realised – beauty is only
   skin deep, and the less attractive boys are often more interesting because they have to work harder on their personalities.

A: I know! Like, Jordan, the really fat boy, he's SO FUNNY! I love
   him!

ME: Well, why didn't you stalk him?

A: Because he was just . . . already there.

ME: So you like the chase?

A: I don't know! Anyway, now I've got Rodney and I don't really want him. It's like that time I saved all my pocket money for that Barbie salon and by the time I got it I didn't want it any more but I still bought it because you'd taken me to the shop.

ME: You could have said! I would have been relieved! All that money on gender-stereotyped pink plastic!

A: Well, anyway, I'm going to go out with him for like, a week, and then I'll dump him.

ME: But you can't really treat people like that. He's not a Barbie salon! You can't just shove him to the back of the cupboard and hope he'll go away. He has feelings too! Honestly, you'll learn one day when someone breaks your heart!

A: Mum! Stop it! It's like you're trying to make me go out with him! You're trying to make me feel guilty!

ME: I'm not. I just want you to be kind. That's all I ever want.

A: YOU'RE SO ANNOYING!

I was quite proud of this conversation. I thought I was doing well, letting her tell me all this stuff I find deeply uncomfortable and saying sensible things back to her, when all the time I just wanted to scream 'get back in your room and play with your Barbies!'

Am I a prude? Is her (ahem) 'awakening' so disturbing to me because it directly intersects with my downward sexual trend? Most days I couldn't be less interested in sex. It's just a lot of bother. Not the act itself – more the mental effort of thinking about doing it, shredding the everyday layers of marital irritation and minor repulsion, crossing the rubicon of necessary domestic distance to reimagine the balding, sweaty man in front of you as a hot young stud.

I don't know what to do with this sharing – on the one hand I'm pleased she feels able to tell me things, and on the other I wish she didn't. Because I don't actually want to know. Where will it end? When she does finally – ugh – lose her virginity am I to expect a blow-by-blow (ahem) account? Will she strap me to a chair and make me listen to how it all went down? Thank God the boys don't seem to be remotely interested in girls yet. They are too obsessed with twatting each other to spare any energy for touching girls. How will I cope when they start hanging out in the park trying to give hickeys to passing strangers?

My phone rings. It's Debbie Downer. Twice in one week. Wow. Things must be really bad out there.

'Hi, Deb.'

'Hi,' she sighs.

'What's up?'

'Oh nothing, nothing, I was just ringing for a chat . . .'

'OK. Erm . . .'

'How are the kids?'

'Good, good. Yes, well I haven't seen the boys today . . . I assume they're still alive. I heard one of them swearing earlier so they must be on their games.'

'Oh dear . . . luckily Meredith isn't into any of that toxic nonsense.'

'Excellent. Well done, you.'

'Well, she won't get her cello Grade 5 wasting all that time killing imaginary zombies will she?'

'Quite.'

'How's Amelie?'

'Yes, she's good.'

'She's got so tall, hasn't she?'

'Yes, I guess so. You know how it is – you don't notice when you live with them . . .'

'I saw her in the park today! She's huge! By the way, I think she might have grown out of that skirt – when she bends over you can almost see her knickers! Ha! She was with a group of boys. I see them a lot in the park actually. Nice little group they have.'

So she's still spying. 'Yes, they seem nice.'

'Have you met them?'

'Yes, yes . . .'

I haven't.

'Amelie is very friendly with one of them. Dark-haired boy. Very friendly! Ha ha ha!'

Oh shut up, Debbie.

'Have you noticed how many gangs of youths there are in the park lately? I recorded it at the local Neighbourhood Watch because you just can't be too careful, can you? And the smell of drugs . . . weed, is it? They all seem to be smoking it now! I had to cover my face with my pashmina walking through it today.'

What is she trying to say – that Amelie is smoking weed?

'I mean, not Amelie's gang, as far as I can tell, but you know, it's everywhere these days. It's like chewing gum for this generation. They don't even try to hide it.'

BLOG 7 – See No Evil

Here's a tip for all parents:

Don't bring shit to my door.

Unless one of my kids has actually murdered somebody (in which case I'd probably know because 85% of murders take place in the home) I don't want to know about it. Parents who report back about other people's kids or pass on rumours/sightings/gossip about them really wind me up. I know they think they are doing the rest of us a service – keeping their eyes and ears peeled for every illicit snog/fag/petty theft from the sweet shop – but in fact I think their motives are much darker. I think they are virtue-signalling their superior parenting skills. They are saying 'I am better than you at this! Look at what I know that you didn't! See how much I have my ear to the ground! YOU'RE SHIT!'

Or maybe I'm just paranoid. Our local Miss Marple for Generation X – let's call her DD – is a very timid, sad little woman with a very annoying little dog – let's call it Fuckwit. DD takes Fuckwit for walks in the park every half-hour just so that she can spy on the local youths. The poor dog is knackered. They're not so much walks as reconnaissance missions. She is a leading light of the local Neighbourhood Watch and runs the community Facebook group where local right-wing retirees can be casually racist at their online leisure. She knows everything before it has even happened. Of course, her own teenager – M, who looks like a creepy child ghost in a horror movie – is absolutely fault-less, mostly because she never goes out (unless it's to cello lessons/extra tuition/Girl Guides). M even visits the elderly in a local care home with DD. Those poor sods – captive audience for all DD's doom-mongering monologues about local mugging statistics, drug abuse in the pre-teens and littering on the high street, not to mention the fright of having M – pallid, frail and hiding behind two curtains of long frizzy black hair – looming into view on a Sunday morn.

DD is always on the phone dropping hints about what my kids have been up to – always with the utmost concern in her voice, of course. I'd really rather not know. And if it's not DD it's her little sidekick M, passing on intelligence like a prison rat. DD can just stick her helpful hints and spiteful glee at their failings where the sun don't shine. Which is most places in her dark little world.

I put the dishwasher on and head up to bed. Martin is reading but puts the book down when I climb in. I turn the light off to signal no funny business. I needn't have bothered; within three seconds he is snoring gently, lying flat on his back. I don't know how he does it. I will lie awake for ages now, trying to block out his wheezes and whistles, trying to block out the flickering streetlight. Trying to block out the persistent low-level hum of dissatisfaction that is my constant soundtrack these days. Trying not to sweat so much that the pyjamas and bedclothes feel like they've just come out of the washing machine when the spin cycle has broken yet again. Trying not to panic about how tired I'm going to be tomorrow because of the menopause's fabulous night-time gifts of hot flushes and febrile dreams.

Night, Mum.

Chapter Five

It's Sunday. I have an idea. It's so long since the five of us went out, I thought it would be nice to go for a drive somewhere, maybe have a pub lunch. I've been awake since 7 a.m., walked the dog, emptied the dishwasher, washed the school blazers, ironed fifteen shirts, scrubbed football boots ready for school tomorrow, bleached the sinks, mopped the floor, plumped up the sofa cushions and dealt with all the paperwork. No one else has turned up downstairs yet, which means they are either still somehow asleep despite my best pan-clattering efforts to rouse them, or they are ignoring me and are glued to various screens. I shout up the stairs.

'Martin? Are you awake?'

'I am now,' he grumbles. I know he was awake already. He just doesn't like to pass up any opportunity to score a few points. Who knows when he might need them.

'Tea?'

'Don't bother, I'll come down.'

I put the kettle on and think about where we might go. Martin doesn't like to go too far away from home at the weekends because he often has to travel a lot during the week and he likes to 'be still' at the weekend. There's a nice pub about twenty miles away – we used to go there when we started going out with each other about a hundred years ago. Maybe we could go there? I look it up on Google. It's open for lunch until 2.30. I ring and book a table for 1.30.

'Who were you on the phone to?' says Martin as he comes in and switches the kitchen lights off. 'Bloody hell, it's like Blackpool illuminations in here!'

'The Stag. I've booked us a table for lunch.'

'What?'

'One thirty.'

'What for?!'

'For lunch! To eat! You know, as a family?'

My determination not to be naggy and complaining is flagging already. Why does it always feel like pushing mud uphill whenever I suggest we do anything together?

'Is it a special occasion? It's no one's birthday is it? The Stag? Our old stomping ground? Oh bloody hell, it's not our anniversary, is it?'

'No, it's not a special occasion, Martin, I just thought it would be nice for a change.'

'But . . . but . . .'

I can sense him scrabbling around his mental shed desperately trying to find an urgent menial task that precludes him from any interaction with his family.

'I've got to cut those roses back! You asked me to do it last week.'

'It's fine, leave them. You can do them next week.'

Defeated, he makes himself a cup of tea, only grumbling twice about having to drive and the cost of five lunches.

I go upstairs to get the kids up. The boys are dead to the world. Lorcan is fast asleep in the clothes he was wearing last night, his earphones still crammed into his ears. If I envy him one thing it's his ability to sleep like the dead. I rouse him gently but he doesn't budge.

'Lorcan! LORCAN! Wakey wakey!'

'Hmmmm . . . what time is it?' he groans.

'It's eleven fifteen. Get up.'

'Why? It's Sunday!'

'We're going for lunch!'

'Why?!' he groans again.

'Just get up. It will be nice. Paddy, get up – we're going out.'

No response.

I pull the duvet off him, and pick up the empty cups and bowls.

I knock on Amelie's door. She is FaceTiming someone – one of the girls in her class who can't seem to be alone ever and constantly needs someone to talk to, first thing in the morning, last thing at night, on the loo, in the shower.

Why do I always feel nervous when I am trying to spend time with my own daughter?

'Amelie – can you get ready please? We're leaving in an hour.'

'What!? Wait! Where are we going?'

'Out.'

'Out? Where?'

She can't disguise her contempt and disbelief, even in front of her friend.

I try to sound nonchalant, like this is normal, like we are the family that is at ease in each other's company, that enjoys trips out together on Sundays and holds hands kicking up leaves in the park.

'We're going out to lunch,' I say, closing the door gently as I leave under a hail of protestation.

This will be a nice family day. If it kills me. I mean, I do all the hard work – where's the reward? Where's the pay-off? Where's the bit where it looks like the adverts?

Midday. No sign of the kids. Martin is chomping on a slice of toast, complaining that he is still full from last night's dinner and doesn't feel in the mood for a big lunch, especially as his bowels haven't been too regular lately. Who says romance is dead?

I shout up the stairs.

'Lorcan! Paddy! Are you up? We're leaving in half an hour!'

They groan.

I can't be sure Amelie heard me because her music is blasting out. I knock on the door and enter. She is still in her pyjamas but has at least started the elaborate eyebrow routine, so we are in with half a chance of leaving in forty minutes.

I go into our bedroom and look for some earrings. I never wear earrings. But in perfect family outings the mum always has nice earrings on, doesn't she? Earrings that her husband and/or delightful children have picked out carefully as a Mother's Day gift. And perhaps a silk scarf that tones tastefully with her neutral-shades casual wear? I look for the small flowery studs I bought with the Next voucher Martin gave me last Christmas. I don't know why I bought them really – they're not me at all, but they seemed like the right thing to buy with a Next voucher from your husband. Real mums shop in Next, they don't wait for the Mutton Police to chase them out of Topshop. I find one earring, but the other is nowhere to be seen.

'Amelie?' I say, going to the hallway. 'Have you seen my earring – the other one in this pair?' I hold the earring up for her to identify.

'Why would I know where it is?'

'Just in case you've seen it while you've been in my room? You haven't borrowed them recently, have you?'

'Why would I do that? They're disgusting!'

I don't take this personally, as Amelie has very binary taste settings – either things are *disgusting* or they are *awesome*. There is no grey area.

Oh well. I'll just have to go without earrings. Time was when I would have just worn one, but those crazy days are over. I'd probably be carted off if I did that now.

12.15. Still no sign of the boys. Martin is dressed, but as usual doesn't seem to have looked in a mirror. He has an old grey thermal polo-neck on under a green shirt, teamed with a blue bobbly cardigan and burgundy cords. He looks like a scarecrow after a fight in a charity shop.

'Martin, your blue jeans are clean – they're in the utility room.'

'They're too tight. I'm comfy like this.'

'But you look a mess!' I laugh, trying to hide my irritation. He has a very passive-aggressive way of deliberately dressing badly because he knows it winds me up.

'We're only going to The Stag, not the bloody Dorchester!'

'I know but . . . none of the colours match!'

'I don't care! I'm comfy.'

Too bloody comfy if you ask me.

'I spend all week trussed up in a suit and tie – I don't care what I wear at home.'

BLOG 8 – Old Slippers

When me and M were first going out, he always looked nice. He'd turn up smelling clean and lovely, with a smart well-fitting shirt and jacket on. At the time I found it amusing – I was more of a boho chic kind of a girl. I loved vintage shops, quirky dresses from Camden market, Levis and DM boots. I found M's formality kind of sexy. His properness was so out there, so different from any of my friends. He was appealingly 'other'. I think I thought that my wackiness, my free-thinking liberal nonchalance as far as clothes went would rub off on him. I didn't exactly think I'd change him, more that our being together would erode his sharper edges, like the lapping of waves can reform the rocks they encounter at high tide.

Instead the opposite has happened. Where once I wouldn't have been seen dead in 'weekend casuals' and pastel colours, now I own several elasticated-waist skirts and what can only be described as 'slacks', plus numerous nondescript sensible tops. Time was when I'd go out with him in a men's dinner jacket and stripy pyjama bottoms, or a vintage prom dress and tennis shoes, and I liked that we were so different. He anchored me, gave me confidence because he fitted in, and after a series of short-lived and disastrous flings with what Martin dismissively referred to as 'arty-farty types', who had trampled all over what little confidence I had with men, Martin seemed like a genuine and, yes, safe bet. He wore a tie pin, for God's sake – who wouldn't feel safe with someone like that? Reader, I married him. Then I was pregnant. Then I was pregnant again. I no longer needed going-out clothes, quirky or otherwise, because I never went anywhere – apart from baby yoga, baby music group, baby gym. Over the past twenty years he hasn't changed his dress sense at all. In fact, he still owns most of the jackets he wore back then. They are a bit tired and fit rather too snugly, but he won't get rid of them because 'they still have plenty of wear left in them'.

Sometimes I feel like one of his jackets – fondly thought of, a bit threadbare in places, old and from another era but too much bother to replace. Or his slippers. A tatty old pair of sheepskin boots he has had the entire time we've been together. I bought them for him on our first Christmas together and he has never replaced them. I kind of bought them as a joke – 'Haha look at us, an old boring couple!' – but he loved them. I tried buying him some new ones a few years ago but he left them in the cupboard. I ended up giving them away. He says his old ones know his feet so well. They fit like a fluffy second skin. He doesn't have to break them in, teach them the contours of his bumpy toes or bend over to put them on – the backs are worn down so much he can just slide his feet in and shuffle along until his heels slip inside.

12.30. Martin is kicking off his slippers and putting on his 'week-end shoes' – a pair of white nondescript trainers he gets every year in the sales. 'Boys! Amelie! Come on! It's time to go!'

Amelie slopes downstairs with her eyes still fixed on her phone.

'Boys!'

'Coming!' shouts Paddy, his voice unmistakably sleepy.

'Don't tell me you're not up yet!?'

'You should have woken us up earlier!' shouts Lorcan.

'I woke you up at eleven thirty! COME ON! Get some clothes on – something nice, not the tracksuits you were wearing yester-day! Hurry up! We'll be in the car.'

We head out and sit in the car with the engine running. Somehow Martin thinks this will transmit a kind of urgency to the boys. It never does. We could literally be on the launch pad for a trip to Mars and they would still move at a snail's pace looking for earphones/socks/a particular hoodie which is liter-ally the ONLY thing they can wear to Mars.

12.45. We are still in the car. Martin has been in twice to hurry them along. The first time he found Lorcan eating a bowl of cereal – 'I WAS HUNGRY!' – the second time he found both boys laughing at a YouTube video of a cat rapping.

Finally they emerge, and after a brief fist fight about who sits in the middle we are all in the car and on our way. It's 12.55. The pub is half an hour away. We should be fine. Ten minutes into the journey Martin takes an unexpected left turn.

'Where are you going? This isn't the way to The Stag.'

'I know. I'm just dropping some garden waste off at the tip.' The bloody tip. Martin is obsessed with the tip.

'Well, hurry up or we'll be late!'

'Relax. It's just a pub lunch, not the Queen's garden party.'

Ten minutes later we are still queuing to get into the tip. The rotten leaves Martin put in the boot last week are starting to hum almost as much as the two thirteen-year-old boys in the back.

'Come on! Get a move on! Bloody idiot!' Martin is, not for the first time, incensed by the absolute inferiority of every other driver on the road. Normally an irritatingly placid man, when he is behind the wheel or when he receives bad service in a shop he changes into a beige suburban hulk. The steam from his ears is almost visible. Today the man in front of him is a very cautious, polite driver who is letting people go in front of him as the queue bottlenecks at the entrance.

Obviously he's a moron.

Another ten minutes of swearing and horn hitting and we are on our way again. The boys have started kicking each other and Amelie is screaming at them. I remember now why we don't go out much. It was bad enough when they were small – faffing about with car seats, clearing up vomit and having to listen to the same nursery rhymes on psychotic loop – but this is pure torture. I play my ace and switch Classic FM on very loudly until they beg me to make it stop. I win. For now.

Five minutes later we are stuck behind a learner driver. 'Stupid cow, why is she so slow?!'

'She's driving at twenty miles per hour, Martin.'

'Exactly!'

'That's the speed limit here. There are schools.'

'They're not open today though, are they? Ridiculous!'

It's 1.35. We're at least ten minutes away.

'Mum, Lorcan keeps saying faggot.'

'Paddy said I'm a Gay Lord.'

'Mum, seriously, can you tell them to stop, I've got a really bad headache.'

'She's pulling over, Martin, just overtake her!' I say.

'I can't overtake on a bend, darling.'

Ten minutes later we pull in to The Stag. It seems to have had a bit of a makeover since we were here last (probably about a decade ago).

There are so many different craft beers, rivalled in number only by the number of staff with man buns, all of whom ignore me while I try to get their attention at the bar. My head is pounding, my shoulders are round my ears and I feel sick with hunger.

'Excuse me! Excuse me?'

'I'm going to the loo,' huffs Martin. The kids are standing by the door, glued to their phones like CIA operatives the moment an international incident has kicked off. All the tables are filled with smiling blonde families, laughing and joshing and all eating their greens.

'Hi,' says the hipster vaguely.

'We have a table booked for lunch? One thirty. Woods.' 'Yeah . . . hang on . . . no, right, yeah . . . I think it's over?' he says, looking vaguely in the direction of the kitchen out the back. Through the hatch I can see several beards wiping empty surfaces.

'What do you mean "over"?' I say, panicking slightly.

'Yeah . . . the chef said that's it, kitchen closed.'

'But we booked a table! Your website says you serve until two thirty!'

'Yeah, I know but, like, all our meat is organic and fresh. We don't buy in bulk so when it's gone, it's, like, gone.'

He says this like it's a massive bonus for me.

'But . . . but . . . we booked! Five of us! I've got teenagers with me! We had to drive here with them!'

'Sorry, that's a bummer.' He carries on pulverising some beetroot in a cocktail shaker.

'Can't we just have something else? I mean, have you got a vegetarian option?' Martin will hate it but it's better than nothing. 'We could go vegan for the day?' I offer. 'Or are your nuts ethically sourced and in short supply too?'

'Yeah, they are actually and we sold out of Nut Loaf at twelve thirty so . . .'

Shit.

Martin comes back from the loo. I shake my head at him. 'What?' he asks, looking cross already.

'Too late.'

'What? Let me talk to him!'

'It's no good, I've already tried. The kitchen is shut. Please don't complain. Let's just go somewhere else.'

'But everywhere will be closed! Honestly, time was you could get a pie and a pint in this place from a bloke who didn't even know what a scrunchie was. Come on, we're leaving.'

The kids troop out after us, not remotely bothered by any of it. They are so oblivious to their surroundings and the company they are in, they wouldn't know if we'd just been turned away from The Wimpey or The Wolseley.

'What now?' asks Martin crossly, like the whole situation is my fault. I snap.

'It wasn't me who wouldn't get up! It wasn't me wouldn't get in the car! It wasn't me that HAD to go to the tip this morning! It wasn't me driving too slowly in front and it wasn't me that DIDN'T ORDER ENOUGH ORGANIC FUCKING CORNFED FUCKING CHAKRA-CLEANSED CHICKEN!' There is the briefest silence.

Paddy snorts. Amelie punches him. Then Lorcan lets rip with a sonorous fart and they all three burst out laughing.

Even Martin starts to smile.

'Come on, love – let's go to the Drive-Thru McDonalds,' he says, putting a hand on my knee. 'We tried.'

There is an outbreak of cheering at the mention of McDonalds, and a brief calm descends while Martin orders McFlurries, burgers and Chicken Selects for all.

We sit in the car eating our food and despite the journey, despite the disappointment, despite the naff food, they are all happy. 'See? We've got the kids, we're all together, we've got food and a nice house to go back to! Who needs a poncy gastro pub anyway? Who needs anything more?'

Me, I think to myself, chewing on a lukewarm, floppy chip, I do.

Chapter Six

Mum? Are you there? I just saw a robin at the back window. Someone recently told me that robins are visitations from the dead. It had a big worm in its beak, but otherwise it kind of looked like you. It stared me down, the way you used to when you knew I was lying. I just wanted to say that I'm sorry. I'm sorry I didn't help out much around the house.

I remember you coming in from your cleaning job and making me feel how cold your hands were.

'It's bitter!' you'd say, pressing your fingers onto my warm cheek, and 'You couldn't do the washing-up, then? Too busy being warm, were you?'

I'm sorry I used to tut and moan about how you never made Dad or Aidan do anything. But Aidan was the golden boy, wasn't he? He got to lie in bed all day because 'He's a boy!' And boys can't be expected to sully their hands with housework. At the time I was so angry at the unfairness of it, I refused to do anything unless Aidan did too. Which, of course, he never did – if you've been handed a get-out-of-jail-free card on the grounds of gender you're not going to rip it up and say 'No, Mum, it's not fair that Ciara should be made to do the washing-up just because she's a girl! Hand me those Marigolds, I'm going in!' are you? All it meant for you was that instead of one entitled, bone idle, selfish child you had two. My emerging feminism didn't really help you much, did it? I suppose I saw you as the last vestige of the female serving class. It was your generation's lot to clean, tidy, cook, iron and make the beds. It was your era's remit, not mine. I was headed for bigger things. I wasn't going to get stuck in domestic slavery, laying my life down for some man and our ungrateful offspring.

Didn't really work out like that, did it? If ashes could laugh, you'd be guffawing now.

I hated the way you argued with me about sexual politics. You committed so many crimes against my belief system, especially when I went to university and came back radicalised. Here are a few of the things I remember you saying that made my head explode.

BLOG 9 – Things My Mum Said That Drove Me Mad That I'd Now Kill To Hear Again . . .

1. 'I used to *love* it when a man wolf-whistled me in the street!'(every time I complained about sexist treatment)
2. 'Martina Navratilova – that *lesbian*!' (*a propos* of nothing)
3. 'It's true that working mums are responsible for teenage alcoholism – I read it in the *Daily Mail*!' (the Bible according to you, Mum)
4. 'I was terrified the first time a black fella spoke to me in a bar!' (no excuse that you came from rural Ireland)
5. 'Trust no one. Look after Number One.' (every time I showed any interest in anything or anyone beyond our four walls)
6. 'Don't vote Labour – the Reds Under the Bed!' (you were so sure that Neil Kinnock was a Russian infiltrator)
7. 'Bloody work-shy immigrants, scrounging off the state!' (this despite the fact that you yourself came over on the boat train in 1948 and lived in a council house for years until your Messiah, Maggie Thatcher, let you and Dad buy it and fuck

the next generation in the process). We would argue every day, in short, furious bursts. It would always end the same way – me telling you that you knew nothing, and that you were a small-minded Irish bigot who shouldn't believe everything she read in the *Daily Fail*. You'd give as good as you got and it infuriated me that you wouldn't bow to my greater intelligence, my superior education and my gift for argument. You'd tell me I was brainwashed by the left-wing BBC. You didn't care that you were obviously wrong – they were your hard-won prejudices and you were damned if you were going to give them up easily. As I got older we came to a truce, which in actuality meant avoiding all subjects prone to provoking fights. As long as we did that, I adored you.

Did you know that?

I think you are the only fascist (albeit in a cardie and slippers) I ever loved.

So I'm sorry, Mum, for not doing the washing-up when you had been out cleaning other people's houses all day. I'm sorry for leaving the washing on the line when it rained. I'm sorry that I never found out how to work the iron. I'm sorry for patronising you and not listening when you had something to say, for always assuming you were going to say something vile. Because actually, now I can see what a fucking legend you were.

Chapter Seven

Martin asked tonight if I would like to go on a Clean Weekend with him, just the two of us.

'What do you mean, a "clean weekend"?' I asked.

'No point asking you to go on a dirty weekend, is there? You're about as sexual as a neutered panda!' He thought this remark very droll, and chuckled to himself at his own brilliance. Wanker. I don't want to go on a clean weekend with him. It will involve listening to him bore on about sport or how expensive everything is. And what would the kids do? He thinks they're old enough to look after themselves for a couple of nights. They're not. They're idiots.

The boys are in trouble at school. Again. I am called in by their form teacher Mrs Tanner, a blonde smuggins in a Hobbs suit with a neat line in inspirational personal anecdotes. I dread the meetings with Mrs Tanner. I wasn't exactly a model pupil at school but I still feel nervous around authority figures, still have the instinct to bow and scrape, concur, defer and generally ingratiate myself. It's easier if you let them win. I think Mrs Tanner means well, but whether it's her decades at the hard coalface of mute indifference and obtuse teendom or whether it's because she is not interested, she has no capacity to *listen*. I have tried on several occasions to tell her my theory that the boys would be much better with a few crumbs of praise now and then rather than the constant barrage of detentions and red comments they bring home daily. She won't let me finish a sentence. She doesn't even seem to hear me start one.

BLOG 10 – School of Hard Knocks

The biggest shock for me in this whole parenting experience has been the education system. History books show blank-faced Victorian children staring dispassionately ahead while a murder-ous-looking hangman in a suit barks at them, their freezing skel-etal hands clutching at stumps of chalk hovering over tiny slates. Not much has changed, except now the kids use pens and the teachers aren't allowed to beat the shit out of them any more.

When you lead your beloved child by the hand on that first day of school you have no idea that you are effectively handing them over to the state for fifteen years. They are no longer your kids. They belong to 'literacy', to uniforms, to assembly, to time-tables, break times, lunchtimes, reports, tests, rigid rules about who gets to sit down where and when. They are prey to bullying, being ignored, being slighted by teachers, being disbelieved if they are sick, being told that the bell is not for them but for the teacher, being made to read things out in front of the whole school, being made to study things they hate and not being allowed to do the things they love. They won't get picked, included, celebrated. If they don't fit the narrow remit of what a good pupil is, they will be left to tread water and they will be told they are failures-in-waiting.

Schools have come on so much in the last hundred years – pupils use computers, teachers run classes via PowerPoint and school canteens no longer serve pink custard. But in many ways they are still the draconian sausage factories of old.

My boys don't fit. Going to school every day, for them, is an exercise in having their sense of self slowly chipped away. They started school whole, but in the past ten years they have been chiselled into smaller, cowed versions of themselves. Sometimes huge chunks come flying off, sometimes tiny barely perceivable chips. They don't get picked to play football for the school because, even though they are good, they fight too much. Chunk. They get mistaken for each other and kicked on the bus. Chip. They get made to pick up rubbish all lunchtime because they briefly danced in Maths. Chip. Chip. Chip.

The state owns your kids. You're not even allowed into the school once they get to secondary. You have to make an appointment. Gone are the days you could pop in to nursery or reception and have a look at their colouring-in. No one tells you about how many chicks have hatched when you pick them up at 3.30, or how beautifully they sat on the carpet at story time. I'm forever having to nip up to the school during the week with forgotten PE kit, homework, lunches, where I'm then made to feel like a disgruntled American teenager tooled up for a shoot-out rather than a weary middle-aged woman with a ham sandwich and a yogurt drink in a Minecraft lunch box. The atmosphere is punitive, forbidding, institutional. So going into the boys' school feels like a parole hearing every time. Even though I know it's largely their own fault for being lazy, disruptive little shits, it's so dispiriting to be told that by another grown-up – especially one as sanctimonious as Mrs Tanner.

Mrs Tanner is on fire today as I sit opposite her in her spartan, freezing office, the boys on either side of me, slumped in their chairs like the most unwilling henchmen in the world.

'Now, Mrs Woods . . . it's L***** and . . . P******, that's right, isn't it?' smiles Mrs T, settling into her swivel chair.

'L and P . . . yes, so I wanted to—'

'Yes, well I've had a word with their Head of Year, Miss

Hertford, and she tells me that both boys were implicated in the altercation in the playground today.'

'Yes, well L said—'

'According to the witness statements we have taken, P pushed a boy, who then pulled L on top of him and all three boys started to fight.'

'L said the boy was calling them gay—'

'Miss Hertford has put them all on report. You will need to sign their sheets every evening so that we're all on the same page. OK? Now, I've had a word with the boys personally. It seems they fight a lot at home, and I just wanted you to know that I had two brothers growing up . . .'

Here we go. I get ready to do my grateful/inspired face.

'. . . and although we fought from time to time, as we got older we came to realise that we would always be each other's best friends. In fact, we recently all went on a mini-break to Bournemouth! Families are forever. As I said to P and L: Boys, one day you will be your brother's closest pal. Perhaps you should start now? You know, you are very lucky to have each other. We have a Chess Club after school – and being twins, you have a ready-made opponent on call twenty-four hours a day! Why don't you give it a try? I'll see you there, boys. It could be the making of you. A little bit of effort and you could be representing the school! We have a half-term Chess Camp planned!'

Waves of panic roll off both boys. Their necks have gone bright red. They would rather be shot with shit than play chess, especially against each other. I haven't seen them this scared since I stood over their PS4 remote controls with a hammer. Perhaps Mrs Tanner is a genius after all.

'Don't give up, Mrs Woods. They will get there, and with a

little bit of application . . .' She goes on about discipline and social media and how these years are so important, but I zone out. I notice one of her carefully painted nails is chipped. A couple of minutes pass. She's still talking.

'Mrs Tanner! For God's sake, let's forget all this dreary bullshit and bugger off to the pub to get pissed!'

OK, so I don't actually say that. But even if I did it wouldn't matter because she wouldn't hear me.

We slope out of the door, the boys shuffling their massive feet and dragging their school bags behind them. Why do I feel like it's me who has been judged and punished? In many ways it is. It's me that's going to have to sign the bloody forms every night. Me who's had to endure the subliminal negative judgement on my parenting skills. Me who will have to – yet again – have the debate about how 'gay' is not, should not, be seen as an insult. The boys are constantly accused of being 'gay with each other' in that twisted teen logic that goes 'two boys look the same, share a room = GAY!'

But I can't tell Mrs Tanner that, because 'bullying does not exist in the school'.

Yes, it does, Mrs Tanner. It's as inevitable as gravity where more than one child is present. Denying it doesn't make it stop. I should know – I have three teenagers at home who are experts in it.

Except there it's me who's the victim.

Chapter Eight

The boys have temporarily gone sullen and quiet. This happens in waves. There will be a few weeks, months even, of peace, relative calm and even some compliance, then it's as if a huge testosterone tsunami comes crashing through the house and all hell breaks loose again. I've learnt not to question the quiet times. I try to just enjoy them. This past week they have hardly fought, they have done their homework and spent evenings in their room doing, well, doing I don't know what but as long as they are not eating all the cereal and randomly shouting 'PENIS' I don't really care what they are doing. They come down for dinner when Martin gets home but there is no bickering – they just eat and go. Our downstairs has turned into a dull diner, a soup kitchen for the die-hard teenage zombies to refuel in. After a day at home pretty much on my own, come 7 p.m. I find myself once again alone in the kitchen with just the dishes and the dog for company – and even the dog looks like she'd rather be anywhere else than sat next to me. My days are bookended by a flurry of activity in the kitchen followed by a ghostly silence. Just now I realised I'd been staring at the grouting for five minutes, idly wondering whether it would be better to try and bleach it or start all over again.

God, I'm bored.

Maybe I should go upstairs and try to talk to the boys . . . I mean, not at the same time, I'm not suicidal. No one survives a conversation with BOTH of them in the room. Paddy comes down for a gallon of milk so I take the opportunity.

I creep upstairs and tap lightly on their bedroom door. Lorcan doesn't hear me because he is always plugged in to some kind of device. I go in and find him lying face down on the bed. 'Are you OK?' I ask.

'What?' he snarls.

'Is there something wrong?'

'No. Go away.'

'Are you sure?'

'Yes. You wouldn't understand.'

'Try me,' I say, secretly delighted with this inroad. Perhaps he's fallen in love? Perhaps he is becoming moody and existential? Perhaps he has finally developed – gulp – a soul?

He rolls over and eyes me angrily.

'Paddy is such a fucking useless spaz! He just ripped my phone charger out of the wall and now it's bust. All because this broadband is shit! I've been asking for weeks for an ethernet cable! Weeks! My game is literally UNPLAYABLE with the stupid wifi in this house!'

'Lorcan, calm down and stop using that disgusting language!'

'See? I told you you wouldn't understand!'

He rolls back over as Paddy walks in with a dozen biscuits stuffed in each pocket. Paddy smirks. Any time one can trigger the other is a massive victory.

'Paddy, don't pull cables by the lead, please, and stop stealing biscuits after dinner.'

'Was that dinner? That was disgusting!' he laughs.

'That's not very nice!' I say, feeling instantly outnumbered as Lorcan turns back to join in the fun, the boys now united in their attack.

'Yeah, that was like a snack for the dog!' laughs Lorcan.

'That was like the snack that the dog puked up!' offers Paddy helpfully.

'That was like the snack for the dog, that the dog puked up then ate again!'

'That was like the snack for the dog that the dog puked up, ate again and then shat out all over our dinner plates!'

'ALL RIGHT THAT'S ENOUGH!' I say, my face flushing with rage. 'I spent two hours on that stew – TWO HOURS OF MY LIFE—'

'Wasted your time there, Mum,' laughs Paddy.

'ENOUGH! How dare you be so rude? How dare you be so ungrateful and hurtful and horrible! I've had enough of you two constantly being cheeky, argumentative and nasty. I would never have DARED speak to my mum like that, and if Grandma was here she'd be ashamed of you!'

'She's not though, is she?' says Lorcan, looking me right in the eye for maximum impact.

My hand flies out before I even know it. There is a sharp slap, and the only way I know it was me that struck him is the tingling in my fingers. Lorcan's hand is cradling his cheek but his eyes burn into mine.

'You made me do that!' I shout, starting to cry.

'Good one, Mum. Well done,' he says, his bottom lip quivering despite his bravado.

Paddy lets out a nervous snigger as I stumble out slamming the door behind me.

'Jesus Christ, Madre, just chill, OK?' says Amelie, emerging from her lair.

Martin is coming up the stairs as I run down them.

'What's going on?' he thunders when he sees how upset I am. 'I'm trying to watch the Channel 4 news!'

I push past him, grab my coat and fly out of the front door.

Fuck them. Fuck the lot of them. Ungrateful, privileged, selfish bastards. My heart is pounding in my chest and my cheeks are wet with furious tears. I am walking, walking, walking and I don't even know where. I need to keep putting space between myself and them. I walk for twenty minutes, half an hour, through suburban streets, past drawn curtains behind which other, nicer families are no doubt huddled around Scrabble boards and educational foreign films, chatting and laughing together.

I storm across the park, the sickly yellow street lamps casting streaks of vomity light across the deserted lawns. Time was this park was a safe haven, a place for the kids to let off steam while I chatted with other mums, all of us lying about how delightful our children were. Not any more. I walk in circles around the streets until my feet start to hurt. I find myself outside the local Wetherspoons pub. I don't think I've ever been in it, in the fourteen years we've lived up the road. But now I'm inside, jostling shoulders with elderly high-functioning alcoholics and students ordering Jägerbombs on a week night.

'Prosecco, please,' I say to the young barman, my voice brittle and cracked.

'Glass or bottle? The glass is four pounds but we've got a special on the bottle—'

'Bottle please,' I say.

'How many glasses?'

'Just one.'

I find a table in the corner. It's filthy and covered with mostly empty pint glasses. Dead soldiers, Dad would have called them. I know how they feel. I pour myself a glass of Prosecco and down it in one. It's cheap, acidic, but it feels medicinal. This place is revolting but at least it's not home. These people are drunk and boorish but at least they are not my family. I pour another glass and take my phone out of my pocket. Time to vent.

BLOG 11 – Is It Just Me or Is Everything Shit?

I just walked out. Not that anyone will notice. I've done it before. I once left halfway through making Sunday lunch. Chicken in the oven, carrots and cabbage in the steamer. Gravy on the go. Left the lot and went into town on the bus. Fuck them. I spent seven hours walking around, browsing in shops, walking in and out of galleries without really looking, had a nice afternoon tea in a hotel. Eventually calmed down and went home early evening. The kids were all upstairs and Martin was watching the cricket.

'Better?' he asked as I stood at the living-room door.

'Not really.'

'Oh well. Tomorrow is another day. There's some chicken left – not much, the boys had most of it. You might have to put it in the microwave.'

And he went back to watching the cricket. Just like that. Sometimes I think I'd have to asphyxiate and drop dead in a pool of my own vomit in the hallway before anyone would notice anything was wrong. Even then they'd probably just step over me, moaning about how inconvenient it was.

I seriously do not know why anyone has children. When I see young women in shops cooing over baby clothes I want to run up to them and scream 'Don't do it! DON'T DO IT! Save yourself! Save yourself a lifetime of heartache and pain! Save yourself thousands of pounds! Don't bother with kids – they're horrible! If you want to feel shit for the rest of your life, cut out the middle man and just stare at yourself in the mirror every day, repeating the following phrase – "You don't matter, you don't matter, YOU DON'T MATTER!"'

I don't do it, of course. No one would listen to me then either. People don't want to know. All those poor souls in fertility clinics spending thousands on trying to conceive – they think that a baby is the only way they will ever feel happy. Wrong. The minute you give birth is more or less the end of your life. I never even wanted kids. What a joke I ended up with three. Ha fucking ha. First one – whoops, accident. Went to the abortion clinic but the old Catholic guilt made me bottle it and I ended up having her. Then a year later fell prey to the old lie 'You can't get pregnant while you're breastfeeding'. WRONG. Turns out you can – and with twins! Isn't that hilarious? I went from a thirty-five-year-old carefree career girl – well, I had a job I liked anyway – moderately happily married to a nice, stable and kind man, to the harassed mother of three kids under two. I literally felt like I vanished overnight. At the doctor's, in playgroups, in the supermarket I wasn't Ciara any more I was 'Mummy'. 'Have you got baby's medical book, Mummy?' 'Mummy, can you help hand out the orange squash and biscuits, please?' 'Are you helping Mummy with the shopping?' It's like your life before babies is written up on a huge whiteboard in non-permanent marker pen, then the minute the kids arrive someone turns up with a big cloth and wipes you away, as if all that was there was just a plan, a rough brainstorm of an idea that would never reach fruition – you.

And him? Who even IS he? I wish there was an ageing app that could predict more than receding hair and wrinkles. I wish you could know in advance if they will revert to type, become their fathers, start snoring, falling asleep in front of the telly, not wanting to go out EVER, suddenly become xenophobic and reactionary. When we met, M and me were pretty much on the same page politically – or so I thought. I remember the precise moment I found out he leant slightly more to the right than I had fondly imagined. We'd just been away for a dirty weekend in Barcelona (even typing that makes me cringe – what happened to sex?). We were at the baggage carousel and he let slip he voted for Maggie Thatcher when he was young. His first vote. 1987. 'Shit. Too late now, I love the idiot,' I remember thinking. I don't know why I didn't run – it had always been a deal-breaker for me if someone was a stealth Tory. I think I assumed I could win him round. I think I even thought he was a deluded pro-feminist who had only voted for her because she was a woman. I made excuses for him. And now look at me. Sitting in a pub on my own with an empty bottle of cheap Prosecco and a family at home who see me as, at best, a necessary irritation and at worst the Death Star in elasticated trousers.

God, it feels good to get all this off my chest. I've never told anyone about going to the abortion clinic. I have never regretted having the kids but at the time I was terrified. I panicked. I never planned to be a mum. I actually thought I was infertile. Martin wanted the baby and tried to reassure me by saying how it didn't mean the end of us as people, as a couple. He said we'd still get to be us and have lives. He said he'd help, he'd earn enough money for both of us, I could always go back to work later. I bought it. I thought we'd live the dream despite the baby. Somehow it never happened and we slipped into the norm.

For a while I actually thought it was kind of cool to be 'normal'. Different. And now here I am – drunk alone and blogging in a bar. Maybe one day I'll print it up and stick it into a scrapbook for my dotage. When I'm dead and gone they'll find it AND THAT WILL SHOW THEM! Yes, this is an excellent idea. But I seem to have run out of Prosecco. It's so cheap it's not really worth buying a glass. Fuck it. I'll get another bottle and I'll write some more. My eyes are a bit blurry and the screen keeps coming in and out of focus but I need to get this out.

Maybe I won't go back this time. There's a Travelodge a couple of miles away. I could go there. I could stay up all night watching telly, drinking and dancing on my own. I'm not allowed to dance at home. Once I tried to make A watch me dance for a whole record in exchange for £20. Even for £20 she couldn't do it. But if Mummy dances in the middle of a hotel room and no one is there to tell her she's humiliating them, did she really dance? No one would ever know. No one would ever care. Yes, that's the problem. Even if I did stay out all night, I doubt they'd notice. Well, they might notice but only in the way that you notice when someone has moved the bread bin – you go to make some toast, but the bread's not there, so you have cereal instead and think no more of it. So they would notice, but they'd register it like 'Oh the school secretary has had her hair cut . . .' and then carry on with their day. And anyway, who cares? Why can't I be rash and carefree and do what I want for a change? I'm no fun any more.

I'm angry and sad and grumpy and just sort of not really there. I hate my life.

I hate my kids.

And my husband makes me feel sick.

No wonder I've turned into a screaming violent banshee. No wonder. The only amazing thing is I lasted this long.

Fuck 'em.

Chapter Nine

Urgh. Stop that noise. There's a horrible beeping noise and a laser piercing my eyes and I think a badger shat in my mouth. I must be in some sort of torture chamber. How did I get here? I remember the pub. I remember the second bottle of Prosecco. I remember poncing a cigarette off a boy called Conor. He told me all about his physics degree and how he hates it. I think I was wise and reassuring. I remember he told me I was hot for an old lady. I remember laughing. Hang on – how reassuring was I? Oh God. Where am I? I didn't, did I? I daren't open my eyes. Slowly I reach out across the bed but my hand finds nothing – just a cool empty pillow. Phew. I pull the duvet over my head while I pluck up the courage to open my eyes.

'Tea?' says a disembodied voice somewhere beyond the covers. Oh God. Who is that? It's not Martin.

Fuck.

It's not Martin.

'Mum? Tea?'

I peer out from my pit and wait for the figure to come into focus.

Lorcan is standing at the foot of my bed.

It's Lorcan. I'm home. I came home.

Oh thank God. I haven't been as pleased to see him since we lost him in that Portuguese supermarket.

'Yes please, darling. That would be lovely.'

My voice is thick with alcohol and fags but I try to sound normal.

'Mum – I'm sorry about what I said last night. I was angry about the wi-fi and I didn't mean to be mean. Sorry.'

He comes to the side of the bed and gives me an awkward hug. He's always been the most difficult but also the more emotionally articulate and the first to try to make up. I hug him back, trying not to gag on the smell of his cheap hair gel. He's ready for school already.

'Did you get yourselves up?'

'Yeah, Dad gave us a shout – he said you weren't well so we had to get ourselves breakfast and that. What's wrong?'

'Oh just a bit of a tummy bug, I think,' I lie, inwardly heaving at the rancid taste in my mouth.

'Why don't you have scrambled egg – that's good for an upset stomach, right?'

At the mention of egg a switch is flicked and I lurch from the bed, pushing past my son and only just make it to the loo in time. About a litre of clear, hot vomit crashes into the toilet.

Oh God. It's been years since I've been sick. I know that once I start I find it very hard to stop. I slump back against the bathroom window, sweat pouring from my forehead, and enjoy momentary peace on the cool floor before the second wave of nausea hits. I hurl again in violent spasms of flat Prosecco. I rest my head on the toilet seat, arms cradling the base like it's my lifeboat.

'Mum?' says Lorcan tentatively from the door.

Bless him. I feel so guilty now. He cares. He does care really. He's just a kid. I'm supposed to be the adult here, and which one of us was is it that struck out, flounced off and got pissed?

'Yes, darling?' I say, trying to sound fine.

'So about that ethernet cable . . .?'

Jesus.

'Not now, Lorcan, OK?' I say, trying to stop the room from spinning.

'Can we talk about it later?'

'Yes, just go to school!'

I sit for a few minutes hating myself before I dare to stand up and stagger back to bed. I hear Martin coming up the stairs and pull the duvet over my head again.

'Good morning!' he says at deliberately ear-splitting volume. 'I've brought you a pint of water and some painkillers.'

'Thank you. I think I've got some kind of a bug . . .'

'Ah yes, the old Wine Flu – terrible, terrible. Poor you!' he laughs, opening the curtains.

'No! Don't – please don't open the curtains!'

'You'll feel better soon. Drink the water, close your eyes. I'm going to open a window – it smells like the barmaid's apron in here.'

'Why are you presuming I was drunk?! I really don't think I'm very well.'

Martin laughs.

'How do I know you were drunk? Because you stumbled in at eleven p.m. when I'd been asleep for half an hour and started ranting on about physics. You really didn't make any sense at all.'

'Oh.'

Shit. Busted. Oh fuck it, he's not my dad. Even though it feels like it.

'Well, if I was so drunk how come I managed to get undressed?'

'Because I helped you. You asked me to undress you, so I did.'

Martin is smiling in a slightly creepy way.

We didn't, did we?

'And then you asked me to put you in your pyjamas – so I did.' I'm dimly aware of feeling relieved.

'. . . after you had your wicked way with me.'

Oh God, we did. I wrack my brains for any memory of a sexual encounter but I can't conjure up a single one, not even a snapshot.

'God, I must have been drunk.'

'Thanks!'

Martin's post-sex glow is dimmed slightly by my accidental insult but I can tell he is pleased to have finally got his end away.

What a horrible expression that is, but I have to admit that after twenty years it feels like just that. Every now and again a married man has to 'get his end away', a bit like a man has to steam clean his car engine or pluck his nasal hairs. I feel vaguely repulsed at the image of myself drunk and naked in front of Martin, asking him to shag me. It must be at least six months since we last had sex. It's not something we talk about, and sometimes we do it more, but if I'm honest I only concur out of a sense of moral compulsion. The menopause has given me many things – permanently soggy armpits, a bright red face, a dry vagina, a moustache and psychopathic tendencies – but it has completely taken away any libido I ever had. A French friend once told me, 'You 'ave to make love wis your 'usband because if you don't, someone else will!'

'Crack on, love,' I remember thinking, 'I'm done.'

Martin pats me on the head and leaves for work. Why doesn't he berate me? Why doesn't he demand to know where I was, who I was drinking with, what I mean by storming out of the house on a school night and crashing back in again blind drunk? And while we're at it, why doesn't he ask me why we don't have a proper, regular, sober sex life? Maybe he just doesn't care. These questions are too big for me right now though – I have a hangover to be getting on with. I sink down into the bed and fall asleep.

I wake some time later feeling much better. The painkillers have kicked in and the water has at least rehydrated my sandpaper mouth. I pick up my phone to see what time it is – 10.30 a.m. I've slept for over two hours. Unheard of. I start to scroll through my social media – the usual FaceBoasts and Insta-lies. Everyone else seems to be so pleased with themselves and their lives. Their kids do nothing but achieve things, win things, pass tests, cook amazing surprise meals for them, pose for family photos and generally enrich their lives. Who are these mums, and do they ever find themselves crying on the floor thinking 'Where the hell did I go wrong?'

I check my emails. I don't know why I bother. Since I stopped working – almost two decades ago now – I don't ever get anything interesting, just endless adverts for bathroom sales since we had ours done last year (how many new bathrooms can one person need?). There are the usual 'MUST HURRY' offers on shower cubicles and vanity sinks, plus an interesting proposition from a man I've never met called Subhendu Jyoti Pal who seems to think I might be able to help him out of a sticky situation in Mexico. I scroll down and stop at an email from someone calling themselves PollyPutTheKettleOn. The subject line says 'LOL!' – another phishing scam?

I open the email.

'OMG you make me crack up! Your kids! All that stuff about the boyfriend! Your kids sound just like mine. Keep on keeping on! Thanks for sharing!'

I'm confused. What? Who is she and what is she talking about?

Underneath her email is another from someone called BellaSignora who writes

'You are doing a great job. Don't let the bastards grind you down!'

A third message from FishFingersMum reads

'Why do we do it?! I'm sorry they were so mean to you – but it makes me feel a bit more normal LOL! Glad you walked out!'

What? I turn red. I feel like I've been spied on. Who has been following me? Who has found my laptop? Who are these people and how do they know about my life?

Fingers fumbling and hands shaking, I log on to my Blog site. There are all the posts, all ten of them, dating back two months now, all still lined up anonymously one under the other. Except.

Except.

Oh God.

Next to each one is the killer word.

'Published.'

At 22.32, after reading through all my posts and chuckling away to myself in the pub, instead of pressing 'Close' I hit 'Publish' and for the past twelve hours the entire world has had access to my rantings and indiscreet ramblings about my entire family. I'm in a blind panic. I try to think who I have slandered, slagged off and shamed. Shit. Shit. The kids. Martin. Debbie Downer. The school – THE SCHOOL! Most of the mums I know are at least implicated.

I've dropped a bomb in the middle of my life with one tiny slip of a drunken finger. How can I have been so stupid? At the back of my mind I dimly recall boasting to Conor about my blog. He wanted to read it but I wouldn't let him. I wouldn't let a stoned nineteen-year-old nobody read it but instead I went and published it to the world! This is terrible. They are going to kill me. I'm dead. Amelie will never speak to me again, the boys will be expelled and Martin will probably divorce me. He'll get the house because the kids won't want to be with me and I'll have to live in a hostel because even Debbie Downer, catastrophe tourist extraordinaire, won't let me sleep on her sofa.

Oh God. What have I done? This is the worst accident of my entire life. I slump back onto the pillow, my head reeling, my guilty heart pounding. I can delete the posts, but is it too late? I check the stats – thank God. Only seven views so far. Seven people have read it, and as far as I can tell I don't know any of them. How did they find me? Maybe the domain name 'Crap Mum' attracted them? All seven have read all ten of my blogs. Still, it's only seven people. Just seven people I've never even met. It's not gone viral or whatever it is they call it. It's statistically unlikely that anyone would know anyone mentioned in the blogs, and I was very careful not to actually name anyone outright. Maybe it's OK. I'll just delete the whole thing and forget about it.

And yet. And yet . . .

Below the last blog someone called CherryTomato has posted a comment.

'I rarely read blogs. I certainly never comment. But I read this through tears and just had to thank you for living it, writing about it & sharing it. Real, honest, fantastically written. You & your family are amazing. Every mum needs to read this. You should publish a book. To you & all the mums out there who are just doing their best to get to bedtime without going crazy, keep going, you are doing great xx'

My eyes fill with tears. I feel flushed with pride. Someone got it. Someone out there felt my pain, heard it, related to it and wants me to write more.

A warm glow spreads through my body and for the first time in months, despite the hangover, despite the worry that I might be caught out, I actually feel . . . happy. Seen. Heard. Valued. Maybe this could be good. Maybe I could do this. If I'm careful, if I can disguise things well enough, I could actually keep going. God knows it's helped me to feel more sane, and if it relieves the pressure, if it allows me an outlet (besides shopping and drinking wine at night) then that can only be a good thing, right?

I distantly remember a university module on Freud. Didn't he say there's no such thing as an accident? That we might be tempted to frame the bad things that happen in life – rear-ending the car in front because you were on your phone, burning your sofa because you fell asleep smoking, getting fired for being perpetually late – as 'accidents', when they are in fact unconscious acts of sabotage designed to reveal our true selves. These things are not accidents, but the results of reckless choices prompted by an unacknowledged desire to tear things down. The choice to be on the phone while driving is an act of latent aggression towards other road-users. The choice to smoke is to self-destruct in the name of pleasure. The choice to be consistently late is to flout authority and declare your time more important than theirs.

Was it an *accident* that my finger hit 'Publish' and not 'Close'? Was it an *accident* that I drank two bottles of Prosecco and got so hammered that I lost all sense of time and decorum? Was it an *accident* that I let rip into the ether and admitted publicly that I am deeply fucking unhappy? No. Perhaps I was actually acting out from a very sad and lonely place, but the amazing thing is that by saying the unsayable – 'sometimes I hate my life and my kids and my husband and maybe this whole set-up is a crock of shit' – I have released something not only in myself but also in at least seven other people. I feel giddy, but unlike last night's cheap fizz this giddiness isn't too much booze.

I'm going to do it.

I'm going to carry on. If people want to read what I have to say, if they can relate to what I'm going through then good. Maybe there's a whole army of us out there – crawling through these parenting teen years in a depressed and desperate stupor, unaware that as we drag our tired and defeated carcasses along the hard shoulder of the GCSE years, we are not alone. Others are just ahead, elbows grazed, knees bloodied, and many are coming behind us, but if we all keep on moving forwards, nodding to each other, offering a hand when it's needed, looking each other in the eye as we pass, we might just make it to the services in one piece. There we will rest, refuel and ready ourselves for the next part of the journey.

I always get philosophical when I'm hungover. It's when I have my best ideas. I'm going to reply to the comments. I'm going to write another post. Maybe CherryTomato is right – maybe I *will* write a book. Why not? What's the worst that could happen?

Chapter Ten

Mum – I'm going to have to take your clothes to the charity shop soon. They're sitting in the garage in seven black bin-bags at the moment. All your lovely cashmere cardigans, woollen skirts and polished shoes. Your silk scarves, jewellery and accessories are in a cardboard box on top of the chest freezer. It took me six months to pluck up the courage to open your wardrobes after you died. I couldn't face it because no matter how ill you got, no matter how tired, thin and weak you were, you always insisted on looking smart.

You told me once that even when you were growing up poor and often hungry, you and your four sisters had one good dress you would wear in strict rotation if there was a dance somewhere. You always loved your clothes. Towards the end it was mostly leggings and nice T-shirts, but always with jewellery, and if we were going to the hospital, a nice scarf because you hated how scrawny your neck had become.

You never understood why I didn't really care what I looked like when the kids were small. Most days it was a major achievement to get my teeth brushed and a bra on. You'd never actually say anything, but I could see you giving my Weetabix-smeared sweatshirts the once-over, and I clocked you eyeing up my roots. It annoyed me. I felt judged in a competition I didn't have any interest in entering. Appearances were important to your generation though, weren't they? It would have been the end of your world if someone had said you looked poor, sloppy, not put together. To see me not coping was a reflection on you, wasn't it? When the kids were little I just couldn't be bothered with myself along with everything else I had to do. Now, when I do have the time, that lack of effort has become so deeply ingrained I find it hard to care. I have the mental space and the money to keep up appearances, but I can't be arsed. Who's going to look at me anyway? I think most women become transparent when they turn fifty – not metaphorically, I mean almost see-through. You would never have let that happen, Mum. You insisted on being seen right until the end, and now all of your armour, your defence against other people's opinions of you, is creased and slowly going mouldy in a dark corner of a garage alongside the rusty garden tools and broken furniture.

I don't know what I'm waiting for. It seems too final, giving your things away, which I know sounds ridiculous – you're not going to come back and ask where your lilac dressing gown with the pompoms is, are you, Mum? I buried my face in that dressing gown and wept the day we finally emptied your cupboards. I'd always scoffed at that sort of thing in movies – I'd never seen anyone sniff the clothing of the dead in real life – but it was so comforting to smell your perfume, your Yardley talc, and to find your tissues and mints still in the pockets.

I can't let them go yet. I will. Soon. But not yet. I still need you around, Mum. I need someone on my side.

Chapter Eleven

My brother has been on the phone. He calls once every six months or so, normally when he's doing something really flashy with his young American wife, Kirsty: scuba diving in the West Indies, skiing in Canada or driving an expensive RV around Yellowstone looking for bears. He doesn't have kids, of course, or he wouldn't be able to take such exciting vacations – he'd be in some miserable faux fun village made of plywood trying to cajole them into joining the Krazy Kids Klub so that he could collapse and get pissed by a freezing pool. He left his first wife, Julie, after ten years because they 'didn't want the same things'– Julie didn't want to run away with a young American woman, grow a bad beard and have her chest waxed and he did. He married Kirsty a few years back after falling in love with America. She's nice but vacuous and says 'Awesome' and 'Have a good one!' with absolutely no irony. She's also about twelve. He doesn't care that he's a middle-aged cliché – divorced, childless, flash car, trophy wife – because he says he's happy. Bastard.

Of course he's happy. He doesn't have to think about anyone but himself. He doesn't have to match up four hundred pairs of socks, bribe teenagers to write shit poems for their English homework or try to remember where he left his supermarket loyalty card because there's £6 off if you spend more than £60. He's minted as well as happy.

What an utter, utter bastard.

He called last night because he wants to know when I am planning on finally releasing Mum's ashes.

BLOG 12 – Bros

Where is it written that men get to body-swerve the care of their elderly parents? My brother is a good guy, really, despite the top of the range car, the condo in Florida and the golf, but when it came to the crunch with our parents he very discreetly did a runner. His excuse was he had to 'get away' to 'clear his head' after a messy divorce (messy because he'd been making a mess with a young American hotty he met at work), so it landed in my lap. Nobody questioned it, nobody asked where he was when there were endless appointments to drive them to, surgeries to be survived, reassurances to be given, shopping to be got in, meals to be cooked, frozen, reheated then finally dumped into the bin, Do Not Resuscitate agreements to be quietly agreed upon in halting consultations with tired doctors.

The load – terrible word to use to describe your father but there we are – lightened a bit when our dad died suddenly eight years ago but, of course, then Mum became even more frail. She also became lonely and kind of needy in a way that really got on my tits, if I'm honest. She would invent wild goose chases for me to go on in order to fulfil some whim or other she'd had while lying in a hot, dull ward for weeks at a time.

I would always ask her if she needed anything – tissues? Sweets? Magazines? Incontinence pads? She'd shake her head, think for a few seconds and then suddenly say:

'I know what you can do for me. I've run out of that White Musk perfume I like – can you get me some?'

I mean . . . why anyone would insist on a particular perfume when they are in hospital and the only place they are likely to be going is to and from the loo (and latterly not even there) was absolutely mystifying to me. It was also annoying because she always seemed to choose something that was difficult to get – a line that had just been discontinued, slippers that no one sells any more, a packet of mints only available in County Sligo between 10 and 2 on a week day.

Of course, I would move hell and high water to get these things for her. Her world had shrunk so much I felt it was the least she deserved, but boy did it irk at the time. Like the few hours a day I had child free were being gobbled up by the demands of an elderly baby with ever more spurious claims on my time. She didn't mean to be demanding – I think she thought I needed to be useful to her – but still, it was hard not to feel a bit irritated sometimes. Now, of course, I'd walk a thousand miles to fetch her the perfect ripe apricot, even if it sat (like most of them did) untouched and rotting by her bedside. That White Musk perfume, sourced and fetched in a two-hour round trip to a hell-ish shopping centre during rush hour, remained unopened for months. It was one of the last things I threw into the bin-bags after she died.

'Are you her daughter?' the nurses would ask. They never asked if she had any other children, but she would brag about him anyway. 'My son lives in America!' she'd tell them, as if living in America was in itself an achievement. But it was me who showed up day in, day out and it was quietly understood that that was the way things were. I'd sit by her bed while she dozed and I'd stare at all the other middle-aged women sat by identical beds, their offerings of homemade cakes, new nighties and women's magazines left idling in their bags. Every so often my brother would video-call me and I'd have to hold the phone up so that my mum could see him. Her face would break into the most ecstatic smile, like she was watching him on a moon landing. I couldn't help but feel even more irritated – there I was juggling kids, a home, my own fractious menopause-related health issues and my mum's chronic illness, and all he had to do was call once in a while and he was a fucking saint. Talk about the Prodigal Son.

How do brothers get away with it?

Now that she is gone he is, of course, the executor of the will – because he's a boy, and boys deal with serious things like probate, solicitors, inheritance and money. I get the shitty jobs like arguing with the Department of Work and Pensions about a £27.40 overpayment because she died in the middle of the week, clearing the house and disposing of the hundreds of medications she stockpiled as she grew more confused, or that the pharmacy continued to send even though she was in hospital for long spells.

And he gets to call the shots about what happens with Mum's remains. I know this sounds weird but Mum is staying with me at the moment. She's in a plastic urn in the wardrobe. It's quiet and warm in there, and she always liked dark places. She had some quite specific requests about what should happen with her ashes. Having never been to America, despite a desperate longing to go to the top of the Empire State Building, she wished to have her ashes thrown off the top of it – she had been obsessed with Fay Wray and *King Kong* ever since she saw it as a child on her first ever cinema trip. She told the funeral directors quite pointedly at the time of Dad's death what she wanted to happen. She told me she knew it would be me doing it because 'Aidan is so busy . . .' and that she would leave a thousand pounds in her handbag to pay for the trip. Sure enough, when I retrieved her handbag from her wardrobe the day after she died, there it was – a brown envelope stuffed with twenty-pound notes.

It's been almost a year and I still haven't managed to do it. Several times I've had the opportunity but I can't face it yet. Most people would probably relish the idea of a fully paid jaunt to New York, but then most people wouldn't have a jar full of cremains as their hand luggage. Imagine going on a mini-break knowing that when you came home you were going to be leaving your mum there – forever. Lost luggage. Excess baggage. I just can't do it. Not yet. Of course, the brother doesn't get that – to him it's simply another administrative task to be undertaken, a box to be ticked in a long list of executor duties.

This is how our conversation went last night:

BROTHER: Hi, Ciara – how's it going?

ME: Aidan! Wow! You're still alive!

BROTHER: Yeah, I know, it's been a long time. I called you at Christmas, didn't I?

ME: You left a voicemail, yeah.

BROTHER: Sure. So, I'm sorry I haven't been able to find a window to join you in NYC yet. We had the snowboarding thing and then I had a heap of problems with our garbage disposal – we think a racoon died in the vent, you know, then it was just really hot and I couldn't think straight because the AC broke down—

ME: Nightmare.

BROTHER: Yeah, right? (Not only does he speak with an irritating transatlantic twang and say things like 'garbage' and 'AC' but he also has had his British sarcasm sensor removed. Ugh.) So listen, have you made any plans yet?

ME: Not yet.

BROTHER: . . . OK . . . it's just, it's been nearly a year and . . . she did say . . . the guy at Robinsons remembers it too . . .

ME: I know. I am going to do it, but I was kind of hoping you would be there too. We did say we'd do it together.

BROTHER: Yes and I really am behind that as an idea, it's just finding—

ME: A window?

BROTHER: Yeah, exactly. Absolutely. So, we are going on a little cruise . . . let me see . . . in May, so that's out, then I guess I'll have to do some work ha ha ha to pay for all these trips!

ME: How awful for you. How has the real-estate business been surviving in Honolulu without you?

BROTHER: Oh they get by, ha ha, I have some good guys in the office now.

ME: Phew.

BROTHER: So we're kind of looking at . . . October? Does that work for you?

ME: October?! That's six months away!

BROTHER: I can't go away during the summer season, Ciara, it's super busy.

ME: Well, if it's half term I won't be able to afford it, and the kids will need me so . . .

BROTHER: How are the kids?

ME: Wankers.

BROTHER: Great, great, listen I have to go – my mojito is melting and you know how I hate it slushy.

ME: Go, go, go!

OK, so he didn't actually say the last bit but you get the drift. I sense – call me old-fashioned – that he wants to leave it to me. Typical – he's not even going to be there but he still has to put the pressure on me to get things done as mum wanted. I don't really care about doing it on my own – I'm sure Aidan would just annoy me anyway. He'd probably slot Mum into a full sightseeing itinerary and tip her over the edge between Tiffany's and a horse-and-carriage ride around Central Park. I always assumed it would be me on my own. All I need to do now is make a date.

That's all. It's all in the 'all'.

Chapter Twelve

I have to admit, since I started actually publishing my blog I've felt different. A bit . . . I wouldn't say *happier* but sort of more . . . fulfilled. I never thought I'd become one of those sad people addicted to social media and affirmation from strangers but I can see now how it could happen. One minute you're ranting inside your own head, putting the world bang to rights, telling it like it is and sticking it to every bastard that wrongs you in the sad, lonely kingdom of self, the next you have a platform, a soap box and an audience of listeners who not only want to hear what you have to say, but leave lovely comments too. I mean, I'm hardly Zoella or one of the other 'YouTubers' my kids venerate but I'm in triple figures for followers – triple figures! One hundred and forty-three people now subscribe to my blog. I don't know any of them – at least I hope I don't. Some of them have written lovely things, some slightly odd things but no trolls so far. Things like:

'You rock. Keep up the fantabulus writing & most of all, keep
being an awsome Mum who they'd never swop for the world.
Doing a fabulus job xx'

I don't even mind that much when they can't spell, as long as they write nice things. In two short weeks I've become a Thumbs-Up Whore – I am living for the little icon of approval. I rely on praise from illiterate strangers. I totally get off on being told how great/funny/sweet I am. They're not all great, sometimes people can be annoying, taking my ideas, my spotlight and using them for their own grief, their own suffering. This one, posted under the last blog about Mum's ashes, really pissed me off:

'Just had to post here and say I am so sorry for your loss. I know what it feels like to have lost someone very close to you and not feel able to move on. Our beloved Millie, the most beautiful Border Terrier in the world, passed suddenly last year and we have not been able to get over it. We are hoping to get a puppy in the summer but to be honest I know it won't be the same. Millie was special. We keep her ashes on the mantelpiece – we even hung her stocking up next to her at Christmas – and I know it sounds silly but it feels nice to have her in the house. It's so quiet without her! She really did rule the roost.

So I can totally sympathise with you about your mum. Sending hugs n love xxx'

Really? Losing a dog is the same as losing your mum, is it? Talk about grief hijack. It's not the same at all. Did your dog give birth to you, teach you to walk, talk, do the *Daily Mail* crossword and knit a jumper? Did your dog provide you with a moral compass, an eye for a bargain and a neat way to dry woollens by rolling them in a towel before hanging them up? Did your dog make the best Christmas cake in the whole world from a recipe she'd copied out of a magazine in 1963, which was so good you can now never eat Christmas cake ever again because it would sicken you to the pit of your stomach to remember how good hers was by comparison? I thought not. You are a fool. Be gone.

I don't write that, of course. I reply nicely – I don't want to alienate any of my new fans. I've only just got them. I have to admit it is tempting to start exaggerating things a bit, upping the drama, just to make sure they stay with me. Click-bait head-lines. But seriously I don't think I need to. These people love me. Literally, they tell me they love me. And more importantly they *get* me.

'OMG you are a bloody saint! Isn't it just horrendous? Everyone says it gets easier as they get older. Well they are big fat liars. Probably the same people that tell you that labour pains feel just like a bad period – yes, in the same way as slamming your finger in the car door feels JUST LIKE being run over by a truck – a truck which then reverses back over you before running you over again FOR TWELVE HOURS. Please please please post more. I sometimes feel like I'm about to go mental, it really helps to know that it's not just me, and that other people's kids are a nightmare too!'

'I don't know how you do it. I've only got one and he's bad enough. I think you're doing a brilliant job, and those buggers should appreciate you more!'

'I am so sorry you're having a hard time missing your mum – it's an awful time of life isn't it? Trying to bring up kids when your own parents are sick and dying. Sending hugs and prayers and hope you get spoiled rotten on Mother's Day.'

Mother's Day? Oh yes, that annual humiliation. I have tried to ignore it so far this year because Mum always loved really senti-mental cards with swirly writing and bad verse, along with some chocolates the kids would eat and a lovely bouquet of flowers. Or two if Aidan remembered to send one (or, more frequently, order me to send one on his behalf). I've steeled myself as I've walked past the displays in the supermarket.

And now it's the Big Day – not that you'd know in this house. Martin has really pissed me off this morning. He's utterly useless. He snored all night, and every time I pushed him to try and turn him over he glared at me indignantly before rolling on his side and promptly falling asleep and snoring again. Then he got up this morning, which I assumed was to bring me tea in bed, and the next thing I knew I heard the front door go. 'Maybe he's gone to buy me flowers?' I thought, chuckling cynically, the triumph of hope over experience. An hour later he still hadn't returned and I had to make my own tea. The dishwasher was still full and the sink was overflowing. I messaged him.

'Where are you?!'

Half an hour later I got a reply.

'Golf. I did tell you.'

BLOG 13 – Mother's Fucking Day

I hate Mother's Day with a passion. It's the perfect example of what philosophers call 'repressive tolerance' – give them one day a year to feel 'pampered', 'special' and 'appreciated' then the next day stuff them back in their box and treat them like shit again. They won't mind! They've had a 'special day'. They'll be so grateful for the garage-bought flowers, the cheap chocolates or (God forbid) the 'spa day' they won't moan for the rest of the year and we can all get on with our lives knowing the mums have got our backs. Hurray!

Spa days. Over my dead body. I hate spas. Sitting around in damp towels looking at all your wobbly bits, trying not to look at other women's equally saggy boobs and inhaling twenty different flu viruses bobbing about in the menthol steam. M bought me a spa trip for Valentine's Day once – early on in our marriage, of course. It was horrendous. The jacuzzi was broken, the steam rooms smelt of cabbage, and the massage was done by a girl called Sooz who kept having to stop to scratch her eczema. I spent the whole time worrying that the kids were missing us (they were very small at the time) and thinking about how much laundry I could have folded while I was sat about doing nothing. By the end of the day I had a cracking headache and a new verucca. I told M never again.

This has since become a catch-all excuse for never taking me anywhere. If I ever complain that he is not romantic or that he takes me for granted he says 'I used to be but you soon bashed that out of me! Remember the spa?' Then he walks off with a smug expression on his face, as if to say 'That's told her!' Nowadays I'm lucky if I get a card on Mother's Day. Today, after getting up to feed the cat, walk the dog, empty the dishwasher as usual (no cute breakfast in bed with undrinkable tea and burnt toast for me. 'Darling! How lovely! Aren't you clever children!?') they all finally shuffled downstairs and said in the most half-arsed manner ever, 'Oh yeah, Happy Mother's Day, Mum.' A said she was going to buy me a card but forgot, 'So I decided I'd make one instead and then it will mean more, right? And Mum – can I have £20, please, because my friends are going to Nando's.' We both know there's not a rat in hell's chance that card will ever materialise, but she thinks she at least says she *thought about it*, then that's good enough. It isn't. M didn't even mention it. He knows I can't stand it, which is convenient for him because he is shit at being nice to me, especially when the calendar dictates it.

So why does it hurt so much that they no longer bother? I

know it's silly, and I hate to be such a clichéd contradictory woman about it all, but I wouldn't mind a little recognition, if only for a day. Maybe it's the fact that I feel unseen, unappreciated most of the time that creates the rancour. If I felt they were grateful and loving the rest of the year, forgetting Mother's Day would feel more like they were making a point ('We love and appreciate her all year long! We don't need to be told to do it on a certain day!'). As it is, a commercial, tokenistic gesture of appreciation would be the apex of their effort on my behalf.

And it's the first year I've not had one to send. Not that they will have thought about that.

I wrote the Mother's Day blog an hour ago. Already it's had one hundred and forty-three views and six comments.

'You poor thing. My kids got me a sweet soap from the chemist – I cannot use it because of my allergies but it was a nice thought.'

Smug.

'I didn't get anything either. That's OK – they won't be getting any dinner! Ha ha ha!'

My kinda gal.

There are a few more general commiserations but the last comment, from someone called Sarah, stings a bit. Not because it is nasty, but because it is a bit too on the nose.

'What strikes me is not the lack of a present or card but the lack of care for you as a person in your household. Too often we become two-dimensional entities to our kids – they don't see us as people with feelings and hopes and dreams. I really feel bad for you that your family is so blind to your obvious pain. Your kids are teenagers – they are selfish and self-serving and self-centred, but they are still kids. What I really think is sad is your husband's attitude – does he really not know that you are struggling? Can you tell him? I mean, REALLY tell him?'

I shudder involuntarily at the idea of REALLY talking to Martin. I think I've forgotten how to discuss anything with him apart from the kids and the recycling schedule. It would feel so awkward to have to face him and say all these things that go round in my head and expect him not to laugh, take the piss or start thumbing through the Screwfix catalogue (which is what he normally does when I start talking). But that's normal, isn't it? I mean, when you've been together a long time and you have kids? What is there left to say? And anyway, I'm not even sure I want his attention. Maybe that's the real problem.

And, oh yes – 'hopes and dreams'? I gave up on those a long time ago. I never really wanted to swim naked with sea turtles off the proceeds of my bestselling novel anyway. Who wants to do that when they could be descaling the kettle?

Chapter Thirteen

Martin wants to talk. Oh God. Has he been hacking into my phone? He doesn't know the passcode. He doesn't pay any attention anyway. Maybe it's something to do with the kids.

He decided to go in late to work today and so hovers around while the kids shuttle in and out of the kitchen looking for PE kit, toast and an argument. It makes me feel very uncomfortable when he's here during the morning rush. It's like someone has parked a broken-down bus right in the fast lane of the dual carriageway. He's always where I need to be, and he moves so slowly. He also does that irritating thing I notice a lot of men do, which is to start trying to boss the situation, even though we operate as a perfectly decent dysfunctional unit without him the rest of the time.

'Lorcan! You're going to be late! Paddy – why don't you pack your bag the night before, then you won't be so stressed! Amelie – is that amount of make-up really allowed? You look ridiculous.'

Finally the kids leave and I stall him for a bit while I go to get dressed. If I'm going to be told off, criticised or patronised I don't want to be wearing a fleecy bunny-rabbit onesie. When I come downstairs he is sitting at the kitchen island staring at his hands. Blimey.

'I think we should go and see someone.'

'Who?'

It's a long time since we've been away anywhere. I can't think of anyone I want to see who Martin would agree to – he even finds Jude, my oldest friend, 'too loud' – but maybe he's feeling sociable.

'A counsellor. Therapist. Shrink. Whatever you want to call them.' He looks mortified. He hates all that kind of 'mumbo jumbo'.

I'm stunned. What on earth is he talking about?

'Martin – what? I mean – what?! Where . . . so, I mean, what's this about? Where has this come from?'

'Look, Ciara, you and I both know that things have been a bit – flat for a while. I'm not blaming you—'

'Good!'

'We are both to blame, but I think it's about time we tried to do something about it.'

'Martin? Hello? Are you in there? Someone help! Someone's taken my husband and replaced him with a hippy!'

Despite himself he smiles. 'I know this must come as a bit of a shock – I've been thinking about it a lot and I want to try to sort things out.'

'"Sort things out"? Like, "make things better" sort things out or "work out how to split the crockery" sort things out?'

'Don't be silly – of course we will sort things out. I just think we could all be happier.'

'Do you?'

I'm not trying to be obtuse, I am genuinely stunned that Martin has had any kind of inner life going on, amazed that 'happiness' is even on his radar. Martin is just . . . Martin . . . he doesn't have *feelings,* he doesn't do *rumination* and he certainly doesn't use language like *sort things out* – unless it's about the garage.

'Martin – let's just have a meal somewhere – have a chat over a nice bottle of wine and some tapas? I could book that place El Toro Loco?' The idea of sitting in a room with a nodding woman and a box of Kleenex is making me feel sick.

'I think it could really help you – you know. Since your mum died you've been . . . distant, and I get that, it's been a tough year, but if we're honest—'

Honest? Oh God, don't let's start being honest. Not now. We've just got new carpets.

'—we've been in a bit of a ditch for a few years now.'

It's true, of course. Ever since the kids went to secondary school and I no longer have to walk them to school, pick them up, take them to karate/ballet/football any more I have felt a bit aimless. I didn't think he either noticed or cared. Obviously it's affected our – oh God – *relationship* but we're not the sort of couple who worry about that sort of thing. It's just the way it is, isn't it? If everyone went around *talking about things* there would be no couples left in the entire world. Marriage can only survive in a controlled environment of buried hurt, submerged desire and sublimated rage.

'Sorry, Martin – just give me a minute. We've been married for almost sixteen years, we've got three kids and a nice house, and we've always just jogged along nicely, and now you're telling me what? That you're not happy? I'm just a bit – incredulous really. I mean, where has all this come from?'

Martin shifts uneasily in his seat.

Oh God. Is he having an affair?

I can't help but smirk at the idea. Martin? Who'd look at Martin? I mean, he's not *hideous* by any means, but on the scale of George Clooney to Boris Johnson he's closer to the corpulent posho than the Hollywood heart throb. More Nigel Farage than Harrison Ford.

Martin clears his throat. I can tell he's practised this. 'It's ever since we had that talk. About my retirement. I've been thinking. We've maybe got twenty years left. Thirty if we're lucky. Give or take a few years. Do we want to spend them scarcely talking to one another, not touching, not having a . . . physical relationship? I told you that I wanted us to have a nice retirement. I've worked hard all my life and once the kids are at university I can cash in my pension. I want us to be happy. We can go on that cruise we've always talked about—'

'YOU'VE always talked about! I don't want to go on a bloody cruise, Martin! Floating graveyards for the terminally dull! You know how I hate large groups of people.' Is this what this is all about? The bloody cruise argument?

The cruise has been a bone of contention for years, but somewhere along the line what HE wants has become what I want too, according to him. And there's the problem right there.

'Well, OK, let's not decide anything yet. First things first. I've got some leaflets. I thought you might like to take a look at them today and we can have a chat about it later? I just thought we could do with some . . . help. I just want to feel like you want me. In some way.'

He nudges some glossy pamphlets with tasteful shots of couples holding hands in pastel sweaters across to me, picks up his bag and, pausing briefly to give me a stilted kiss on the top of my head, leaves for work.

Jesus, what fresh hell is this?

I sit at the kitchen island flicking through the pamphlets. They promise 'a neutral space' in which to 'reconnect' and 'really hear' each other. I glance down the list of 'issues' most commonly presented:

Money (no)
Communication (yes)
Sex (YES).

BLOG 14 – Couple Trouble

I've always assumed that if a couple need to go to therapy they
are really just trying to find a way to split up without anyone
throwing anything. It's the expensive and excruciating way to
'uncouple' that makes you feel like less of a failure. A load of
waffle about 'growing apart','changing desires' and 'unmet
needs' which really means 'I'm bored of you/I never really liked
you anyway/I've realised I'm closer to the grave than the cradle
and I fancy one last spin of the wheel.' And now here we are – M
wants to 'get help' with our marriage. I don't understand how
anyone can 'help' with a marriage – it's not like packing groceries
at the supermarket, it's not like some Girl Guide can put your
marital problems in a Bag for Life in exchange for 50p towards
their camping trip.

I also feel pretty insulted. How dare he? How dare he, after
this many years of fairly dull but comfortable domesticity, decide
that suddenly that's not good enough? Who does he think he is
– Princess Stéphanie of Monaco? Suddenly he's special and
needs to feel 'Blissfully Happy' instead of 'Not Quite Bored
Enough to Shoot Myself in the Mouth'?

I have never liked the idea of therapy. I tried it a while back
but it wasn't for me. It felt like letting someone look in your
underwear drawer – all those grey pants, embarrassing baggy
bras and ill-advised purchases in Ann Summers that you bought
in a desperate attempt to ignite some kind of libido. A complete
stranger rooting around in all that and asking you to talk about it.
Yuk. The minute you have to pay someone to sort out your

marriage, that's kind of it, isn't it? It's like calling in the bailiffs when you've maxed out your credit cards – they'll just come in and dismantle everything, take a few good bits away and leave you with the mess. I don't want to go. The idea of it is making me dry heave. Maybe I just need to get my hair done, buy some posh knickers, take him out for a nice dinner then shag him senseless?

Now my stomach is in knots at the idea of that. Oh dear. That's not good, is it? But should you honestly be expected to carry on 'dating' one another when you've been together for twenty-odd years? Who says? Can't you just live parallel lives in relative peace without having to ramp up the romance every now and then? What's so wrong with silent, distant companionship with no touching and very little talking? What's so wrong with that? Isn't that what most marriages are? Those couples you see in pubs or restaurants, especially on holiday – the couples who sit opposite one another not speaking, looking as though they are willing a tsunami to crash in and save them from an eternity of staring at each other. That's normal, isn't it? How can you find the same person interesting forever? You can't. But marriage therapists make a mint out of trying to tell us there's something wrong and that we need to 'save' our marriages, as if marriage were some kind of endangered species of water vole and not just a man-made construct with an excitement shelf-life. If anyone reading this is in a long-term relationship, has teenage children and wants to tell me that I should be 'trying harder' with my man, please – resist the urge to let me know. Nobody likes a smart-arse.

Of course, the minute I post this I receive just such a comment from Sarah, the one who came over all 'sorry about your life' a few days ago.

'I have to say I think it's a wonderful thing that M wants to go to counselling. Please don't assume it's the beginning of the end. It can be a very rewarding process, and you never know – you might end up feeling much happier than you are right now. Me and my husband went for six months and it really helped me to feel heard. Admittedly we did split up in the end but still . . .'

Oh great. Perfect.

Is there a part of me that would like to make things a bit . . . nicer? I really don't know. What would that even look like? Would we go on mini-breaks and hold hands on Las Ramblas? Go to the cinema in the afternoon? Join a Swingers club and exchange bodily fluids with other disaffected oldies?

I take the dog for a long walk and think about how I can try to avoid therapy. Despite my apparent snarkiness and gobbiness, I am actually very shy. Always have been. My idea of hell is having to meet new people and talk to them, so the thought of spilling my guts to a total (paid) stranger is enough to bring me out in hives. And a cruise? I think I'd spontaneously combust. Every time I have to meet new people or do anything out of my comfort zone I remember my ill-fated attempt to start working again. It was a couple of years ago, when the kids were all at secondary school and the days had got longer and lonelier. I volunteered in a charity shop for a short time, only one day a week, but the manager was a horrible little man who bullied all the old ladies there. I tried to stand up to him and he said he didn't think it was going to work out. I felt humiliated. It really knocked my confidence, which was already in short supply. I decided that the rough and tumble of working life was too much for me if I couldn't even handle the politics of a little charity shop. I'm 'not good with people', as Martin puts it. He knows this, so asking me to go and talk to someone is borderline sadistic.

How can I get out of it?

I could just say no. I could refuse. I could make more of an effort to be chirpy and receptive when Martin comes in at night. Maybe that would make me happier, and then Martin could be happier? I must have been a miserable cow this past year. But I can't help it. It's grief. I've found myself staring at walls. Sitting in the same spot for hours. Talking to an urn. And yet I'm starting to realise that my mum dying is not the only grief I carry. I miss her terribly, but in a way her death uncorked years of sadness. Her passing was the rug of complacency being pulled from underneath me. It's almost as if, while she was alive, we were both invested in the lie of my happiness. I had to be a good wife, a loving daughter and an all-suffering mother just like she had been, because it's what she expected of me. She never actually said 'Just put up with feeling a bit bloody low all the time, it's normal!' – but she implied it in a million tiny ways. That's the sort of shit you subliminally learn from your mum – how to bear disappointment and regret. Mum did love Dad but it was dutiful rather than doting. They didn't really talk, or do anything together. I thought that was what a marriage was. Your life – such as it was – happened outside of the marriage. I thought I was OK with that. Maybe I'm not. It seems Martin isn't either. Maybe I should go? Fuck.

My phone pings. A text from Jude.

'Hello doll – long time no hear? Are you coming to see us this summer? It's been tooo long! xxx'

I let Sadie run off the lead and reply.

'Don't know yet. No plans. Things a bit weird here as of this morning x'

She calls me straight away.

'Weird? Weird like what? Tell me EVERYTHING!' she orders. She's the only person in my life who doesn't bother with the preamble. I'm normally very candid with her because she demands it.

'Martin wants to go to couples counselling.' There is a stunned silence at the end of the line. Sadie is sniffing a massive dog's balls. How easy dogs find it to interact on an intimate level straight away. 'Hello? Are you still there?'

'Yes, I'm just ... so, hang on, *Martin* wants to go to *couple counselling*?' She says this like it's the most unlikely thing in the world. Which, fair play, it kind of is.

'Yep.'

'What the actual fuck?' she laughs finally. 'Why? I mean, I know you two aren't exactly Exciting Couple of the Year but you've always been good together, haven't you? Is something going on? Is he having an affair? Oh my God, are YOU having an affair?'

'No, no, of course not. I mean I know I'm not, I think I might have noticed if my nightie was being interfered with, and he doesn't really do anything apart from football and golf, he just sits in the spare-room office twatting about on the computer.'

'Well, what the hell is going on, then?'

'I have no idea. He says he thinks we could be happier.'

'Could you?'

'Of course. I don't know anyone who couldn't.'

'Are you going to go? To therapy?' I can hear the amusement

in her voice. She knows how awkward I would find it. At school we once went on a religious retreat and I spent the whole weekend trying to pretend I had the shits so that I didn't have to do the group soul-searching sessions. I'd rather people think I have explosive diarrhoea than have to tell them anything about my 'soul'.

'No! Of course I'm not! Absolutely out of the question!'

Chapter Fourteen

'So I'd like us all to just take a minute to be with ourselves, and think about why we are here. And maybe perhaps, how we came to be here.'

We're sitting opposite a nice woman in a beige room on a Tuesday night in March. I'm assuming she's not being literal – she doesn't want to hear how we got in the car at 7.15 p.m., earlier than we needed to leave because Martin doesn't like to drive with less than half a tank of petrol so we had to pop to the garage on the way. She doesn't want to know about the fit of the giggles I got as Martin solemnly rang the wrong buzzer and we almost went for a tax audit tutorial instead. The three of us – Celeste, Martin and me – sit in a triangle on Ikea chairs, a small box of tissues on the floor between us. Celeste looks like she's only about ten years younger than me but has obviously enjoyed more 'me' time than most of us. Her face is smooth, tanned and relaxed-looking. She is slim, draped in an earthy linen smock, and her blonde/grey hair is piled up in a messy bun at the back of her small head.

No one says anything. Celeste looks quite pleased with this. I bet she is. That's a fiver already for basically saying 'Everyone shut up for a minute.' I'd be a millionaire by now if someone paid me to say that. It's excruciating. I haven't been this mortified since I farted during a smear test. I haven't ever sat in a room with Martin to discuss 'why we are here'. All for the bargain price of £75. Martin is paying. Martin, who baulks at putting the heating on when it's minus ten outside. Martin, who gets so upset when he forgets his shopping bags at the supermarket that he packs all the items into the boot individually rather than buy more. Martin, who won't join in with rounds of drinks in the pub 'because some people take the piss and order doubles'. He must be really unhappy.

Celeste smiles at us both. 'Martin, perhaps you'd like to start by saying something about why you called me? I'm interested in what you hope to achieve here.'

'So am I,' I think. But I don't say it. I'm all ears.

Martin is fiddling with the frayed cuff on his cardigan. He tugs on a loose thread and it starts to unravel. He clears his throat and looks up.

'OK. Well, um . . . yes . . . it just seemed to me that there might be a way for us to be happier.' He laughs nervously and inexplicably I want to hug him. He hasn't looked this vulnerable in years.

'OK, so what I'm hearing you say is you feel as though there might be a way for you both to be happier?'

That's what he just said. Jesus, I could do this. I glance at all the framed certificates on the wall behind her in the lengthy silence allotted to allow us all to 'hear' what Martin and then Celeste just said. What are all these qualifications – Diplomas in Parroting Back What the Miserable Sucker Just Said, awarded by the Institute of Coining It In?

'Ciara? How does it make you feel to hear Martin say that?' asks Celeste, cocking her head to one side for added empathy.

'Feel? Erm . . . OK, yes, sorry. Erm well – I don't know really ha ha ha!' I always laugh when I'm nervous. How does it make

me feel? FEEL? How the hell do I know? I'm too bloody embarrassed to feel anything apart from bloody embarrassed!

'I notice you're laughing?'

Well done, Columbo.

'Yes, sorry, I get a bit giggly when I'm nervous ha ha ha!'

'So I hear that you feel nervous and that's why you're
giggling?' She's doing it to me now. That's a tenner gone.

'Yes, it's just a bit odd, sitting here.'

'It's odd,' repeats Celeste.

'Yes, I mean, different.'

'Different? It's different.'

Bloody hell this is going to be a long fifty minutes. 'Yes, well,
we don't normally sit in silence with a stranger staring at a box
of tissues ha ha ha!'

God, I'm annoying myself now.

'You don't often sit in silence.'

Thankfully Martin steps in and breaks the circuit.

'We don't really talk that much any more. I mean, I fully
confess I'm not much of a talker and Ciara has tried in the past,
I freely admit that.'

'No one is on trial here, Martin – we're not looking to lay
blame,' soothes Celeste. 'Ciara – how do you feel the communication is going between you two?'

I know what she wants me to say but I feel curiously stub-
born. I don't want to get into it. Not here. Not now. Maybe not
ever. I have the very strong feeling that if I pull on a loose thread
of this cosy jumper, the whole lot will end up on the floor in one
big pile of acrylic yarn.

'How does it feel to hear Martin acknowledge that he doesn't
talk to you about things he is feeling?'

'Fine! I mean, he doesn't have to talk to me. We get along just fine. Well, I thought we did ha ha ha!' I risk a glance up at Martin and he catches my eye.

'We do,' he says smiling gently. I feel warmed. Emboldened.

'So why *did* you want to come?' I ask.

Martin clears his throat again. 'Well, I guess there is something that's been on my mind that I wanted to tell you about but it didn't seem the right time.'

'Go on,' says Celeste.

'It's not something I'm proud of and it's caused me quite a lot of upset really. I mean, there's nothing to confess to as it were, but it's just . . . For the past few years, you know, you and I have hardly . . . made love at all . . . and I know you've had problems, the menopause and so on, and what with your mum dying and everything it's been tough, especially this last year . . . well, I've been going online a fair bit and . . . looking at a lot of things . . . porn, I suppose, and it just sort of snowballed, and after a while I started entering chat rooms, and talking to people – women – and I found I really . . . liked it . . . liked the company. And sometimes I . . . did things while I was chatting to them . . . not on camera, never on camera, just . . . you know . . . talking. There's one woman in particular that I've talked to a lot, and she encourages me to . . . do things. And even though I've never met her I started to feel a bit confused – things have become a bit muddled. And I suppose I just felt increasingly sordid and sort of . . . sad . . . and I wondered that maybe if I told you about it we could . . . sort ourselves out?'

There is a long stunned silence.

Celeste shifts in her seat. Shit just got real. 'That's a lot, Martin. Well done. I know that can't have been easy for you.'

CAN'T HAVE BEEN EASY FOR HIM? FOR *HIM*? How do you think it was for me? I'm mortified. My head spins.

Martin is staring at me, willing me to speak and take the spotlight off him. I open my mouth but no words come out.

'Ciara? That's a lot to take in, isn't it? How are you feeling right now? Just check in with me and let me know what's going on.'

I stare at Celeste. Did she know he was going to say this? Is she in on this? I look back to Martin, who's got the same relieved look on his face as he has when he comes back from a long toilet break. I certainly feel a bit shat on.

After what feels like an age I realise that the only way out of it, out of this hour and this room, is to say something. I don't know what I'm going to say but I start anyway.

'Well, I had noticed that you were spending more time on your computer in the spare room. I suppose I just thought you were looking at sheds ha ha ha.'

Oh shut up.

'Sorry. I don't really know what you want me to say, Martin,' I continue. 'Do you want me to be angry?'

'That's an excellent question, Ciara. Martin, Ciara wants to know if you want her to feel angry?'

'Yes, I heard that,' snaps Martin, who is clearly keen to get to the bit where I express sadness and blame myself, then promise to do better on the sex front. 'I don't know what I want you to feel. I think I just thought I should tell you because it's not a very good sign, is it?'

'"Not a very good sign", Martin? What do you mean by that?' asks Celeste.

'Well, it doesn't look very good for the marriage, does it? If we don't . . . and then I . . .'

Martin has never been good at talking about sex. He is worse than me. I will let him squirm.

'Ciara, would you like to say something about your sexual feelings towards Martin?' asks Celeste, as if it's the most casual, normal thing in the world to enquire after.

'Would I like to say something about my sexual feelings towards Martin?' I counter. Two can play at her game. 'Not much.'

'Not much? You don't want to say anything much?'

'No, I don't have much sexual feeling towards Martin.'

Martin throws his hands up in the air as if to say 'See? See what I'm dealing with? It's no wonder I have to tug myself off online with some strumpet.'

'That's a big thing to say, Ciara. You look angry. Are you angry?'

My face flushes. Yes, I am. I am fucking livid.

'Why are you angry?!' says Martin incredulously.

BLOG 15 – 'Why Are You Angry?'

Why am I angry? Why am I fucking angry? There's nothing that makes me angrier than someone asking me, normally in an indignant manner, why I am angry. The question is the problem, not the answer. It always comes after some particularly CUNTISH behaviour that ANYONE IN THE WORLD would find challenging. Yet here I am being questioned about my (totally understand-able) angry response as if I am the one being unreasonable/rude/difficult.

Most of the time I just suck up the bullshit and get on with it. Push it down. Don't let anyone see. The odd occasion I do let rip and shout, I am rage-shamed like I'm some outrageous harridan, and the whole family embarks on an infuriating 'don't upset the beast' pantomime, rolling their eyes at each other and becoming oddly familial against me. This time, though, he's not only taken the biscuit, he's iced it, covered it with sprinkles and put a big fat cherry on the top.

I ask you this, dear reader, if you were to find yourself opposite your partner of almost twenty years, in front of a complete stranger, and they suddenly announced that they are so dissatisfied with your sex life that they have taken to bashing one out in an online sex room courtesy of some busty bird called 'Scarlett' – would you be a tiny, weeny bit cross? Do you think you might, I don't know, feel slightly betrayed? Humiliated? Appalled? Let's say you are nodding your head, dear reader, and saying that, yes, you can understand why that might sting just a tad. Would you then also feel a little bit surprised to be asked WHY you feel ever so slightly blamed? What's the opposite of slut-shamed – prude-pilloried? Would you be riled by the insinuation that it was somehow YOUR FAULT for not 'putting out' enough? Like sex is a buffet that you have wilfully under-catered?

I am beyond fuming. How dare he? He walks around in his baggy old pants, hair growing out of every orifice, farting, being boring, dressing like a colour-blind hobo and behaving like a grumpy old codger, then has the nerve to say I'M UNSEXY! Is it any wonder I don't want to rip his clothes off and have him up against the tumble drier when his idea of foreplay is to pat me on the head because I patched up his golf trousers? It's no surprise that our sex life has dwindled to almost nothing when he treats me like a cross between a housemaid and a Golden Retriever. Somehow, I'm supposed to shrug that off and turn into his willing, up-for-it fuck bag at night. I don't think so, mate. I really don't think so.

So yeah, for those of you asking, therapy went really well.

Chapter Fifteen

It's been two days since we went to counselling. We are still speaking – just. Martin is edging around me like I'm a bomb that might go off at any moment, which is both pleasing (because it means he feels guilty) but also supremely annoying (you try getting anything done when there is a cowering figure almost constantly in your peripheral vision). We haven't discussed what was said in counselling. Celeste has advised against it because she feels we should 'sit with it' for a while and then bring it back for the next session. Of course she does. She'd be out of pocket if every couple went away and actually talked about their problems – best to keep all conversation strictly on the clock. Her clock.

I don't know what I feel now. I was furious at first, but now that there is a bit of space between me and Marriage Ground Zero I find myself having conflicting emotions. Mostly, I have to confess to a background sense of relief. Relief because if Martin is getting his jollies elsewhere – albeit a virtual 'elsewhere' – it lets me off the hook both morally (because I'm the 'innocent party') and physically (I won't have to have sex with him). I know that sounds bad but there you are. I remember Jo Brand once said, 'Once you've had sex with the same person three hundred times, what's the point of having sex with them again?' and it strikes me as so true, even down to the specificity of the number. Let's assume that in twenty years most couples' sex lives are on a downward curve in terms of frequency. The first year you'll probably clock up at least a hundred shags. Possibly more. After that once a week for a couple of years, then it tails right off after about five years – sooner if you have kids early on in the relationship. Three hundred times would take most couples to around year five, after which you're in the sexual desert with nothing but your memories and a good book at bedtime.

One really positive thing to come out of all this is my blog now has almost one thousand followers. I don't know where they all came from but they are loving all the recent stuff. I started out writing about kids – everyone wants to read about other people's parenting hell, don't they? – but since I've been writing more about me, about our relationship, the views have doubled daily. It seems there are a fair few women like me out there – feeling a bit lost, a bit desperate, a bit on the edge. Yay. Generation Living Dead. They vary wildly, from the 'string him up' to the 'get a grip, sister!'

'Sorry to hear about your husband doing this to you. Sounds like he is pretty unhappy but basically a decent guy. Maybe the problem is you? Maybe you need to find some excitement elsewhere in your life? I was in an abusive relationship for four years; when I came out of it I eventually started dating this lovely man, and the relationship was good. But because there wasn't all the stress and drama of the previous one I thought it was dull. I broke up with him after a year, dated someone else where there was plenty of passion but we broke up almost every month and it was exhausting. And that was when I realised that things with the other guy weren't boring and without passion. It's just supposed to be easy like that. The sex thing is something that you can fix,

HE even wants to. So if you love him work through that. But don't throw away a good thing because you don't know how to deal with it.'

'Poor you. Why are men such pricks? Why do they think with their pricks? How come he didn't tell you about all this until you were in the therapy session? Sounds like a douche. Bin him now before he starts with the prostitutes.'

'Get out while you've still got your own hips! Seriously, your marriage sounds dreadful! Personally I couldn't be in a relationship with zero intimacy. You're basically just friends – and by the sound of it friends who don't really like each other that much.'

'I could have written this post myself. It's a tough one. On the one hand I think "Why do we all feel, in this day and age, that one person should be able to satisfy all our desires? What's wrong with your hubby having a little fun online, especially if your libido has taken a bashing during the menopause?" On the other hand I think "what a cheek – making you go to therapy to tell you he's been doing things behind your back with other women online!" You've got three children who need you both, and you seem to have had a good marriage up until recently. Give it a chance with the therapist and don't make any rash decisions – you have too much to lose. Sending hugs, hun.'

I mean, I don't remember asking for opinions or advice but it seems if you offer this stuff up online people feel entitled to give you it anyway. Almost a thousand views, though. Never mind the quality, feel the width! I don't know if it makes me happier or sadder to realise that I'm not alone, that dotted all over the

UK, the WORLD, there are probably hundreds of thousands of women screaming into the abyss of domestic loneliness.

It's been a welcome distraction from the real world, where the kids are still doing my head in. Lorcan and Paddy have been fighting. Again.

BLOG 16 – Twinagy

My boys hate each other. They can't even be in the same room any more. And yet they are attracted to each other like magnets. One will accuse the other of pulling a face, then the other will deliberately trip his brother up. Before we know it, tea time has turned into World War Three; there are chairs tipped over, pasta spilt on the floor and walls kicked. So far this year Lorcan has broken a banister, smashed his phone screen and knocked a chunk of plaster off the hallway wall. Paddy has punched a hole in his desk (desk? Who am I trying to kid? He never does any work on it. It's a stand for his PS4 keyboard), knocked the bulb out of his bedside lamp and broken two pieces of stained glass in the front door. Why should I have to put up with this?

They are getting so big now too – I've started to think it will be me they are smashing next. Two big angry lumps thumping around the place, holding us all hostage with their violence and their mood swings, and their weird twin mutual obsession. One cannot bear to hear the other praised in any way – it feels like a criticism of the other. If I say 'Well done for doing your home-work, Paddy,' Lorcan will chip in with 'He copied it off the inter-net.' If I praise Lorcan for making me a cup of tea (after nagging him for twenty minutes) Paddy will say 'He spat in it.' They can't let each other have one moment of glory without trying to rip it to shreds. And what I've come to realise is – I'm actually furious about it. I know it must be difficult being a twin – having someone who looks just like you always there as an instant comparison – but my God, they would try the patience of a saint, as my mum used to say. They ruin any rare moment of calm in the house with their selfish twin-teen bullshit.

And if it isn't them it's Amelie, or the Queen of Fucking Sheba as I've taken to thinking of her. Entitled doesn't cover it. She wafts in and out demanding money/data/special food that we haven't got, turns her nose up at everything I offer, disses me in front of everyone, spends all her time on the phone to girls she saw only half an hour ago and to top it all seems to have become Hickey Queen of Haringey. Disgusting purple and yellow bruises that appear all over her neck every time she goes out with Rodney. She tries to hide them but I can spot them a mile off. If they're doing that, what else are they doing? What happened to my sweet princess-loving baby girl who kissed her twenty best toys goodnight every night? She's given up the Brownies for some weird teen version where she competes against her friends to see who can get all the badges first – the Hickey Badge (tick), Alcohol-induced Vomiting Badge, Spliff-Building Badge, Fingering Badge and the most prized of all, the Absolute Cunt Badge (hard to earn but she's well on her way). Where did we go so wrong?

Although, I guess Martin and me are not the best examples. Maybe the kids sense our unhappiness.

Nah. They don't sense anything that's not about food or money. Fuck the lot of them.

Chapter Sixteen

It's our second session with Celeste. She starts with the same nodding-and-smiling routine, warming up no doubt for her stating-the-bleeding-obvious nonsense. I must admit I feel nervous. I don't know what I'm going to say. I don't know what I feel.

'How have you both been?' asks Celeste, after about seven quids' worth of silence.

'It's been fairly quiet at home,' says Martin, trying to catch my eye for support. I don't look at him. I can't.

'Ciara – do you still feel angry with Martin? I remember you left our last session feeling angry.'

'Erm . . . no, no I don't think I do feel angry. I was a bit shocked I suppose. But on balance – I don't think I feel angry now. I mean, it's not that bad, is it? It's not like he's had an actual affair, is it? It's just a bit sordid and a bit humiliating, but hey – that's my life these days – feeling humiliated by everyone I live with. Feeling unseen, uncared for, an irritating afterthought ha ha ha!'

'You sound hurt,' offers Celeste with her signature head tilt.

'You think?! Yes I suppose "hurt" is about right. But I'm sure I'll get over it.'

'You'll "get over it"?'

'Yes. Keep on keeping on, as my mum would have said.'

'Your mum. Yes. Martin mentioned in our first session that you lost her last year. I'm so sorry.'

My throat tightens.

'Thank you.'

'She encouraged you to keep going, did she?'

'Yes. She was old-school. She sacrificed a lot for us because she said she loved being a mum. But I know she didn't have much of a life.'

'How do you know that?'

'Because she always looked a bit sad.'

My eyes start to fill with tears.

'Was she depressed, do you think?'

'No, she didn't believe in depression. She said she had too much to do around the house to be depressed. She just didn't do anything apart from look after us. She didn't have any friends. She always looked nice but she never went anywhere.'

Now I start to cry. Celeste leaves a respectful silence around my sobbing, and, mortifyingly, Martin reaches across and pats my knee.

'I know it must be very hard raising a family and losing your mum. Sounds like she was a very strong woman. I wonder if you could allow yourself to let go of the "keeping on" for a bit? Allow yourself to feel sad, to not cope, to be vulnerable, like you've just been here with us? It's a powerful message, what your mum told you, and I'm sure it's invaluable, but there are times when we can't cope, we cannot just trudge on. Maybe losing your mum is one of those times?'

'What's the point in cracking up? The dishes still need doing, the kids still need feeding, the washing doesn't do itself. I could sit on the floor and cry or I could just get on with it. I choose to get on with it.'

'And how's that working out for you?' asks Celeste, looking me right in the eye for once.

'Not great,' I laugh.

'"Not great",' repeats Celeste, and hearing her say it back to me I know it's true. I have the sensation of a bag of wet sand sitting on my chest, weighing me down. But it's not mine. It doesn't belong to me. Whose is it? As I focus on it I realise I've been carrying it for years. Years. I'm so tired all of a sudden. I close my eyes and sleep through the rest of the session.

Chapter Seventeen

Mum – how did you stand it? How could you have been so bloody subservient and so easily satisfied? I actually feel quite annoyed with you. Thanks. Thanks for making me feel like a failure by comparison. Less of a woman. Less of a real mum. You always did the right thing. You hated it when I came back from uni spouting 'feminist nonsense'. You were an Irish immigrant, dirt poor, uneducated. When you got off the boat you were treated like shit by the country you had come to help rebuild – No Irish, No Blacks, No Dogs in all the lodging windows – but you fucking stood up every time you heard 'God Save the Queen'. What kind of republican were you? I have always been proud of my Irish heritage. A plastic paddy, you called me. You never lost your accent but you loved England. You were so grateful for it all. It annoyed me. Crumbs from the table. You gobbled them up. Well, I'm not happy with crumbs any more, Mum. I can't carry your sadness any longer.

Chapter Eighteen

'Hi, Debbie,' I sigh, unable to disguise my instant deflation at seeing her name flash up on my phone. I'm at the supermarket on a Saturday morning picking up a few bits, while everyone else enjoys a lovely and, of course, well-earned lie-in at home. Bastards.

'Hello, Ciara,' says Debbie rather more crisply than usual.

What have the little twats been up to now? Tripped Meredith up at the bus stop? Looked at her in a funny way? Not offered her a crisp? 'Is everything OK?' I ask, settling in for the long haul.

'Not really, no. I just thought I'd better warn you.'

Oh God, here we go. She's had an alert from the local neighbourhood watch about fly-tipping, or someone claiming to be a reformed prisoner is going door-to-door trying to sell knock-off dish cloths, or an Irish family in a caravan has been spotted either having a picnic or obviously trying to annexe the local park for two hundred of their cousins.

'It's about you. What you've been doing,' she says darkly.

What? For a moment I can't think of a single thing I've been doing that might have irked Debbie Downer. Mixing my plastic recycling with cardboard? Not sweeping my path? Forgetting to toot every time I drive past her house (a charming habit of hers I refuse to reciprocate).

'I haven't been doing much, Debs, apart from developing an unhealthy obsession with Dark Chocolate Digestives and

Alexander Armstrong on *Pointless*,' I offer lightly, chucking pre-packed vegetables into the trolley.

'Your . . . writing. What you've been writing.'

My heart stops for a brief moment. I drop the cucumber I'm holding and it rolls casually under the shelves. 'What? Writing what?'

She can't possibly have seen it. She doesn't have any interest in blogs or social media or thinking or *anything* that isn't to do with making everyone else feel as depressed as she is. Even if she has seen it I have taken pains to disguise people's names. I haven't used the kids' names in full, or Martin's, and everyone else wears a disguise, admittedly a thin one. My head starts to spin.

'Your online thing. Your . . . blog.' She spits the word out.

Shit. Shit shit shit.

Deny, deny, deny.

'What "blog"? What's a blog? Why would I be writing a blog?! What would I have to blog about? I don't do anything! I've got nothing to talk about ha ha ha!'

'Well, it seems you do. There's not much point trying to deny it, Ciara. There are far too many coincidences. I have to admit you were very careful at first. But in the last one you slipped up a bit. I went back and checked, and in the rest you refer to them as P, L and A, but in the last one you must have been so annoyed you forgot and used their full names. I'm sorry, but I don't know many people with kids called Amelie, Paddy and Lorcan, and a husband called Martin, who go to a school where there is a *very nice* teacher called Mrs Tanner, and who have a *very caring* friend called Debbie!'

At this, her voice cracks, and she starts to sniffle.

I can't speak. Shit.

'How could you? I mean, how could you? I can take it but poor Meredith . . . and your poor husband, being humiliated like that? Didn't you think about that?'

I have to front this out. Quickly.

'Oh look, Debs, I know what it must look like, but it's all made up! You know I was thinking of doing that creative writing course, I was just trying out some of my fiction skills! Yes, I know some of the stories might sound a little bit like real life but you know, it was just a starting point! Come on, as if you're anything like "Debbie Downer!" And me and Martin – that's not *really us*! Ha ha ha I think I'd be in a loony bin if that was my real life ha ha ha!' How quickly can I get her off the phone and delete it all? I'm half walking, half running towards the exit, dodging the various bucket shakers and RAC salesmen. I have to get home. Now.

'I'm not stupid, Ciara. It's your kids I feel the most sorry for. You've done the worst thing a mother can do. You've betrayed them. Publicly.'

'Look, OK, I get it, you have put two and two together and made about four hundred and fifty. There's really no need to be upset, Debs. It was just a bit of fun, making up stories about family life, you know, to pass the time! I know, I should get out more! Ha ha ha! I've always had a vivid imagination. But you're probably right, I should probably just take it down – before anyone else sees it and jumps to the wrong conclusion! Ha ha ha!'

'Well, that's just it, it's probably too late.'

'What do you mean? I know I've got quite a few followers now but . . . I mean, it's one of millions of blogs out there! I mean, how did you find it?!'

'I have Google Alerts on all my friends.'

Creepy fuck.

'OK. What do you mean "too late"?'

She's worrying me now.

Debbie sighs theatrically, almost regretfully. 'I wasn't a hundred per cent sure, so I showed Meredith this morning just to check a few details, and she wasn't a hundred per cent sure so she took screenshots and sent them to Paddy . . .'

I drop my basket and run.

Chapter Nineteen

I've forgotten how to drive. I stall the car three times trying to get out of the car park. I'm sweating. I feel sick. Oh God. Calm down. Maybe Paddy isn't up yet. Maybe if I can just get home, get his phone and delete it all I can laugh it off as another stupid Meredith stunt. No one will be any the wiser. Of course, they'll all still be in bed – Paddy doesn't normally wake up until gone lunchtime on the weekend. It will be fine. I get out of the car park and step on the gas. Bang. A sickening crunch as my car prangs the car in front, which, for some reason, has stopped at an amber light. Idiot. Shit. The guy gets out of his car, theatrically inspects his bumper and approaches my window. I put the handbrake on. Not now. Please not now.

'Bit too close there, love!'

'The light was green! Why did you stop? It was green!'

'Amber, love. An amber light warns you to stop. And anyway, what if there had been a child wandering in the road and I needed to make an emergency stop?'

'Was there a child in the road?'

'No, but there could have been. You went into the back of me. Nothing I can do about that.'

He's one of those. I can already see there is the tiniest dent in his nice shiny bumper but he's going to do this the hard way.

'OK, I'm sorry, I'm in a bit of a rush, look, just give me your details and I'll reimburse you for any work.'

He eyes me suspiciously. He's about sixty, driving gloves, acrylic cardigan, blazer on a Saturday.

'Don't you want to exchange insurance details? Is that a problem?' He thinks I'm not insured.

'Well, we can if you like but the excess is ridiculous so let's just do it privately, shall we?'

I'm aware that my panic about what might be about to detonate at home is making me sound suspicious. I try to smile but my lips stick to my teeth and I grimace at him apologetically.

'Let's go the official route, shall we?' says the man, his eyes turning steely. 'I'm a retired copper so I like to keep things above board.' Of course he is. Of course. Just my luck.

With an almost sarcastically slow amble he heads back to his car and reaches into his glove compartment for his documents. I scrabble around in mine but all I find is an empty tin of travel sweets and a hundred old tissues. The man places a hazard triangle on the outside edge of our cars and starts directing the, by now, tetchy queue around us.

'Have you got your documents there, love?' he says, clearly enjoying himself, back in the saddle.

'I don't seem to have them in the car. I was sure I left them here.'

The man smiles. 'Well, who are you insured with?'

'Admiral. I think. Or was that last year?'

'I don't know, love, was it?'

'It's just that we switch every year so I can never remember . . .'

'Shop around for a more competitive quote – don't blame you, love.'

'Look, I really do need to get home—'

'Yes, I can see you're a bit flustered – probably why you weren't paying attention. Whatever it is – can't be that much of an emergency to warrant all this expense now, can it?'

Ha. If only he knew.

'Here's my number, my address,' I say, scribbling my details on his pad. 'Call me later and I'll look up my insurance details. There's no problem. Honestly. Please – can I just go now?'

The man considers his options for a minute.

'I'll be in touch,' he says finally, and strolls back to his car. After spending about five minutes adjusting his mirrors, fastening his seatbelt and doing experimental neck rolls to check for any lucrative whiplash, he pulls off at a stately pace and I crawl after him. Of course he is taking exactly the same route as me, and is driving well below the speed limit. Occasionally he pulls up sharply as if to test my concentration. I will never bloody get home at this rate! Finally, he makes a left turn and I zoom up the last stretch of road desperate to get hold of Paddy's phone. My hands are shaking as I put the key in the door, my heart thundering in my ears.

Quiet. Not a whisper.

Thank God. All is not lost. I can delete everything. Thank God for teenage sleep patterns. I'm about to creep upstairs to Paddy's room when I hear a chair being pushed back in the kitchen. Who is up? If it's just Martin he won't know anything so long as the kids are still asleep. I creep back down the stairs and open the kitchen door.

Shit.

The entire family is seated around the kitchen table. All of them. Paddy's phone is in the middle. Martin has his arm round Amelie, who is sobbing. Paddy and Lorcan look ashen-faced. The door creaks as I push through it and Martin looks up at me, stricken. Fuck.

'Hello?' I say weakly, as if there might be a way to pretend this isn't happening.

Amelie looks up and at the sight of me bursts into a noisy crying fit. Paddy scrapes his chair back noisily and barges past me before thundering up the stairs. Lorcan keeps his head down. Only Martin looks at me.

'I think we need to talk,' says Martin gravely.

'Is it about the blog? Because honestly it's just a joke, I mean it's not really us! I mean, it is, but it isn't either, it's kind of based on the truth but it is massively exaggerated and embellished!'

Martin shakes his head. Amelie stops crying and looks at me.

'How could you, Mum? How could you do that to us? All those horrible things you said. About me. About Dad!'

'Oh darling, I didn't say anything horrible – I didn't mean to upset you—'

'MUM! You called me a CUNT!' she roars. And she's not wrong. 'Well, yes and no, I didn't actually call you a C-word, I said sometimes it's *as if* you're a C-word. That's different.'

'Oh stop it, Mum, you're pathetic. If you hate us so much why are you even here?!'

'I don't hate you, don't be ridiculous!'

'Ciara – I don't think there's any way round this – the kids have read it all, I've read it all, and we're all pretty stunned, to be honest. I know we've had our issues but we've always been quite a tight unit, and it is pretty devastating for us to learn that you don't actually like being a part of this family any more. Pretty devastating. So no matter how much you try to distance yourself from what you've written, it's clear to us that you wrote all of this because it's how you actually feel.'

Martin looks quite pleased with his speech. He puts his arm back around Amelie and she rests her head on his shoulder.

Why do I feel like the errant child all of a sudden? The outsider in my own marriage? It's always been a bit like this – Daddy and Amelie, Amelie and Daddy.

Lorcan speaks.

'Do you have any idea how much we are going to have the piss ripped out of us, Mum?' His voice shakes with anger.

'Nobody will know!' I say, hoping to at least get him on side.

He laughs a hollow, dry laugh. 'It's already gone round our year group. Meredith made sure of that. So now everyone knows all about our fucked-up family. Cheers, Mum.'

Paddy has sloped back in. 'Everyone knows our dad watches porn!' he hisses.

'That's not true, kids! That bit is not true! I don't know where your mother got that idea from but it is categorically, one hundred per cent untrue!' says Martin, flushing bright red.

'It doesn't matter if it's true or not, Mum, everyone thinks it's true,' says Lorcan.

'Lorcan, I'm so sorry, I really am. It's all been a bit of an accident. I never meant to publish it and then when I did I just sort of enjoyed the space . . .'

I feel terrible. Lorcan, for all his idiocy, his crapness and his lazy indifference to the world, has always been the child I feel closest to. He looks crumpled and defeated.

'I didn't know you hated us that much, Mum, that's all.' He gets up and shuffles out of the room. Amelie jumps up and runs after him.

There is a long silence.

'I'm going out,' says Martin, finally.

'Martin, I—'

'I don't think I need to hear any more from you. I'll take my fat, balding, boring carcass out of your way so you can spend the day crafting some more hilarious observations about family life for your little gang of fans.'

'Where are you going to go?' I ask weakly.

'I don't know. Somewhere I won't run in to anyone we know. I don't think I can deal with any pity or sniggering. It's bound to be all over the place by now.'

'Martin, you're overreacting! Yes, it's . . . unfortunate that the kids' school friends know but nobody around here will!'

'Debbie didn't tell you?'

'Tell me what?'

'One of the parents has posted it on the school's Facebook page – the stuff about Mrs Tanner is going down a storm apparently. Debbie rang just before you got back. She says a lot of people feel sorry for me. Great. I'm a local celebrity saddo. Cheers. Excuse me.' Martin gets up and leaves. I can hear him trying to get his shoes on. He huffs and puffs, pulls on his jacket and is gone, slamming the door behind him.

I sit staring at the wall. I feel . . . numb. I thought the house would tumble down around my ears if I spoke everything out loud. I had imagined a nuclear cloud would envelop the whole street, sirens would go off up and down the road, wailing and gnashing of teeth would be heard for miles around. But it's silent. Deathly silent. I've laid it all out on the table, all the things I've bottled up for years, all the disappointment, hurt, anger, confusion and irritation, and instead of the cathartic shit storm of my nightmares, there is this. This . . . nothingness. I am aware of a slight sense of relief – no matter how upsetting it is for everyone today to have read some of the things I wrote, maybe tomorrow they will have calmed down a bit and they might actually find it in their hearts to have some sympathy for me. Nobody said getting heard was pain free, but perhaps in the long run it will be a good thing? Maybe they will realise that they need to up their game, stop taking me for granted, show me some love and respect as if I'm another normal human being instead of just 'Mum'.

Maybe.

Chapter Twenty

It's gone midnight by the time I hear Martin return. I've spent the day holed up in the spare room. The kids won't speak to me. Amelie spent most of the day on crisis conference calls with her friends, loudly criticising me and reading out the worst extracts about her she could find. For someone who claims to be mortified she's making quite a big noise about it all. The boys stayed in their room all day. I haven't heard any of the usual shouty banter they normally take part in with their online school friends – they are clearly too embarrassed to go online today. I've brought Mum into the spare room with me for moral support – not that she would support what I've done. She'd never let anyone know her private business – not even her own kids. She was paranoid about anyone hearing anything about her. She whispered when she was gossiping about people who live in Australia.

I've been going over my blogs. I can see how I let too much slip, got a bit too cocky. I can see why the kids are embarrassed and upset. I totally get why Martin is mortified. I really went for it. Especially towards the end. Because it is the end. It has to be. How can I carry on now that they all know? How can I carry on at all?

Some things, once said, can't be unsaid, can they? I don't know how me and Martin will come back from this. I feel sick to the pit of my stomach. But if I'm honest, underneath the nausea, the shakiness and the scorching shame, there is a new feeling bubbling away. What is it? I'm not quite sure. It feels a bit like . . . hope? Not for us, the family, but for me. Something has shifted and I don't think I can shift it back, even if I wanted to.

Whatever happens now, we will have to go forward in the full knowledge of what I have very publicly said. What to do with the blog now? My finger keeps hovering over the delete button but I cannot quite do it. What's the point of closing the stable doors after the horse has bolted? Everyone in the local area will know by now. Debbie has seen to that.

I don't want to delete it. I've deleted most of me over the years – I want to let this stand so that at least I have something to show for the last decade.

Martin doesn't come to find me. I can hear him shuffling around in our bedroom next door. He sounds like he's been drinking – he keeps crashing into things and muttering. I'll leave him to it. Maybe in the morning we can talk.

Perhaps this is the wake-up call we needed. I try to console myself with positive aphorisms. Everything happens for a reason (apart from all the random dreadful things that happen every day for no reason whatsoever).

Things can only get better (apart from when they just keep getting worse).

There's no such thing as a mistake (oh piss off, Freud).

Finally I drift off to the sound of Martin snoring drunkenly in the next room.

It's late when I wake up. The sun is blasting through the flimsy spare-room curtains; it must be at least ten o'clock. The house is quiet. I lie staring at the peeling wallpaper – we never did get round to decorating this room. It was going to be my study. Ha. I was going to write a book once. I can't remember what it was going to be about. Now the 'study' is home to the Christmas-tree decorations, the hoover, the laundry baskets, the ironing board, Martin's home computer, piles of towels and bedlinen and several boxes of the kids' old toys. That's the story I wrote.

Mum is perched on top of the laundry I have yet to iron, like a chiding reminder of all my domestic failings. I've placed a crucifix on top of her. It's what she would have wanted.

You would never have let that pile get so out of hand, would you, Mum? You could set the clock by your ironing schedule – 5 p.m. every Saturday in front of the football results, so that you could check your pools entry. I can still hear your voice 'No-score draw . . .' as you ticked and crossed the results off your sheet, your legs going blotchy from the gas fire. All our school clothes, threadbare but neatly pressed and folded, Dad's shirts hanging pristinely from the dryer; sheets, pillow cases, even towels crease-free and soft. My ironing pile is a depressing heap of wrinkled, shapeless garments that, no matter how hard I try, look just as bad after I've ironed them as they did before. Sorry, Mum. Sorry for everything. I've messed it up a bit.

I am dying for the loo but I'm scared to open the door. It feels like the start of something. The morning after the night before. There is the plastic Christmas tree bucket in one corner but I can't pee in that. I will have to leave the room eventually. I can't stay holed up in here for weeks, hoping it will all go away. I pull back the covers and tiptoe to the door. With my hand on the handle I listen to hear if anyone is up. Nothing. I turn the handle slowly and open the door. Nobody there. They are all still sound asleep. I make a dash for the bathroom, crash straight into something and fall flat on my face.

A suitcase.

There is a suitcase on the landing. What's going on? Attached to the suitcase is a Post-it note.

Maybe you should go away for a bit.
M

I sit on the landing floor, rubbing my sore knees. Go away? Where? Where would I go? Who with? I haven't been anywhere on my own since that Swiss penpal exchange trip, and that was a bloody disaster. I spent a week not eating and crying myself to sleep. I don't really do alone, especially not abroad.

'Go away'? Wow. He really is taking this badly.

From my vantage point on the floor I look around at the scuffed skirting boards, the stained carpet and the dust dancing in the shafts of light. Suddenly my imperfect little world doesn't look quite so awful.

Go away?

Then a shaft of sunlight glances off the crucifix on top of Mum. Mum.

She always wanted to go to New York. I still haven't done what she asked us to do. Is it now? Is now the time? I'm being absurd.

I creep downstairs and sit with a cup of tea in the Sunday morning quiet. The clock ticks aggressively and, not for the first time, I feel the pressure of the nothingness in this silent house. Would they even miss me if I went? I mean, they would, because there'd be no one to find the shin pads for football, no one to shout at when there are no tights, nobody to blame when the cereal runs out. Martin would be a bit lost for about a day but I'm sure he'd adapt, helped along no doubt by the attentions of some busty bint online. He could wank himself silly in the spare room and go to sleep with a smile on his face for once.

It's not like it's the first time I've considered what it would be like if I wasn't here. I'm always amazed at funerals when, in the depths of grief and loss, people eat sandwiches, laugh and chat about inconsequential things. I remember staring hard at my mum's neighbours, the ones who bored her rigid on their almost daily visits any time she was not in hospital, and thinking 'Look at you! Laughing and stuffing slices of pork pie in your mouths! It will be you next! And we'll all be here stuffing our faces with pork pie, and you'll be dead, and then it won't seem so funny!'

Life goes on. We stumble forwards, shielding ourselves from the inevitable destination. Pretending we're not all treading the same path. I've never fooled myself that I'm anything other than dispensable. I've set up a good system here. It works, more or less. Maybe I could move on. While there is still time. Men do it all the time, don't they? Do a runner, leave the kids, the wife, the flatscreen TV behind and start a new life, often with a new woman. They buy themselves cars, start wearing blouson leather jackets and dyeing their hair. They get their teeth fixed, go on nice holidays with their new woman and treat her a bit better than the crying wreck they've left behind to pick up the pieces and dry their kids' eyes. Why can't I do that? Who says women have to stay behind? The kids like Martin more than they like me anyway. I always told him 'If things get hard, I'll race you to the front door.'

Things are hard. So why not now?

Why not?

Before I even finish asking myself the question I am heading for the laptop. My hands, seemingly without permission from my brain, are looking up flights. My bank card is out, my passport packed, the suitcase stuffed with whatever items I can find in the laundry basket. I always wanted to go shopping in New

York anyway – I can buy stuff while I'm there. Two weeks. It's not much of a Mum Break but it will be a start. Two weeks to sort my head out and come back with a master plan on how to crawl out from under this wreckage.

I wrap Mum in a towel and stuff her in the bottom of the suitcase. She's paying for this, she might as well travel in comfort. I take the thousand pounds in cash Mum left me from the tin under the sink. There's no time for permissions, special certificates allowing the transport of cremains, no time for ceremony. I can get my visitor's visa at the airport. I haven't sailed this close to the wind since I almost missed the last posting day for Christmas.

I have three hours to get there. I scribble a reply on the Post-it note.

OK. X

It looks a bit arch so I add a PS.

Sorry x

And I go.
I go.

Part Two

Chapter Twenty-one

'Which terminal, love?' asks the Uber guy.

Terminal. Certainly feels like it.

'I'm not sure. I'm going to New York. BA.'

'Very nice. Going on your own? Work?'

As if.

'Yes. Work.'

I suppose it is in a way. What do the Americans say? 'I'm taking time out to work on myself,' like the human psyche is a car you can hoist up and tinker with from underneath. Maybe it is. Maybe I'll come back from New York with some great new jeans and a bright new positive disposition. If I come back.

As we turn into the high street we get stuck in traffic. It's the monthly Sunday 'Farmers' Market', so the place is packed with people who enjoy paying twenty quid for a loaf of sourdough and a slither of waxy cheese despite the fact there are no farmers, no sheep, no maidens with milk urns and snowy, heaving bosoms tripping along the cobbled square. The only thing remotely farmy about any of it is the stench of bullshit.

I slip down into my seat in case anyone I know sees me. I watch the precious mummies oblivious to their children ramming their scooters into the heels of pensioners queueing for bread, marvelling at the way intoxication with their offspring makes them blind to any wrongdoing. The park is already packed with them, these yummy little families with nice clothes, yoga pants and scruffy 'just out of bed' hair. Why do middle-class children always have scraggy hair? My mum always made sure our hair was clean and neat. It rubbed off on me; I'd be mortified if my kids ever went out with dirty hair. But these kids . . . big bushy bird's nests on top of their skinny middle-class bodies, boys with hair longer than the girls, as if to say 'We don't need to look smart – we've got money!'

I'm so full of scorn. What's happened to me? I used to be one of those mummies. Even though I always fucking HATED the playground, I still went. Hours spent applauding bravery on the climbing frame, pushing little bodies backwards and forwards on creaky swings, admiring tenacity climbing up slides. I hated every moment but I did it because they loved it, and I loved them. Are these mums secretly just like me? Do they feel the existential void sucking them in every time they enter the park? Does the continuous and never-ceasing motion of the roundabout make them reverberate with the pointlessness of the human condition? I doubt it. They all look very happy. Time was this would have warmed my heart, this picture of familial bliss, fun in the spring sunshine with the novelty of Daddy during the daytime. Now it just makes me snarl. I am the grinch of parenting.

'You wait,' I think, looking at the walking Boden catalogue pushing designer buggies. 'They love you now but in ten years' time you'll wonder what on earth you did so fucking wrong.'

The taxi crawls past the park and we come to a stop again near the Co-op. A group of women are huddled around a central figure. They are all peering at something in the middle of the group.

Shit. Debbie. It's Debbie. She has her phone out and she is showing the group something. The women tut and shake their heads. She's showing them my blog. She looks shaken but curiously invigorated. I think she's been waiting her whole life for something this terrible to happen. She can die happy now. I duck down in my seat and pull my jacket collar up around my ears.

I'm out of here.

Chapter Twenty-two

Terminal five is heaving. I am jittery and anxious. I always am in airports, but today I have a better reason than just the normal 'Am I about to die?' fear-of-flying grandiosity. Today I am leaving my family behind, the centre of my universe, my *raison d'être* for the past fifteen years. What's more, when the lady at the baggage drop asks me if I have anything I need to declare in my suitcase I will have to look her in the eye and say 'No' when in fact I should really say 'Well, I've got no guns, bombs or drugs but I do have my mum's ashes in a tub – is that a problem?'

I think it's actually illegal to travel with a dead person, even if they have been reduced to a bag of gravel. I daren't look it up because if I find out it is illegal, what can I do now? Dump her in the bins near Pret A Manger? Flush her down the loo? Scatter her along the multi-storey car park? I'll just have to tough it out. I could pop her in my hand luggage but she'll stick out and draw attention to herself. And just imagine the awkward conversation at the security gate! 'Any liquids in your bag?' 'No, my dead mum is particularly arid these days.'

There is no queue at the baggage drop. The check-in woman on the left looks more relaxed than the bearded guy on the right. I head to her.

'Hello there, madam, where are you flying to today?'

'New York,' I say, my voice catching in my throat. I am a terrible liar and she's about to test me. I suffer from severe Catholic guilt and often dream I am confessing to something I haven't even done. I once dreamt a mass murderer was on the loose and I falsely confessed to burying hundreds of bodies along the motorway hard shoulder because I couldn't stand the pain of the police officer who couldn't solve it.

'Travelling on your own, madam?' smiles the nice middle-aged British Airways lady.

'Yes,' I smile nervously.

'Did you pack your case yourself?'

'Yes.'

'Anything sharp in there?'

'No.'

'Great. And has the case been with you the whole time?'

'Yes.'

'Super. That's all checked in for you, then, madam,' she says, staring at her screen intently.

Oh God. Why is she frowning? Is there a police warrant out for my arrest? Has Martin got wind of my destination and phoned ahead to tell them I am mentally unstable and therefore unfit to fly? Can she see my mum through my suitcase?

'And I have some good news for you, madam – I'm able to offer you an upgrade this morning. You'll be flying Business Class with us today! Enjoy!'

I could kiss her. I burst into tears. I've never been upgraded. Ever.

'Thank you so much!' I say, mortified by my crying.

'You're welcome!' she smiles. 'You look like you could use a break.'

No shit.

Chapter Twenty-three

'Good morning, madam, and welcome on board. May I take your coat for you? Would you like champagne or orange juice?' asks the mature, glamorous flight attendant.

I've never turned left on an aircraft and it's another world. No shuffling along kicking your hand luggage in front of you, sweating under all the layers you've worn to cheat the baggage allowance while other scum passengers block the aisles carefully folding their coats, which they'll then fill all the overhead lockers with. No emergency scanning the seat numbers to make sure you're not next to a morbidly obese over-spiller or a crying baby. No passive-aggressive elbow-room wars.

'Champagne, please,' I say as she takes my coat and my bag and leads me to a massive seat on its own by a window. All I'm left to deal with is a chilled glass of bubbles.

I can't stop grinning. Things like this don't happen to people like me. Or at least they didn't. Maybe this is my luck now? I feel a flicker of momentary guilt that Mum is in the hold, in a towel, in the dark while I am lording it with the poshos. She'd have loved this. She would have put her best English accent on and pretended she did this every day. Oh well. Sorry, Mum.

I sip on my champagne and push my seat back. It reclines so far that I spill my drink down my top, which I've noticed has egg stains down the front. Quick as a flash the attendant arrives with a fresh glass of champagne. As she dabs at the seat I can't stop myself from bursting into tears again.

'It's OK, madam, these things happen. Please don't be upset. We're here to look after you.'

'Sorry, I'm just a bit emotional.'

'Family bereavement?' she asks kindly.

'Yes,' I say. 'My mum.'

'I'm so sorry, madam. I lost my mum two months ago so I know how you are feeling.' Then she bursts into tears and the two of us start to laugh.

'This won't do, will it?' she giggles as I hand her a tissue. 'I'm supposed to be looking after you! Don't worry, I'll keep you supplied with drinks. Just try to relax.'

I want to tell her that it's not a recent thing, that my mum died over a year ago, and that in fact she is in the hold because I've run away from my horrible family who now have a really good reason to hate me other than the fact that I exist. I want to tell her about couple counselling, about Debbie Downer and my blog and all the lonely years I've spent with no one to tell all this to. I want to sit at a bar with her and swap horror stories about the menopause, compare night sweat symptoms and discuss vaginal dryness. But I can't. She is called away to deal with a peanut allergy warning. I feel pathetically grateful for her kind words, her noticing me, and it occurs to me that it has been so long since anyone has really attended to ME that I have forgotten how to receive. Another attendant comes by with warm hand towels and I almost weep again.

We take off and I peer down at the tiny houses disappearing beneath the clouds. I imagine Martin and the kids sitting sullenly at the kitchen table, wondering where I am. Martin will tell them that I've gone away for a break to think about my actions – like a prolonged, expensive naughty step. When I land I will text him to let him know where I am.

Or maybe I won't.

If I don't, I will have to be sure I am withholding my whereabouts for my own reasons – to feel free and unreachable for once – and not out of some vain hope that it will send them all into a spin of concern, panic and guilt. It won't. If being a mum to teenagers has taught me anything it's that my inner world, my hopes and dreams and joys are second to absolutely everything and everyone else. No point walking out just to make them suffer because they won't. I once tried a cooking strike to teach them that it's rude to pretend-gag at every meal I make, but they just ate cereal and soup for a week, and all the vegetables and meat rotted in the fridge.

I have to be sure that what I do now is for my own benefit and not theirs. These are my new rules. I'm going to spend two weeks doing what I want, when I want. If I want to sleep all day and eat Chinese food at midnight I will. If I want to talk to drunk men propping up the bar and have the rules of NFL mansplained to me on a Tuesday afternoon I will. If I want to sit in Central Park in a vest top while eating a warm, salty pretzel I bloody will. They're not such big dreams, are they? Even someone like me deserves as little as this. Don't I?

Chapter Twenty-four

I wake up with drool pooling on my Business Class pillow. We are nearly there. Suddenly I feel scared. I realise with a jolt that I have been riding an adrenaline wave and I've just been slam-dunked onto the shore of my own rashness. What the hell am I doing? I don't know anyone in New York. I am awkward and shy. I talk nonsense at the checkouts when I try to make small-talk, and end up saying things like 'You're lucky you are in here sitting down, because there is rain tomorrow!' and they look at me blankly like I'm a lonely nutter. Maybe I am.

I don't even know where I am going to stay. The nice flight attendant is coming around with landing cards. She offers me one and hands me a warm face cloth. Can she see the drool? I start filling it in but have no idea what to write in the section that asks for your 'US street address/hotel/destination' – I just assumed I could pitch up and find a hotel when I got there. In a panic I grab the BA magazine and frantically flick through it. There is an NYC section with the Top Ten Boutique Hotels. I run my finger down the list with my eyes closed. I come to a stop and open my eyes. The Hotspot Hotel, East Village. The photo shows a dreamy wood-panelled lounge room with the most inviting whisky bar I have ever seen. Perfect. I have no idea if they have rooms but 242 2nd Avenue, NY 10003 USA is going to be my street address. East Village. I've heard of that. Isn't that something to do with the Village People? OK, so I'm not a young man and I'm sure it's more expensive than the YMCA but I feel reassured. It's bound to be really pricey but I don't care right now. I have been sitting on the money from Mum's house for a year now, and I have the thousand pounds she left me (I'm sure that won't go far but anyway . . .). We were going to go on a family holiday with some of the money. The kids wanted to go to Florida again. Martin did not. I wanted to go to Italy. The kids did not – 'Walking around old ruins all day, BORING!' Martin wanted to go to Malta. Malta! Me and the kids did not – 'Malta is full of retired Brexiteers! You'd do just as well to pop on a Tena Lady and lie down in the dark all week for the amount of excitement there is there!' I remember saying.

'I don't want excitement,' Martin replied, looking at me as if I was mad. 'Who wants excitement on a holiday!'

I'm sure I can afford a few nights at least in a nice hotel. I don't want to come back from NYC with a suitcase full of bed bugs because I stayed in a flea pit to save money and then have to spend thousands on pest control – false economy. Really I'm doing them all a favour back home by splashing out a bit. They'll thank me in the end.

I allow myself to think about how furious Amelie will be when she finds out I'm in New York. She's always wanted to go there. My mum showed her pictures of the Chrysler building, the Empire State, Tiffany's on Fifth Avenue. She was besotted. It's been her dream to go shopping in Manhattan. She's watched so many films and TV shows set in NYC, her map of the city is made up of settings in *Gossip Girl* or *Friends*. She thinks there really is a coffeeshop called Central Perk. I feel momentarily guilty that she is not beside me. She'd be so excited now. Then I remember that moments like these are always better in your imagination. In the Disney version she'd be looping my arm, resting her head on my shoulder and loving every minute of the anticipation of a shopping trip with Mummy. In reality she'd be grumpy and moaning about how little spending money I'd allowed her and why it's so unfair that she couldn't have a tongue piercing for the occasion. I sit back and allow myself to feel glad that I am alone.

I am alone. I haven't been alone for twenty years and yet I've always felt alone. I only realise that now. Maybe this trip is not going to be so hard after all – I've done the groundwork. I wonder how Mum is doing in the hold? Is she cold? Is she lonely? I bet she will have struck up a conversation with any pets that have been crated in there. I must be mad. She is gravel. She can't feel or talk. I'm so used to thinking of her as still here somehow in her old form. I have talked to her every day since the urn arrived back from the crematorium, as if she has ears, as if she can process what I am saying. Of course she can't. She is dust. My stomach lurches at the realisation of this. I knew it all along – of course I did – but at the same time I chose not to know it. Somehow it has taken being thirty thousand feet above the ground, soaring through heavenly clouds, to ground myself in the undeniable truth that my dear mum is no longer with me, and in fact is as inanimate and insentient as the Argos suitcases she is currently piled in with. It's sobering. Bang on queue, the flight attendant angel arrives with a glass of champagne for landing. My head is already thick from the last three, but I accept it and quietly raise my glass. 'To Mum,' I whisper.

Chapter Twenty-five

International Arrivals. It sounds so glam. I expect everyone to be wafting in with floaty dresses, exotic headwear and matching deluxe luggage. Instead there are hundreds and hundreds of tired, arsey people snaking their way to the bad-tempered officials at Customs. Everyone is trying to get into America.

I shuffle along with my hand luggage between my feet, trying to block out the screaming children, the bad travel smells emanating from almost everyone and the gnawing sensation of panic growing inside me. Everybody looks purposeful – they have meetings to get to, family to be reunited with, someone waiting beyond the baggage carousels with a 'Welcome Home' sign, or even just their name on a small taxi whiteboard. I went away with Mum once some years ago and Martin picked us up from the airport. I was so looking forward to having someone to wave to as we emerged into the arrival hall, but he hadn't come in because 'it was too expensive to park up' so he was waiting with the engine running in the drop-off area. Mum muttered all the way home about how he'd made us walk a mile through the airport with our luggage to save himself £3.50.

It takes ninety minutes to reach the front of the queue. A tired, chunky man with an accent straight out of the movies reaches for my passport.

He flicks through it silently, checks my visa and glances at me in a perfunctory way.

'Your first time in America, ma'am?'

'Yes!' I smile.

'Welcome to the United States,' he says, handing me back my passport.

And it's as easy as that. I'm in America.

I find the baggage carousel and stand behind the mental people pressed up against the conveyor belt. What do they think is going to happen if they don't grab their suitcases the first time they pass? Are their cases going to leap off the belt and scuttle across the shiny floor to a life of freedom with no more cruel post-holiday banishment to the lofts of the world? Finally the board indicates our flight number and the bodies at the belt lean forwards eagerly. Not long now till I'm reunited with Mum. She never did like to hurry. She'll tumble down the shute in her own good time, but I know I'll feel better somehow when she's with me again. Half an hour passes. The people grab their bags and pile them onto trolleys. The crowd thins. I'm starting to get anxious now. Finally my case is vomited from the depths of the baggage area. I jump up to grab it. It's open. Or at least partially. Shit. Mum. Mum. Are you there? A few grey pairs of pants are hanging out of the gaping split where the zip used to be. Oh Jesus, Mary and Joseph and all the saints, as Mum would have said – please please please don't let this be happening. I drag the case off the belt and wriggle the broken zip free with my finger. I grab at the towel I had wrapped her in. She's there. She's there. I burst into tears and sit on the floor trying to stuff everything back inside. What the hell am I doing? I've run away from a perfectly decent life in a nice house with a pretty nice man and three (admittedly annoying but essentially normal) children to sit sobbing on an airport concourse clutching the ashes of my dead mum. What the hell was I thinking?

I sense somebody stopping next to me. I peer up at a tall elderly black woman who is staring down at me with obvious pity and a whiff of disdain.

'It's just a suitcase, honey, ain't worth gettin' all upset over! Jus' claim it on your insurance! It's jus' *things*, and they can be replaced!'

If only she knew.

Chapter Twenty-six

'Good afternoon, ma'am, welcome to The Hotspot Hotel, may I take your name?' says a young man with a massive Edwardian beard and a topknot. His jeans are so skinny I can see what he had for lunch and his ankles are bare. This place is so cool – retro armchairs and leather sofas are artfully arranged against a backdrop of wood-panelled walls, trailing ivy and huge palms. An out-of-work actor in a top hat and red waistcoat has just opened the door for me outside. It's another world. My first day in New York.

'Ciara Woods,' I say, my face turning purple. I've always hated saying my name out loud.

Topknot peruses his handheld device and frowns.

'I can't find your reservation here, Miss Woods . . .'

'Oh, I don't have a reservation. Sorry. I just saw the hotel in the magazine and thought it looked nice.'

Topknot peers at me ruefully.

'We are very busy at the moment, ma'am, but let me see if I can find you something . . .'

I'm sure I'm not imagining him giving me a judgemental once-over. Do his eyes rest on the egg stains? Do I stink of stale booze and regret? I look around for any reassuring signs that I'm not a massive misfit here. A young gay couple are fussing over their pug, a fat snorty thing in a stupid dog jumper that says 'Princess' on the side. A roaring open fire crackles at one end of the lounge area. An impossibly glamorous leggy blonde is draped over an oversized armchair flicking through a style magazine. The bottles in the boutique bar glint invitingly in the spring sunshine. It's beautiful here, and it's full of beautiful people.

I definitely don't fit in.

Topknot eyes me again.

'We have such limited availability, ma'am, but I have managed to find something. How long do you want to stay?'

'Two weeks?' I ask nervously, as if he might know better than me.

'Hmmm . . . the only room I have for that duration is a Deluxe King, ma'am.'

He looks at me as if daring me to ask the price. Stuck-up twat.

'OK, that sounds fine,' I say. I don't even want to ask the price.

'Awesome!' says Topknot Man, taking my credit card. 'We'll keep an imprint of this until you check out. And I'm pleased to let you know that as a super-valuable customer I can give you fourteen nights for the price of twelve!'

'Lovely!' I reply. I'm super-valuable all of a sudden.

'So that will be a discount of $1200,' he smiles.

Jesus H Christ. I try not to do the mental arithmetic in front of him. He's staring me down waiting for my reaction, so I do my best poker face and take the trendy 'olde worlde' brass key on a big red tassel from his cool slim fingers.

'Enjoy your stay, ma'am!' he smiles, going back to his screen. A young man in what I presume is an ironic bellboy outfit grabs my suitcase and guides me towards the elevator.

'How is your day going?' he smiles as he presses the button to the fifteenth floor. Americans are not remotely embarrassed by inauthentic curiosity.

'It's been fine, thank you, but I'm rather tired now,' I mumble, aware of how British I am suddenly becoming. I never say 'rather tired' – I've turned into Hugh Grant.

'Awesome!' says the bellboy, tapping on the brass handrail absentmindedly.

We arrive at my floor and he walks ahead with Mum in my case. I can feel her loving every minute of this. I hope the dead can't do sums – she'd be screaming at the price.

'Here we are,' says the bellboy, opening the door to reveal a white linen heaven. The bed is huge. The whole family could fit in it. The soft, smooth cotton sheets are edged with a tasteful red trim, and in the bathroom, just visible through the open oak door, gleams a sunken marble bath tub with gold taps, and the fluffiest towels I have ever seen. They almost purr, and so do I. I can't wait to get in the bath and luxuriate in the complimentary bubbles before spreading out on the massive bed-big-enough-for-the-entire-family, COMPLETELY BY MYSELF.

I self-consciously hand the bellboy a five-dollar bill and he scuttles off. I tiptoe around the room like I'm not meant to be here. Maybe because I'm not meant to be here. Down on the streets below the taxi horns honk but up here it's peaceful and calm. I go into the bathroom and pull back the white curtains – the view! I can see skyscrapers through the leaded windows! I fill the tub, get Mum out of my battered case and pop her on the window sill.

'Get a load of that, Mum! New York City!'

I steel myself to switch on my phone. Seven WhatsApp messages on the family group. My stomach lurches. I don't want to hear from them. Not yet. But now I know the messages are there ... I steady myself with a swig of the Irish whiskey I bought on an impulse in the duty-free shop – Mum never travelled without a litre of hard liquor.

The first message is from Paddy.

'Mum? Where are you?'

The second from Amelie.

'I hope you're happy – because we're not!'

The third from Paddy again.

'MUM!!!'

Then Martin.

'You've gone then. I thought you might. Can you at least let us know where you are? Thank you.'

Bloody hell. I almost wish they hadn't messaged me. I know I never imagined the aftermath of my leaving would be nuclear, but if I had stopped to think about it I would have hoped for something a bit more seismic than 'You've gone then.' He bloody suggested it! Typical, now he's acting the martyr, like I've just waltzed off on a whim. It was him that drove me to it – or at least dropped me off at the bus stop. How can he play that wounded-soldier routine NOW? Too little too late. I take another swig of whiskey and scroll down. Paddy again.

'Mum – since you've gone away and left us – can I buy some V Bucks for my PS4?'

Guilt-tripping mercenary little shit.

Nothing from Lorcan.

Martin again.

'At the risk of invoking further flouncing, can you please tell me where you keep the dishwasher tablets?'

Paddy again.

'MUUUUUUUMMMMM? Can I?'

I take another swig and hit reply.

'Dear family

In response to your recent queries, here are my replies in order.

1. I'm in New York City.
2. Yes, I have gone away for a bit – see 1 for whereabouts.
3. No you can't. I'm deleting my card from your account.
4. Under the sink next to the bin-bags.
5. Still no.

I have taken Grandma on a trip. I will be back in two weeks.'

I pause before I hit send. Do I need to explain any more? I'm so tired of explaining. I try to stay calm but all I hear is a naggy old bag in my head. Maybe the kids deserve a bit more? Martin is big enough and ugly enough to work it out for himself. Or if not he can go and have a cosy one-on-one chat with Celeste the nodding head-tilting therapist? They can sit and slag me off for fifty minutes and then he can go home and do all the washing.

I decide to throw them an olive branch.

'Just for the record, I love you all, kids, but you drive me absolutely mad and I just couldn't take it any more. I know to you I'm just "Mum" and I should be able to take all the crap I'm dished out on a daily basis but actually I am a person, just like you.'

I take another swig. A flash of inspiration comes along with the flush of the whiskey. I suddenly remember the boys are studying *The Merchant of Venice* at school. I used to love that Shylock speech. I type again.

'I am a mum.
    Hath not a mum eyes? Hath not a mum hands, organs, dimensions, senses, affections, passions? Fed with the same food, hurt with the same weapons, subject to the same diseases, healed by the same means, warmed and cooled by the same winter and summer as a teenager is? If you prick us do we not bleed? If you tickle us do we not laugh? If you poison us do we not die? AND IF YOU WRONG US SHALL WE NOT REVENGE?'

Are the capitals too much? Is that what I'm doing – revenge? Am I taking my pound of teenage flesh? I sit on the bed trying to decipher my own heart. Am I flouncing? I don't feel very flouncy. It feels more fundamental, more vital than that. I feel like I'm trying to come up for air. It's an involuntary thing, breathing. I need to do it. The outcome is almost immaterial. It will have to take care of itself.

I look out at the skyscrapers and think about those wretched souls who, trapped by fire, smoke and no hope of rescue, jumped to their deaths from the twin towers. They didn't get the luxury of consideration, choice, options. I blush at the grandiosity of likening my family abandonment to the 9/11 victims' fate. I'm lucky. I'm alive. I jumped and landed on a bouncy bed. I'm so lucky. I delete the line about revenge and hit send.

If only the buggers did their homework – my parody will probably be totally lost on them. I take another swig. This stuff is good. I can feel my shoulders dropping to somewhere near normal. They are usually up around my ears. I lie back and close my eyes. The bed is so comfortable and the covers so smooth and cool.

I'm woken by loud banging. For a second I have no idea where I am.

'Ma'am? Ma'am are you OK?'

I scan the room for clues. It's dark outside and I left no lights on. A siren blares from far below. New York. I'm in New York.

'Just a minute!' I say, leaping up to get the door. Squelch. My foot hits wet carpet. The rug is sodden.

Shit. The bath.

I run to the bathroom and turn off the trendy mixer tap. The overflow is partially blocked by the fluffy towel I threw there in readiness. The water is seeping over the rim and onto the flooring. A small but creeping puddle has formed, and has already reached the bedroom rug.

My door bursts open and Topknot stands hands on hips in the doorway, the master key dangling by its tassel from his tight trouser pocket.

'Ma'am, you can't overfill these tubs – they don't like it. There's been a leak in the room below,' he says accusingly.

'I'm so sorry – I must have dropped off!'

I reach for the whiskey bottle and try to hide it under a pillow. Too late. He's clocked it. He purses his lips as his eyes flicker over the room. My head is pounding. I grab at the spare towels and start pressing them onto the rug. Topknot rolls up his sleeve and reaches in to release the plug.

'The water is cold. Some nap,' he says, drying his arm with a flannel.

'Jet lag. I was so tired. I'm terribly sorry. If I can reimburse you for any damage please do not hesitate to furnish me with a bill,' I witter. Hugh Grant's here again.

'I think we're OK, thank you, ma'am – just a small damp patch in the ceiling – but in future please pay attention when filling the tub. Is there anything else I can help you with?' he asks. His tone is so passive aggressive I actually smile.

'No, I think I can manage now – I'll try not to electrocute myself or set fire to the place ha ha!'

Topknot cracks a flicker of a smile. Cheer up, love, it might never happen.

'Well, you know where we are if you need us,' he says as he leaves, closing the door almost sarcastically carefully.

I sit back on the bed. I feel sick. Whiskey on an empty stomach. I haven't eaten for ages. What time is it? 10 p.m. I must have been asleep for a few hours. I need food and painkillers and water. But it's late and I'm in New York and if I go to find a diner or whatever I'll probably get stabbed or gunned down in the street. I reach across the massive bed for the room service menu. Apparently I can order 'ethically sourced smashed avocado crowned with happy, lightly poached eggs on a bed of power spinach'. What is an ethically sourced avocado? A happy egg? Maybe not. How about some 'foraged wildflower risotto curated with a sea salt air reduction'? As Amelie would say, WTF?

My phone pings. Paddy.

'Wait – Mum? So are you Jewish now?'

Oh God. He doesn't get it. I sit on the edge of the bed, stomach growling, head throbbing, my feet damp from the bath debacle, and wonder what the hell I am doing here. It's not big or clever. The room suddenly feels stupid, pretentious, lonely. Outside, the city still honks and flashes. I'm not an adventurer. I'm not brave or honest or deserving. I'm just a middle-aged woman alone in a strange city. I reach for the complimentary kale biscotti. I could murder a Hobnob right now. I chomp miserably on the cardboard slice and consider my options.

I can go home in the morning, I think. They won't mind. Maybe one night is enough.

Chapter Twenty-seven

I don't know how long I've been asleep but it's light outside when I open my eyes. I feel better. The headache has disappeared but my stomach is howling for food. I'm not risking the room service menu again, so I will have to brave the mean streets of East Village before I pack my things back into my knackered little case and head home with my tail between my legs.

I pull on a pair of dirty tracksuit bottoms, grab my key and my purse and head to the elevator. Elevator, not lift. Already acclimatising. Not.

The lobby is busy. Topknot is bowing and scraping to some tattoo-covered young men in black leather jackets and interesting haircuts. He clocks me heading for the door and calls out 'Have a good one!'

I pretend I didn't hear him. 'Have a good one'?! What the hell does that mean?

The pavement – sidewalk? – is throbbing with commuters. It's 8 a.m. on a Monday morning and I am in Manhattan. It's still night time back home. I wonder if Martin will manage to get them up and out to school. Does he even know how to top up their dinner money accounts? I do it every Monday because if I put a month's worth in at a time they spend it in ten days on absolutely essential things like pizza at morning break and chocolate milk for the bus home. He won't know how to do it because I set it up and I don't think he has ever even accessed their school accounts.

Should I just do it? I could top them up now. Or I could do what I came here to do: focus on me for a change and let them sort themselves out. They won't starve – the boys would chew each other's arms off before they'd go hungry, and Amelie is an expert food bully who can extract a samosa from any shy Asian girl in her class. I'll let them work it out. I wonder if Martin knows about food tech ingredients, about how they have to take an apron, a tea towel and a container to bring things home in. I wonder if he knows where the boys' shin pads are for PE – they are not allowed to play football if they don't have them. Does he know that Amelie has a netball match on Wednesday and her permission slip needs to be signed or she'll not be allowed to travel home alone afterwards and instead will have to make the miserable journey all the way back to school in the minibus, prompting several days' recrimination about his failings as a human being. Is he aware that their six-monthly dental check-ups are due in a week? Will he even think to look at the family calendar? Does he even know where it is? I have to hide it because the boys like to scrawl things on various dates like 'Paddy's period due' or 'Lorcan's boyfriend's birthday!'

Has Martin realised that we are almost out of pasta and tea bags and hand soap and that special conditioner that Amelie MUST have? If he goes shopping does he know where the bags for life are (his hilarious favourite nickname for me) and will he remember to take them?

Oh well, this will be an interesting week in our household. I wish I had a spy cam so that I could watch them all crash and burn. They'll be begging me to come back by tonight, if only so that there is bread and milk and clean pants.

I take a deep breath and start walking along the sidewalk, dodging people glued to their phones. The city is beautiful. The sharp, cold spring morning sends shafts of sunlight low along the street. Every New York cliché is here – the steam rising from the subway manholes, the buildings reaching up to the heavens that make your neck ache, the gridlocked yellow taxis, the delis on every corner, the speed and energy of the place.

I love it.

I spot a diner across the two lanes of stationary traffic and get shouted at as I weave my way between the iconic yellow school buses, the taxis and the cars all bumper to bumper. A diner! Like in *Happy Days* with the Fonz (my first big crush). I hope a bored waitress will be wandering up and down pouring weak, luke-warm coffee from a glass pot. As I reach the door I realise with a thrill that the diner is actually called Happy Days! Oh, wait, that no doubt means it's an awful ironic place, referencing the TV show for tourist mugs like myself. I push the door open. It looks authentic enough. Some men in suits are sitting up at the counter eating eggs and reading the paper. A group of younger men in overalls are sitting in a booth silently shovelling pancakes into their mouths. I take a seat up at the counter. I am grinning. I have literally always wanted to do this. A fat man in a very greasy apron wordlessly asks me for my order.

'Can I see the menu, please?' I ask in my best British accent. He is unimpressed, and slides a laminated card over to me. I peruse my options. So many. Omelettes with about fifty differ-ent fillings. Eggs served with bacon, patties (?), burgers, slices of yellow plastic cheese, grits – what the hell are grits? – granola with fruit and yogurt, pancakes served long or short order (what-ever that means), milkshakes, salads, fries. My head spins. In the end I point to the plate of the man sitting near me.

'Can I please have that?' I say, smiling charmingly to the greasy man.

'Sure. You want coffee?'

'You bet!' I say. He doesn't smile. Why am I so socially awkward? Why did I have to do a silly American accent?

He shouts through to the kitchen, 'Short stack with a side of bacon and eggs over easy!'

He pours the coffee into a mug and pushes it across the counter.

'Is the bacon crispy?' I ask. I hate flaccid bacon.

' "Crispy"?' asks the greasy man, clearly irritated. He doesn't offer any insight. He moves on. Oh well. I'll take it as it comes.

I add some 'creamer' to my mug and take my first sip of real American diner coffee. It's disgusting – acrid, burnt, bitter. It tastes like it was made last week and has been stewing ever since. Probably was. What a let-down! I always imagined diner coffee to be kind of nice – everyone always gets refills in the movies. It's not. But I don't mind. I'm in New York. Two minutes later a pile of fat round pancakes appear.

'Short order pancakes,' says the greasy man sliding a sticky bottle of maple syrup along the counter. There is a stack of three flabby-looking pancakes the size of tea plates, accompanied by two greasy fried eggs and some incinerated streaky bacon. A paper ramekin of butter balances wantonly on the side of the plate. I dollop the whipped butter on top of the pancakes and drizzle the syrup over the whole lot. It's a cardiac arrest on a plate and it looks fantastic. I haven't eaten anything like this for . . . well, forever. I've always been so careful with what I eat as I can gain a stone just walking too close to a Greggs, and before we got married Martin let slip that he would hate for me to get fat. At the time I scoffed at him and probably told him off for his sexism, but something went in. I have never allowed myself to eat anything like this, and I dig in with gusto. It's disgusting and delicious. I eat the whole lot, gulping it down with swigs of tepid dishwater coffee. When I look up the greasy man is staring at me in admiration.

'Somebody sure was hungry!' he says, smiling finally.

'I sure was,' I smile back. I sure am. Hungry for everything. I suddenly feel gloriously happy. I want to run out into the city and gobble it up. I want to go to the Museum of Modern Art, ride around Central Park on a hundred-dollar horse and cart, drink cocktails on top of the Rockefeller Center and shop till I drop. I don't care how clichéd it is, I have been so bored and so alone for so long, putting everyone before me without even realising it, like a sad Stepford Wife with bad hair. How does that happen? One minute you're a bright young thing full of your own dreams and hopes, determined to live life on your terms no matter what, convinced that having a family will not define you or limit you – the next you're cancelling the one night out you have planned in a year because one of the kids needs to build a bloody fortress out of Weetabix boxes.

'You here on your own? On vacation?' asks the greasy man.

'Yes,' I say, unsure if I'm lying or not. It's sort of a vacation. Sort of a pilgrimage. Sort of a bunker.

'How long you got?' he asks.

'Well, I'm not sure . . . I was going to go home tonight but . . .' I wasn't even aware I was debating this now.

'I could show you around,' he says, wiping the counter with a cloth even greasier than his apron, 'I like a woman who can eat. New York women don't eat.'

Wow. I haven't been hit on in years. Who knew all it takes is a stack of pancakes?

'Well, that's very sweet of you, but I'm sort of on a mission. I won't be staying long.'

'Your husband doesn't mind you being here on your own?' he asks, eyeing my wedding ring.

I laugh. 'He won't even notice!'

The greasy man shakes his head. 'Crazy guy. I lost my wife two years ago. There ain't a day goes by I don't miss her.'

'Well, then you were very lucky.'

I take a twenty-dollar bill out of my purse and place it on top of the grease-stained 'check' in front of me.

Greasy man waves it away. 'On me. Go enjoy your holiday, lady,' he smiles sadly.

My eyes fill with tears as I thank him and stumble out of the diner. I thought New Yorkers were notoriously rude and tetchy. I can't cope with people being so nice to me. First the lovely flight attendant, now this guy. I'm much more comfortable with being treated like an irritation, an embarrassment. Topknot is kind of my comfort zone when it comes to dealings with people.

Am I really going to go home so soon? Won't that make them think I wasn't serious? That I'm not really unhappy? I stand on the sidewalk. The pedestrian crossing in front of me flashes Walk/Don't Walk. What do I do?

Back at the hotel I make a beeline for the elevator before Topknot can have a go at me about something. In the suite the bed has been turned down, and a replacement kale biscotti is propped up against the complimentary 'glacial mineral water'. All is calm, clean and beautiful. The bathroom has been spruced, the soggy rug removed and replaced with a fresh one. Mum is still propped up on the window ledge enjoying the view.

Mum. I haven't thought about Mum. She's meant to be my reason for coming here. I will at least have to go to the Empire State Building today and cast her ashes off the top. It's what she ordered, her last wish. She even had a meeting with the funeral director to make sure he knew what she wanted. She wouldn't leave it to me or Aidan to sort.

'What do you reckon, Mum?' I ask. 'Do you like it here? Do you really want me to sprinkle you over the edge of the Empire State Building?' I don't even know if it's legal. I pick up my phone and Google flight times. There is a flight home at seven thirty tonight. I could be home in time to make them breakfast tomorrow morning. The thought sickens me, but what can I do here for two weeks once Mum is gone?

'Mum? Should I stay here or go home?'

Mum is in a taciturn mood today.

'Are you sure about this, Mum? This could be our last proper conversation. I'd like it to be better than our last "last conversation", about whether or not you wanted an apple turnover. Nothing to say on the matter? Are you sure?'

Idiotically, inexplicably, I wait for some sign from Mum. Nothing.

'OK, then,' I sigh. I go to the Empire State Building website and pay $80 for an express ticket. I message Aidan, for what it's worth.

'I'm in NYC. Doing Mum thing today. Just to let you know x'

He won't mind – I suspect his busyness is a cloak for his uncomfortableness with the whole thing.

He messages back.

'K. Cool. Sending love x'

And that's it. That's his goodbye. It's now or never.

'OK, let's do this,' I say, popping Mum into a tote bag. No point waiting for Aidan – he'll be kayaking in a manatee lake or something.

Chapter Twenty-eight

It's a long way up. I've already had to fight my way through all the roped-off queues, the jaunty corridors lined with pictures of Minnie Mouse admiring the view from the top, the ridiculously officious uniformed staff herding the backpacked tourists through like lambs to the slaughter. The elevator chugs along, hauling its load metre by metre until we reach the 86th floor. On the way we are treated to a jolly video played on the ceiling of the elevator – hundreds of animated carpenters and scaffolders re-enact the creation of the building floor by floor. It appears above our heads as we ascend. It's meant to be entertaining but it unsettles me. I'd like to think, as we climb this enormous, terri-fying tower in the sky, that it has been here forever and wasn't just made by ordinary people – but by the gods. People building it is too worrying.

We are spewed out onto the observation deck. The view is astonishing. Manhattan laid out in its gritty glory, Central Park a lush rectangular oasis amidst the soaring skyscrapers. A 'suicide fence' pens us in on all sides as we shuffle along taking photos, selfies, videos of the vertigo-inducing panorama. I feel dizzy. We are so high up. In the distance the new World Trade Center stands alone as a monument to all those that fell there. A guard patrols the perimeter of the deck, warning people not to lean too far in case they drop their cameras. He looks friendly enough but how am I going to get past him to tip a couple of pounds of bone fragment over the edge? They are so vigilant about everything here. It's risky.

I find a small gap in the fence and slip my arm through testing it. The urn is big, but the opening will just fit between the bars. If I angle it right I should be able to tip Mum out in a few seconds, and with a friendly wind beneath her wings she will sail over those rooftops and out towards the Hudson. I will need to time this right. I wait until I feel the guard brush past me on his walk around. I fumble with the handles of the tote bag and heave the plastic tub out. A quick look around – it's still early in the season and miraculously no one is about. Gingerly I unscrew the lid. I haven't ever dared opened it for fear that her spirit will fly out, or that the banshee will howl her mourning song right in my face. I lift off the lid and take a quick look around. No one. I take a deep breath and look into the urn – I want to see Mum one last time, even if it is just her powdered skeleton. The fine grey/white grit is so impersonal it's hard to believe this is all that is left of my twinkly, silly, maddening mum. But here she is.

'Bye, Mum,' I say, my voice catching in my throat. I tilt the urn experimentally. A tiny cloud of dust – a finger? A toe? – puffs into the air. Then something catches my eye. A small piece of paper. Tucked just under the top layer of the ashes. Gingerly I pull on one corner. I shake off the dust and open the A5 sheet. What is this? A certificate of some kind? The coast is still clear so I unfold it with my free hand. My heart stops. Mum's unmissable shaky swirl reaches out from the other dimension. She has written.

One word.

'Live!'

I gasp. Why? How? Is this note what her secret chat with the funeral director was about? How can she have organised this?

How can she have known that this directive from beyond the grave would be exactly what I need right now? I press the paper to my mouth, kiss it and sob silently for a moment.

'Excuse me, ma'am,' comes a gruff voice from behind me. Oh God. Not now.

I slam the lid back on the urn. The tall guard peers down at me from under his big hat.

'I just saw something on the breeze there. What did you throw from the bag?'

'My mum. Well, a bit of her,' I smile sheepishly. No point in lying. Better to tell the truth and risk a fine than get arrested for suspected anthrax terrorism.

The guard considers me for a moment. 'Is that your mom in the urn?'

'Yes. Yes it is.' I wipe the tears from my face.

'Was it her wish that she be scattered from here, ma'am?'

'Yes it was, very specifically.'

'Then I ain't seen nothin',' he says, and he stands, a silent sentinel behind me as I cast Mum out onto the glimmering New York skyline, her note burning into my palm.

Chapter Twenty-nine

Live. That's what she said. Live. I have been dreading the aftermath of getting rid of Mum's remains. She has always been there for me, even in death, and I feared that if I let go of her physically that sense of her presence would go. But here she is, right here in the pit of my stomach, the centre of my heart. I can feel her all around me. I can almost see her.

'Live!' Even though we were close I never really felt seen for who I was. Perhaps that's an impossible ask. For a mother to really know her daughter. Or maybe the closeness that a woman can have with her daughter is blinding in some way. Do we go out of focus because we are too close, too near to be able to see properly? I knew my mum loved me and that was all I thought I could expect. But to be *seen*. She knew. She knew all along that I wasn't satisfied, that I'd stopped myself from believing there could be something else, something more. She knew that I wasn't like her, that sacrificing myself on the altar of motherhood was never going to do it for me. Her note has struck deep into my heart and for the first time in my life I feel totally visible – like someone has brought me sharply into focus for the rest of the world. It's a gift from beyond the grave. I know she could never have said it to my face while she was still alive – she would have felt it was an admission of some kind, an acknowledgement that I wanted more than she had chosen, and therefore a slight. It means the world to me to know that she saw this, no matter how crazy her method seems. That she saw *me* and that she was generous enough to make sure I knew.

I float down in the elevator, clutching the empty urn against my full heart. Out on the street I look up at the sky and wonder where she is now. She is gone, but I have never felt her more present. I jump in a taxi and head back to the hotel. My head is spinning, but not in that anxious, sickening way – I feel alive with energy. I beam at Topknot as I cross the lobby, and he even smiles back. Up in the room I sit on the bed and look at my suit-case. 'Live!' Am I really going to go home? What for? To give in to their version of me, the one that puts up and shuts up, the woman who doesn't mind merely existing to facilitate the more important lives of her husband and children? The wife who demands little and gets even less? Shouldn't I at least take these two weeks to do something for me? Live! That's what Mum meant. Despite her protestations that being a wife and mum were her life's ambitions, I can't help feeling that Mum is want-ing me to fulfil some of her dreams too, and that in letting her go I am taking on a promise to give her some vicarious thrills in the afterlife. There is just the smallest whiff of regret about that one word – 'Live!' Even though she would never have abandoned us for two weeks, I feel I owe it to us both to stay in New York.

My phone pings, bursting back into life via the free wi-fi.

A message from Amelie. A LONG message from Amelie.

'Mum – I just can't believe you did that. I know that you get sad sometimes and that you must get fed up with us but the things you said were really personal. I'm so fucking embarrassed. How could you publish all that? All the stuff I told you in private, all over the internet. Everyone was laughing about it at school today. I had to hide in the toilets with Tanika at lunchtime and I had mascara all down my face. Just because I'm your daughter it doesn't mean you own me, that you can chat shit about me online. I'm not your property. Thank God you don't understand about social media or you'd probably have posted pictures of my first tampon on Instagram. Are there no secrets? What next – will you publish this message on Twitter with laughing emojis? "Look at my stupid c**t daughter trying to tell me off"? Where does it end? I might be a drama queen, a typical selfish teenager in your eyes but don't you think I at least deserve some privacy? I do love you, Mum, but you've really fucked it this time.'

Wow. I can't really be angry about the casual swearing – I think we've crossed the rubicon on that one. I know she has a point. My mum would think nothing of telling my most embarrassing secrets to the neighbours, but at least that was only across the garden fence. Have I turned into Gwyneth Paltrow, oversharing every aspect of my own family fuck-ups to please my adoring followers at the expense of their dignity? Do our children really deserve privacy? Or are they just an entitled bunch of self-serving despots with a pumped-up opinion of their own importance in this tough old world? And yet for all my counter arguments, beneath her usual rage I detect Amelie is hurt. I know I've let her down. She felt safe with me at least – like slipping on an old cardigan feels safe – and I've blown it. I need a drink. First I will message Martin. Then I'll drink.

'How are things? Are the boys OK? Give Amelie a hug from me. PS bins go out tonight. PPS Amelie has netball tournament on Wednesday – don't forget permission slip x'

His reply arrives as I'm putting on my jacket.

> 'All good here. Boys fed, doing homework, Amelie fine –
> just flexing her muscles don't worry – bins out, note already
> done. Take care x'

Bloody hell. He's only gone and stepped up. This is huge. I feel vaguely pissed off. He's doing it deliberately – acing it to show me I'm being dramatic. He could at least have had the decency to flail around for a week. But oh no. Well, if it's so easy why couldn't he have stepped up before now? Why does it take me buggering off to get him to realise how rubbish he's been? Passive aggressive coping. The worst. I reply.

'Great! x' and head out for my first Manhattan in Manhattan.

Chapter Thirty

I can't face the bar in the hotel. Although it looks gorgeous there are too many wannabe novelists sat with laptops and topknots. Everyone is about twenty-five, plus I had a peep at the cocktail list and everything is nigh on fifty quid. I plan on having a few so I need to find somewhere a bit less 'special occasion' and a lot more 'keep 'em coming till I fall over!'

I head out into the spring evening. Despite my irritation with Martin's annoying 'coping' strategy, designed no doubt to make me feel guilty, and despite my gnawing sense of shame at betraying Amelie, I find myself excited by the prospect of a few cocktails in Manhattan. Will it be just like in *Sex and the City*? I wish I'd changed out of my dirty fleece and old trainers – I'm less Carrie Bradshaw and more *Carry on Camping*. Oh well. But hey, who's looking at me anyway? A middle-aged female tourist with eyesight so bad she can't see the tuft of whiskers appearing under her chin until they are waving at her? Greasy Man was an exception. Invisible is OK. No one to bother me or hijack my evening with pathetic flirting – sometimes being a dowdy old bag is like having a super power.

There's a bar a few blocks down from the hotel. It's just past the Happy Days Diner, so I turn up the collar on my fleece as I go past in case Greasy Man fancies a second go. I duck in and out of the crowds pressing along the sidewalk to the subways on their way home from work.

It's dark inside the bar. It's a nice place – not too flashy but not a pool table and TV sports kind of joint either. They should serve a decent Manhattan. I pull up a stool at the bar and a young woman with everything pierced places a napkin and a bowl of crisps on the counter for me.

'What can I get you?' she smiles, her tongue stud clacking against her soft palette.

'Can I get a Manhattan?' I ask, attempting a nonchalance I have never been able to pull off.

'Sweet or perfect?'

Wow. I didn't know there was a choice . . . I'm so provincial.

'Erm . . . perfect?'

'Sure,' she says, and gets to work mixing sweet and dry vermouth in a cocktail shaker along with rye whiskey and ice. She adds a dash of angostura bitters and strains the russet nectar out into a V-shaped glass before popping a maraschino cherry in to finish it off.

It's almost a religious experience, that first sip. I close my eyes in anticipation and let the cool deliciousness slip down my throat. I drain the glass in one and place it back on the counter. I open my eyes and the pierced girl is smiling her approval.

'Same again?' she laughs. 'It's Happy Hour, so two for one!'

'Why not?' I smile. 'I could do with a happy hour.'

'Like that, is it?' she asks, picking up the shaker and getting to work again. 'Well, let's see what we can do.'

I sit and drink one, two, three, four cocktails. The bar is filling up with New Yorkers finishing work and coming for a drink before heading out to dinner. No one seems in a rush to go home. I know I'm not. I haven't really eaten so I cram in mouthfuls of crisps with decreasing care. The crumbs fall into my lap and I pick them out absentmindedly. I'm drunk. I'm alone in New York. I don't know what to do. I think I'll stick it out for the two weeks. They are coping OK. I'm coping OK. I know where to get pancakes and where to get Manhattans. I've marked out my territory in the neighbourhood. This would be great for the blog. Is that a step too far? I've already upset them all, I might as well have some fun with it. It will be a way for me to document my trip as well as keep in touch with my followers. 'Followers'? What am I, some internet parenting guru? More like 'How NOT to parent teens/run a family/please your husband'. Right now it seems like a decent idea. I'll keep it light. Fun. Escapist. Who wants to read about depressing arguments and stale relationships? Where's the fun in toxic teens and monosyllabic marriages? But first I'm going to find somewhere else to drink. Somewhere illicit and cool and so NYC. A speakeasy where I can speak.

BLOG 17 – NYC BABY!

Hi there! I've escaped! I have been let out of jail for two weeks! So I thought I'd take this opportunity to carry on my little blog to show you suckers stuck in parenting teenager prison what you are all missing! There is nothing that doesn't look better after a few Manhattans. I hate bourbon and rye, and I don't have the sweet tooth needed for red vermouth, but together they make the perfect couple. The only true perfect partnership I know – forget Ruth and Eamonn on *This Morning*, Carrie and Mr Big on *Sex and the City*, or Michelle and Barack Obama in the White House – those swirling, oily clouds in an iced, V-shaped glass of Manhattan are the tops. I have to admit I've had a few. I started early in a bar somewhere near The Hotspot Hotel, now I'm in this whacky 'speakeasy' – you access it by going through the front of a dry cleaner's. You have to squeeze into this retro phone booth and give them the password. I didn't know it but the helpful girl on the line let me in anyway because of my English accent. Yes! It really is still a thing here!

It's very dark and I'm drinking some weird raspberry gin concoction out of a chipped teacup. A bloke at the bar is drinking a beer from a bottle wrapped in a paper bag. It's incongruous alongside his obviously high-end suit. We are all getting off on the prohibition vibe, harking back to the days of the alcohol ban, the great depression and Al Capone. I may be an old bag in a dirty fleece but right now I'm living my best life as a '20s flapper in a roaring jazz bar, getting tanked on illegal booze.

I order another cup of gin and carry on tapping away at my phone.

It's Monday night. Back home the boys and the old man will have been to football tonight. There will be sweaty T-shirts and boots discarded all over the hall floor. Normally I'd be there to pluck them up, washing and tidying after everyone while they all move forwards in their lives. Instead I'm going back in time, to an era when women had only just got access to public drinking – ironically after it had been banned. The little leaflet on the table tells me that women liked the speakeasy culture because there were tables to sit at, and you didn't have to compromise your lady manners by sitting up at the bar with all the men. I like this speakeasy culture, it's helping me to forget; forget that I'm not a flapper, that I should be at home fulfilling my maternal duties, that I don't want to be at home and that I'm miserable.

Oh dear. What happened to keeping it light? I think this gin is depressing me. I settle up with the waitress and lurch back out through the dry cleaner's. It's gone 10 p.m. now but the city that never sleeps is wide awake and I'm hammered. Food. I need food. The fresh air hits me hard and my head starts to spin. I've had A LOT to drink. I stumble into a retro burger joint and slump at a formica table, forcing a fancy burger in a brioche bun down my face. The curly fries are covered in that weird plastic orange cheese they seem to love here. It doesn't taste of anything recognisable but it's delicious. My face is covered in ketchup and gherkins. I don't care. It tastes so good.

Back on the street I'm confused – do I turn left or right? E12th Street – is that up or down from the hotel? I stumble in one direction and then the other, convinced both times I'm heading the right way until I realise I don't recognise anything. I sit down on the steps of a Halal food store. A woman at the checkout eyes me with irritation – another drunk westerner who should know better. I'll just sit here for a bit until my head stops spinning and then I'll ask someone. Oh God, I feel ill. The strong liquor and the greasy food is coagulating in my stomach, compounding the quiet churning of low-level anxiety I realise I've had for years. I belch loudly. I feel really bad. I'm going to be sick, but I can't do it here in the nice lady's clean shop doorway.

I pull myself to my feet and stagger to the corner, where I sit on a water hydrant and vomit prolifically over my trainers. It comes in spasms, and I break out in a hot sweat instantly. It's over quickly, and I raise my head experimentally to see if the world has stopped spinning. I catch sight of my reflection in the shop window opposite. My hair is stuck to my face, I'm white as a sheet and I'm covered in sick. 'Live!', she had said. If this is living you can keep it. I run my sticky fingers through my hair and bend to wipe the burger puke from my trainers.

'Are you OK?' asks a female voice from above me.

Oh God, the last thing I need is a good samaritan. She

probably thinks I'm a hobo or a local alcoholic. Maybe I am. I am certainly of no fixed address.

I look up. Standing over me is a tall woman with neat dark bobbed hair, wearing a crisp white shirt and a leather jacket. She looks so clean and kind that I burst into tears.

'Sorry,' I mutter as she hands me a tissue, 'I had a bit too much to drink.'

'Happens to the best of us,' she says as she roots around in her pocket for more tissues. 'You on your own?' she asks, producing another neat pile of tissues.

'Yes,' I say, 'I am.'

'Let me guess – you're on holiday? Where are you staying?'

'The Hotspot Hotel – just down the road.'

'OK, well, that's just a hop and a skip away, let's get you back there.'

'Thank you. Thank you so much.' She heaves me to my feet, links my arm and we totter the few blocks back to the hotel. I can't be sure but I think there is sick on my sleeve.

And that's how I meet Gina.

'Where did you put your key?' I'm dimly aware of Gina rummaging around in my pockets. The walk back to the hotel has done nothing to sober me up. I'm slumped against the wall outside my room.

'I don't know,' I slur, trying to remember what the key looks like. Is it one of those key card things? It could be anywhere.

'Ah! Here it is!' says Gina, pulling a fancy tassel from my back pocket.

She lets us in and sits me on the bed while she pours me a glass of expensive water.

'Drink this,' she says. Her manner is firm but kind. I feel mothered. It's nice.

I obey and drink the whole glass in one. I feel queasy as hell but I know I need water. I lie back on the bed and let her take my puke-stained shoes off.

'Are you OK?' asks Gina. I open my eyes and peer up at her. She's standing by the door. Tall, tanned, healthy-looking. At least ten years younger than me. I bet she hasn't had kids.

'Do you need anything else?' she asks.

'No, no, I'm fine . . . thank you so much. You're very very kind. Very kind. Thank you.'

The room starts to spin again so I close my eyes. I hear the door click gently and I fall into a fitful sleep, dreaming of netball matches and muddy boots and bins full of rubbish spilling out onto the street.

*

It's light when I wake up. My mouth is dry but my head, miraculously, is not pounding. I tiptoe gingerly to the bathroom and marvel at the dark amber of my pee. I'm really dehydrated. The expensive water is vile, so I stick my head in the sink and drink straight from the tap like a house cat. I'm still in my sicky clothes. I peel them off and step into the shower.

Under the stream of hot water the events of last night start to creep accusingly into my consciousness. Oh God. So many cocktails. This is becoming a bad habit. And the burger. And the vomit. My stomach turns at the memory of it. There are chunks in my hair. How did I get home? The woman! Yes, there was a woman. I think she told me her name was Gina. Did I meet her in a bar? I know she helped me get home. I think she gave me water. Oh the shame. I let the hot water wash away the stench of stale alcohol, fried food and vomit. I'll get clean, get dressed into some clean clothes and try to focus on how I get myself out of here.

What has become of me? Tuesday is my ironing day. I should be at home trying to stop the eleventh iron this decade from spitting brown sludge all over the kids' fifty school shirts. You can set your clock by my ironing routine. How I hate it. But it's a routine. I'd love to be inhaling the smell of warm linen right now.

I pull on clean clothes and sit on the bed, combing out my tangled hair. I need some fresh air. It's obvious I'm not going to be able to hack it here without risking serious liver failure. I'm not meant to be here. I'll go to Central Park – I have to go there before I head back home – then I'll head to the airport.

My phone beeps. A message from Martin.

'Good to know you've been having some fun out there. Amelie says you are blogging. Manhattans, eh? I made do with a gin and flat tonic. We didn't have ice because Paddy left the freezer open again but don't you worry about that. You just carry on enjoying yourself. Sorry to be a reminder of your 'miserable' life back here in 'jail' but I just wanted to let you know that we are OK all things considered, and we hope you are OK. That's all.'

No rage, no exhortations to rush back. He thinks I'm on a massive jolly, when really it feels like I'm having a late onset tortured adolescence. Or a nervous breakdown. Or I'm sinking into mid-life alcoholism.

The blog. I blogged again. I didn't think I was going to. I log on to see what I wrote. Not too bad, apart from the last bit about not wanting to go back to my miserable life. Oh dear.

I scroll through the comments.

'Wow you really did it! I am SO jealous! Can I come visit? Ha ha
ha – my husband would never cope without me – he doesn't
even know how to boil an egg ha ha. You have fun love!'

Does he really not know how to boil an egg or is she telling
herself that to make herself feel indispensable?

'They will soon miss what they took for granted. I'm impressed
you are able to leave your kids without worrying about them!'

Mum-shaming.

'You must go to the secret burger joint, the Dead Rabbit, the
cafe in Central park! Don't waste a minute of your special trip
– who knows when you'll get another chance like this? Not until
the bastards leave home, which, with the current housing market,
could be NEVER!'

I let out an involuntary groan at the prospect of picking up a
twenty-five-year-old's pants. She's right. They probably won't
move out, will they? They're not likely to choose high rents and
no maid service over a clean and serviced home funded by Bank
of Mum and Dad, are they?

I pull on my jacket and try to slip out through the lobby unno-
ticed. Topknot clocks me and beckons me over.

'Ma'am, how is your stay going so far?'

'Great, yes, great!'

'Are you feeling better today?' He smiles knowingly.

'Yes, yes, I'm very well thank you!'

Oh God, what did he see? Did I do the hokey cokey all around the
oak-panelled bar? Did I moon an 'influencer' in interesting glasses?

'Glad to hear it, ma'am, you have a great one!'

There it is again – the pressure to not merely put one foot in front of the other and survive each bloody day, but to have a '*great*' one. How do depressed Americans ever make it out of the door? The sense of failure they must feel every time they buy a coffee, a newspaper, a drink and are subliminally told they are not trying hard enough if they are merely getting through the day?

Chapter Thirty-one

Central Park is big. I've already walked for an hour and I don't know where I am any more. The winding paths all seem to lead to the same stretch of inner road, which loops around the entire park providing rollerblading fitness freaks with the perfect runway. Cyclists, joggers, skateboarders and children on scooters, all giddy with the rare freedom of movement and speed the park allows, steam along the road screaming at anyone stupid enough to get in their way. There are people with dogs, of course, but there are also people walking their cats on leads. This is bizarre and irritating and wonderful in equal measure. I have never seen a cat on a lead in the UK, and this is going straight in the mental file of American weirdness alongside Cronuts and alligators in the sewers. Or is that L.A.?

I find myself in a leafy glade where several twitchers have gathered to point their cameras at seemingly empty bushes. A solitary red bird hops from branch to branch close to the ground. It's about the size of a large sparrow and has the most fabulous black mask across its eyes. It's stunning. I sit on a bench to watch it and consider my next move. It's incredible to be sitting in the middle of the city watching a bird I have never seen before.

'Excuse me – what's that bird called?' I ask a snooty-looking birdwatcher.

'Oh that's just a Northern Cardinal,' says a bearded guy in a large anorak. 'There's a bunch of them around here.'

A Northern Cardinal! I've always wanted to see one! There it was right in front of me and I didn't recognise it. It's beautiful.

'And what about that paler, beige one?'

'That's the same bird. The female.'

Of course. Everyone knows the females are always duller. Is it something to do with males needing to attract a mate? The males have to put more effort in so that they get to bag a female and procreate? Someone should tell Martin. He might not be on his own scraping dried cereal remnants into the bin if he'd chucked out some of his old brown cardies.

'Hello again!' comes a voice from behind me.

I turn my head and look up. A tall woman in a grey shirt, khaki trousers and a straw hat is smiling down at me.

'Hi,' I say. I recognise the face but the uniform is throwing me off. Is she from London?

Gina. It's the woman from last night. I can feel the blood rush to my cheeks.

'Small world!' she smiles.

'Yes, yes . . . Gina, right?'

'Correct. I'm impressed you remember – Ciara.' She says my name with a slight wink. I blush again. 'You were kind of in a bad way.'

'Well, of all the birdwatching areas in all the world, you had to walk into mine ha ha ha!' I jabber.

She laughs. 'Feeling better, then?'

'Yes, yes – I think I ate something . . . you know . . . dodgy?'

She laughs again. She has beautiful teeth and her skin is lightly tanned. 'Dodgy?! That's a new one. Looked to me like you'd had a few too many.'

'Well, I had a couple but . . .'

'No, sure, sure. Something "dodgy" you ate, sure . . .' she smiles.

'So why are you here dressed like a massive Girl Guide?' I ask, eager to turn the conversation away from last night. 'Did you follow me ha ha ha?'

'Excuse me? Girl Guide?'

'The kit? You look like a Girl Guide.'

'Thanks, I think! It's my uniform. I work here.'

'Here? In Central Park?'

'Yeah – I'm a ranger.'

I have no idea why, but I blush again. She looks sort of silly but also impressive. I wonder if she rides a horse. Some of them ride horses, don't they?

'Ooh how lovely,' I coo, genuinely impressed.

'Sometimes. Summer is nice. Winter not so much. Mainly trying to stop folk from getting major head injuries on sledges or drowning in partially frozen lakes, but you know, we get by.'

'Do you ride a horse?'

This makes her laugh.

'I wish. I have a golf buggy sometimes but no horse.'

She sits down next to me and we stare at the bushes for a few beats. I have no idea what to say now that we've covered the obvious topics of my being sick and her being here. For some reason I feel like telling her everything. I have had no one to talk to since Mum flew over the rooftops yesterday. No sounding board. Just the same thoughts running round and round my head all night and all day. It might help to tell this almost stranger the true story of last night, of my escape from domestic servitude, my grief, my panic that the years haven't just aged me, they have rendered me transparent.

'I have a lunch break coming up. Do you want to grab a bite?' says Gina.

I'm stunned. Why would she invite me to lunch?! After my hideous display last night. I mean, she's seen me in a worse state than most other people that know me well. Does that make us friends? This simply does not compute. I may have been brought up by Irish parents but I am what Mum would have called very 'English' when it comes to social interaction. I prefer anonymity, I decline all food, drinks, conversations and small intimacies – the very cornerstones of Irish culture. It's just not the done thing in London to speak at any length to strangers. It's actually highly suspect. It's weird.

'Ooh. Food. I haven't had any food today yet. I'm fine, thank you very much.'

'I didn't ask you how you were! Let's go get something to eat – it will do you good. Come to the Tavern on the Green. It's nice – we can grab a sandwich at the counter, you don't have to sit down.'

She has read my suspicion and smiles at me as if to say 'I dare you!' I squirm awkwardly. What if she is trying to recruit me into some cult? She doesn't look culty (Girl Guide uniform notwithstanding) . . . What harm can it do?

'OK. It was on my bucket list anyway.'

'Really?! Why?! Most people go for Niagara Falls or the Pyramids but sure – sandwich in Central Park!'

'I'm a simple girl.'

'I doubt that very much,' she laughs, and I dip my head to hide my treacherous cheeks, which once again are burning up. What is that? I feel like such an idiot next to Gina. She exudes confidence, capability and ease. She doesn't look like she crashes around strange cities vomiting on corners. I bet she's never accidentally betrayed her whole family with slanderous public take-downs on the internet. I bet her husband is really cool and kind and they have amazing sex where they kiss and look each other in the eye, and don't just roll over in the dark and fart.

'I'm heading there for one p.m. if you feel like ticking one off that bucket list.'

And she goes.

Have I just made a friend? I haven't made a friend in years. I lost contact with all my university friends soon after the kids were born. It was hard work having three toddlers, and on the rare occasion I did make it out of town to visit them I took the kids with me and it was so horrendous for everyone that we all made a silent pact we'd never repeat it. The weekend in the countryside with three childless mates was wrecked by the Norovirus. I spent all night mopping up children's vomit – first Paddy's then Lorcan's, who was sharing his bed and had rolled in his brother's sick before succumbing himself. In and out of the shower we went, rinsing regurgitated fish fingers off the bedding and hosing down mattresses. In the morning, bleary and nauseous myself, I had detected only hostility at the broken night everyone had had to endure in the small cottage. No one said anything but it was clear that me and my noisy, sicky family were a blight on the rural idyll.

Things cooled a lot after that with my friends. They soon stopped calling altogether when I could never get the energy together to go for drinks. By 6 p.m. I was usually far too shagged and covered in excrement to have the energy to wash, find clean clothes and throw on a bit of slap. I had nothing to say anyway – while they jawed on about their latest promotion/new dress/ trips to art house cinemas, I would sit quietly trying to work a toddler tantrum into an amusing anecdote for childless adults. Any time I did open my mouth I could sense everyone mentally going on pause until I stopped and they could resume their much more amusing chat. In the end, by mutual but unspoken agreement, we all just drifted apart. Occasionally I see them pop up on Facebook, and some of them have even got children themselves now. Now they know what it's like! But it's too late for us to reconnect. Too much amniotic fluid under the bridge.

There's Jude, of course. I'll message her. She'll know what to do. I take a picture of the lake with the skyscrapers behind it and send it to her.

'Guess where I am?'

She'll be up by now, tending her orchids and wafting around in an expensive kaftan. She replies straight away.

'In Ikea buying some skyline wall art?'

'Ha ha. Nope. I'm here. I'm actually here. NYC!'

'Whatttt????'

I explain that I've run away. I tell her about the blog. She's gobsmacked.

'Babes – I always knew you had it in you! It's like when we bunked off double science. Except now you're bunking off your life! Wish I was there. Go have lunch, you weirdo – she's not going to KILL you. Probably not. Xxx'

I've missed this. Jude tells it like it is. I've got Debbie Downer, of course. And a handful of other mums I've been friendly with over the years, but more out of necessity than choice. They were all very nice but we were more like cell mates than genuine chums, with our only common ground being our delightful offspring. When the only other adults you see during the day are the spectres with hollow eyes and vacant smiles pushing buggies like zombies in the Mumsie Apocalypse, you cling to them. You can have a nice time with a gang of mum chums, none of whom really know you or even share your world view but who are bonded to you via your mutual struggle to make it to the school and back every day without either falling down dead from frustration and exhaustion, or accidentally killing anyone. It's quite the glue, that 'mothers in arms' thing, even though it's largely predicated on our children's – often precarious – friendships. Gina? Where does she fit in?

I don't make friends any more, I wouldn't know how. As a rule I refuse to befriend people on holiday. We once went to Tenerife and I got chatting to a German woman by the pool, who I foolishly invited to stay if she was ever in the UK. Most British people would take that for what it was – a disingenuous invitation designed to fudge the intimacy of a permanent goodbye – but not Mattea. Oh no. She turned up for a long weekend three months later and when we weren't round a pool with our clothes off we no longer had anything to say to each other. I came out in awkwardness hives.

Should I meet Gina for lunch? A bright red Northern Cardinal hops out of a bush onto the path in front of me and eyeballs me impassively. 'Go on,' he seems to say. 'Live a little.'

Chapter Thirty-two

I see her as soon as I walk in. The restaurant is perched on a lake and full of tourists who don't mind paying stupid money for a salad just to say they had lunch in Central Park. Gina is in the takeaway cafe right at the front of the queue. A gaggle of poorer tourists and savvy Americans push up against her in a disorderly rabble.

'Hey!' she says, seeming genuinely happy to see me. Like we're friends.

'Hello!' I say.

'What can I get you?'

'Oh nothing, you sort yourself out and I'll wait in the queue.'

'Oh OK, and if you wouldn't mind sweeping the floor and cleaning the counters while you're waiting?' she laughs.

'Sorry?'

'What do you want? Forget it, I'll get you something.'

I wait at the door and marvel at her ease ordering things. Americans don't say 'Please may I have . . .' or 'Could I possibly trouble you for . . .' – it's all 'Gimme a tuna mayo sub, hold the salad' and 'I'll get a cheeseburger with fries, easy on the pickles'. She pays by throwing a twenty-dollar bill on the counter and we head outside. The tables are full of people enjoying the spring sunshine so we sit on the grass by the lake. She hands me a paper parcel.

'Here – enjoy!' she says.

'What is it?' I ask, peeling back one corner of the paper suspiciously.

'Pastrami on rye. It's a local delicacy. You'll love it.'

'OK. Thanks.'

I try not to look at the flaccid pinkish meat flopping out either side of the dark, hard bread as I put a corner of the monstrous sandwich into my mouth. It's unexpectedly good, and my stomach wakes up to its hunger. I take another huge bite.

'So what's your story?' asks Gina as my jaws lock around a large chunk of crust. I try to speak but I can't unclamp them, and I start to choke with the effort. Gina laughs and claps me on the back. She hands me a can of Coke and waits for my coughing to subside.

'Sorry,' I gasp, 'I'd just bitten off more than I could chew.'

'Bad timing,' she says kindly.

My story. She wants to know my *story*?

'Not much to tell, I'm just out here having a little break. Some "me" time,' I say, putting the quote marks around 'me', as if my concept of self is ironic.

'OK, sure,' says Gina, like a detective who has just heard the shittest alibi ever and is waiting to reveal she already has my prints all over a nervous breakdown.

We eat our sandwiches in silence. I'm not sure what I'm doing here.

There it is again – that urge to spill the tea, as Amelie would say, and tell her everything. That's what would happen if this were a romcom. But life isn't a romcom, as I've found out the hard way. I decide to avoid my own misery and ask her about herself.

'So how long have you been a park ranger?'

Gina smiles again. I find it disconcerting, this constant wry amusement at everything I say.

'About two years.'

'Did you always want to work . . . outdoors?'

Gina laughs again.

'What's so funny?' I say. I feel embarrassed but I'm laughing along anyway.

'Nothing, I'm sorry, it's just . . . you're so freaking awkward!'

We barely know each other and she feels comfortable enough to point out my extreme social ineptitude. I kind of like it. It feels like being at school again, like when you have a plaster over a grazed knee that needs to come off but it's clinging on to the dried blood and pus, so your friend waits until you're not looking and just rips it off for you – it's sore, but it cuts all the crap. No softly softly here. Jude would do the same.

'I am. Yes. I am,' I laugh, and it feels good to be seen, that she seems to want to get past the barriers. It's like she's walked up to my icy windscreen and poured a kettle of hot water all over it.

She answers my question anyway. 'It wasn't my childhood ambition to work as a ranger, no. I guess I just fell into it.'

'How do you fall into a job like this?'

'It's a very long story.'

'The headlines, then.'

'I grew up in care, I ran away at fifteen, I almost drank myself to death while living on the streets, I got sober, I met someone special, moved in and got a job in a store and things were good for a while but then she threw me out two years ago.'

I don't know what to say so I just say 'OK' and look down at my half-eaten sandwich. Here I was feeling sorry for myself because my husband and children, in my neat, clean, warm home 'don't understand me', and here is this woman with her terrible childhood, her struggle with serious addiction and her sexuality to deal with and it's *her* picking *me* up off the floor?

'It's all right, you don't have to feel bad for me. It's all good. I'm working here now and I love it. I'm outside every day and I have a warm bed to go home to. I'm sure whatever it is you're going through is tough in its own way.'

I look up at her and she is smiling directly at me. What does she want? What does she see in me that makes her want to talk to me, eat lunch with me? Try to get to know me? I feel a wave of anxiety. I always feel this when I suspect someone is trying to get to know me. Panic. I feel bad for them, that they are probably wasting their time, thinking that I am something I am not. Perceiving my reticence as intellect or depth, when in fact it's just shyness masking a massive sense of emptiness. Normally I can just scuttle away muttering something about having to pick the kids up or put the dinner on, but here there is nowhere to run. I look out at the ducks waddling along by the lake. I wonder what to say next. Gina seems to sense my intense discomfort.

'So what are your plans for your holiday, then? You've ticked off one thing now – what else?'

'Oh well, some friends mentioned a few things . . . a secret burger joint?'

It sounds so silly now. So teenage.

'Oh sure yeah, I know that place. It's not so secret. It's in every guide book and it's almost twenty bucks for a burger and fries but sure, it's fun, I guess.'

'Shopping, you know, the usual. Maybe a drink on top of the Rockefeller . . .'

I'm such a cliché. I bet Gina knows some really cool places to go. Not just the usual tourist checklist.

'Amazing view of the park apparently – if you can get up there.'

'Yes, I've heard. Have you never been?'

'No, never. It's different when you're always here, you take it for granted. I mean, have you been to see Buckingham Palace?'

I laugh then. 'No. I haven't. Fair point.'

Gina looks at me for a long beat. She seems to be assessing something. Is she a religious nut? Is she going to try and recruit me? Scientologists are big in the States, aren't they? Will she try to make me take a personality test? She'll have a job finding mine.

'Why don't we go tonight?' she says finally.

'Go? Where?'

'To the Rockefeller? You want to go, I've never been – it's a match made in heaven!'

Tonight? What will we talk about? I almost made this casual sandwich into a living silent hell – never mind a match made in heaven.

'OK,' I say, before I have time to say no. 'Why not?'

We agree to meet at the Rockefeller at 6 p.m. Gina says she will book the tickets, and with that she says goodbye and strides off into the woods, swinging her hat between her thumb and forefinger.

What have I just agreed to? As far as she is aware I am a lone middle-aged woman with a very pedestrian tourist checklist taking a holiday in New York. What on earth is she seeing in me? We have nothing in common. She's at least fifteen years younger than me, she hasn't mentioned any children and she's a lesbian.

It occurs to me that most women of my generation would probably ascribe a sexual motive for this interest she is showing in me. I despise that. I had plenty of lesbian friends at college and I remember them raging at straight women who assumed that because they were women ALL lesbians would fancy them. I remember fierce exchanges between Jodi, the performance poet, and Shula, her rampantly heterosexual friend.

'Oh my GOD, why do you always try to snog me when you've had a few ciders? I am NOT INTERESTED IN YOU! Just because I'm gay it doesn't mean I'm going to want to sleep with every woman I ever meet! I do have some taste you know!'

'Charming!' Shula would say.

'I'm not being rude but you're not my type!'

'What do you mean, "type"?! Are you objectifying me?' she'd say, pouting a little.

'I'm not objectifying you – I just don't want to sleep with you!' Jodi would wail, exasperated.

'WHY NOT?!'

'BECAUSE I AM NOT YOUR EXPERIMENTAL SEXUAL GUINEA PIG! I AM NOT YOUR RIGHT-ON, "TICKED THAT BOX" BADGE OF HONOUR! BUT MOSTLY I DON'T WANT TO SLEEP WITH YOU BECAUSE YOU'RE BEING A DICK!'

I'm wary of that heterosexual arrogance. I know it's not a sexual thing. How could it be? I think I have the opposite of pheromones – I emit 'leave me alone' chemicals that would repel even the most determined leerer at saggy-faced old women like me. I never assume anyone is interested in me, male or female. Martin always joked that it was like trying to coax a deer out of the forest, getting me to agree to a date. Absurd now to think that I was so demure, but at the time I couldn't stand any more of the exposing, torturous pain of getting to know someone new, of them getting to know me. I'd have preferred an arranged marriage, or a CV selection process whereby all interested parties could access my history, read it and then decide if I was a contender or not. It never occurred to me that maybe I could pick someone. I've only ever been the one being asked. And that always ended in disaster. And here I am again, coyly accepting an invitation which is bound to make me sick with anxiety. And yet ... something about Gina is reassuring. Maybe she just wants to be nice? Maybe it's not true that all New Yorkers are rude and unfriendly. I'll go. It will be fine. I'll have a drink and admire the view then go home. No harm done.

*

I have nothing to wear. I'm sure trainers and casual clothes are frowned on in places like the Rockefeller Center. I haven't really bothered much with clothes in the last decade or so. My roots are greying and I only have one (beige) lipstick to my name, which makes me look like I've had a cardiac arrest (as Paddy so gleefully pointed out the first time I wore it). I walk back down Central Park and head for Saks Fifth Avenue.

The usual snooty cows with too much make-up on look me up and down as I enter on the ground floor and quickly decide I'm not worth much effort. I head up the escalators and shuffle apologetically though the ladies fashion section. Everything seems so expensive and I don't know what to buy. I hate shopping for clothes. I feel like Mr Benn, trying on different characters. Am I a Weekend Casual linen-wearer who favours pastel shades and carries a basket full of daffodils? Am I a well-put-together career woman with careful tailoring and a neutral colour palette? Or am I a hippy earth goddess in flowing silks and floral patterns? I'm none of these things. Which is why, I guess, I favour the blank canvas 'don't notice me' navy slacks and T-shirt non-look.

If Amelie was here she'd be going crazy, running up and down the displays declaring she 'had to' have this or that, her passion for clothes making her breathless and unselfconscious for once. She'd know what to put me in. She's always on at me to make more of myself and stop dressing 'like an old bag lady'.

I could call her. She'll be at home now, probably failing to do her homework because of the hours of grooming her pet eyebrows demand.

I try not to overthink it. Maybe if I just call her and try to normalise things she'll forget that I've run away and will just be excited that I'm in a department store in New York.

I perch on a small sofa next to a terrifyingly fashionable mannequin dressed in what looks like plastic bags.

I hit Amelie's name on my FaceTime app and chew my lip as I wait.

She answers.

'Hi, Madre,' she says in that familiar depressive tone designed to garner maximum attention. I smile. It's good to see her miserable face. Familiar.

'Hello, love. How are you?'

'I'm good.'

'That's good to hear. How are you all getting on?'

'Fine. When are you coming home?'

That's progress. She wants me home.

'I wasn't sure you would want me home,' I say, fishing for forgiveness.

'I didn't say I did. Obviously I'm still really pissed off.'

She pouts at herself experimentally in the camera. None of the kids ever look at me if I video call them. Amelie poses, plays with her hair. The boys pull stupid faces and press their noses up against the screen.

'I know, and I understand. But you have to know that a lot of it was just silly exaggeration.'

'So you don't think I'm a cunt, then?' she says lightly, tossing her mane over one shoulder.

A well-dressed woman walks past.

'Shhh!' I hiss. 'I'm in public and they don't like the C-word in America.'

'Why have they got one in charge of the country then?'

She doesn't say this as a joke but I laugh. She's pleased to have amused me and her face relaxes.

'So what's it like then, New York? Seeing as I'm obviously NEVER going to go now.'

'You will. We will. It's . . . OK. Lonely. I'm thinking of coming back in a day or two.'

'OK. Well, you know maybe you should stay a bit longer. We're OK. Dad is actually a pretty good cook and he's done all my blouses for the week. He's really good at ironing, you know. And he's being really nice. He gave us all twenty quid last night. I think he feels a bit bad.'

'He hasn't done anything wrong, you know, Amelie, not really.'

'Ugh, I don't want to hear about your relationship with Dad, Mum. That's weird. Oh and I broke up with Rodney.'

'Why? Are you OK?'

'Yeah, it's all good. We just realised we were making each other sad and we're too young to meet the demands of a romantic relationship right now.'

Wow. She's growing up.

'Well, that sounds like a very mature and healthy decision,' I say.

'Yeah. Plenty of time for boys anyway. Don't want to be tied down. Not like you and Dad. What's it like to know that you're going to be with each other forever?'

I blink. Why is she asking about us? Is she testing me? Does she think I've left for good?

'Well, I don't think anyone really thinks like that. You just plod on and hope for the best. It's a bit daunting to think like that.'

'But to know that there isn't anyone else out there for you ever again, that you've found the one? Ugh.'

'I don't really believe in "the one", Amelie. I think relationships are like night buses – you wait and wait for the right one until you get sick of waiting and jump on the one that will get you closest to home.'

'Romantic much?! Mum! Dad is not a bus.'

'It's a metaphor, Amelie. It's just a metaphor.'

'Mum, can you just wait a sec—'

She pauses our conversation and the screen shows her blurry silhouette as she attends to an incoming Snap message. Whatever it is we are trying to patch up here – our mother/daughter schism – will just have to wait while she views a pointless message from someone she saw half an hour ago. Business as usual then.

She's back.

'Hi, Madre – so did you want something?'

'OK, I can see that you're busy. I'll let you go.'

Why did I think that anything would have changed? I'm still the least important thing in her world right now, even though I've left them all. What would I have to do to get top billing – set fire to myself outside Topshop?

'No, don't be like that, Mum – I've got a couple of minutes.'

'It's nothing important – I thought I might buy myself something nice to wear while I'm here. I'm in Saks.'

'You're in Saks?!'

Now I have her attention.

'Why are you in Saks? Why do you want to buy something nice? This all sounds very dodgy, Mum.'

'Dodgy? Why is it dodgy? I've got my own money and I wanted to buy myself something. I'm going to the Rockefeller bar tonight.'

'Why?!'

'Because someone asked me!'

'Who asked you? Mum – are you having an affair?!'

Her face is right up close to the camera and her nostrils flare with indignation.

I sigh.

'No, I'm not having an affair. Look, I just made friends with a woman called Gina and she suggested we go.'

'Oh a woman. OK. That's a bit weird. You don't make friends. But anyway, OK. So you need to be on trend. But a bit posh. But not too middle-aged. I'd suggest a Bodycon dress – black – with spaghetti straps. You're a slim/thick shape so you can show your bootee. Wear it with gold hoop earrings and maybe some Gucci trainers.'

'OK and now in English, please? What is a Bodycon dress and why would I wear trainers with a dress?!'

'Trust me, Mum – this is my area. Go and ask someone to help you. A dress with trainers is cool – the dress does the hard work but the trainers say "I'm not trying too hard", because that is DEATH.'

'No one can ever accuse me of trying too hard on the fashion front, Amelie. OK. Thanks.'

She smiles at me then. She likes to feel useful after all.

'And Mum?'

'Yes, love?'

'Please may you buy me something?'

'OK. What do you want?'

'Some Anastasia Beverly Hills Dipbrow Pomade in taupe. And a Nike fanny pack. And some Nike Airforce 1s. And a Huda Beauty #FauxFilter Foundation. And an Anastasia Beverly Hills Modern Renaissance eyeshadow palette—'

'Sorry, you're breaking up, I didn't quite catch that,' I lie. I'll be here all day and I'm damned if she's going to hijack this shopping trip.

'Mum? MUM!'

I hit the end call button and go off in search of a sales assistant. A young, beautiful woman is loitering near a display of what look like plumber's overalls.

'Hi,' I say, grinning nervously, 'I wonder if you can help me?'

'Sure!' she smiles.

'I need an outfit – do you call it an outfit? – I need something nice to wear for this evening.'

'OK,' she says, looking me up and down quickly, 'What sort of thing do you have in mind? What's the occasion?'

'Well, it's not really an occasion as such, I'm going for drinks at the Rockefeller Center and my daughter says to not try too hard, so maybe a black Bodypack something or other with a fanny con or something?'

Is that right? I think I remembered it wrong.

The assistant tries to suppress a smile.

'A Bodycon dress? Sure.'

She leads me through a labyrinth of rails and we arrive at a beautifully lit evening-wear section.

'This all looks quite . . . erm . . . I'm not sure I really suit this kind of thing,' I gulp, as she pulls a thin tube of black elastic from a rail and steers me towards a fitting room.

'Maybe take this one too, if you think black might be too formal?' she says, handing me an identical peach-coloured elastic tube.

She ushers me into the cubicle and pulls the curtain closed. I stare at myself in the full-length mirror. I feel sweaty, dirty and tired – the perfect frame of mind for trying a completely new look. I pull off my jumper and leggings and stand face to face with my poor old carcass. It's a sorry sight, not helped by the morgue lighting. My knickers are grey and baggy – I can't remember when I bought them. Probably in a supermarket ten years ago. My bra is digging in around my chest, leaving a red welt ring around my ribcage. My stomach is alive with silver stretch marks, like a stream full of sticklebacks, and my C-section scar is raised and faded to an antique rose. The skin on my belly is wrinkled and sad, a deflated balloon. My legs look like a pair of tights filled with porridge. I turn away from the mirror in an act of defiance and denial. If I don't stare at it, it isn't there.

I pull the peach dress from its hanger and pour my body into the tiny elastic bandage. It's tight. I heave at the hem, which has come to a stop around my middle. I tug and tug, and eventually it gives. I drag it over my hips, pulling it decisively over my reluctant thighs. I dare to look up. Jesus. Bodycon is cruel. Staring back at me is a gigantic flesh-coloured sausage. I pivot experimentally, morbidly fascinated by the horror in front of me. My knickers have bagged up around my bum, and my back fat spills over the top of the rubber band around my boobs. I don't think I'll be teaming this with trainers – more like a binbag. I tug at the straps, desperate to release my body from it's elastic prison. I pull desperately but the dress is glued to my body. I start to sweat and panic. What if I die here?

'How is that working out for you?' asks the nice assistant from beyond the curtain.

'Erm . . . I don't think . . . actually, erm, I can't seem to get it off.'

She pulls back the curtain.

'Oh. OK. Here let me help you.'

She pulls expertly at the hem and peels it off over the top of my head. My knickers are halfway down my bum and one boob has popped out under the exhausted elastic of my bra strap.

'Let me see if I can find you something more . . . you,' she says sweetly, mercifully averting her eyes from my disgrace.

She disappears and I slump onto the floor of the changing cubicle. My phone pings and I pull it from my pocket. A message from Martin. Impeccable timing as usual.

'You say you feel invisible. It's not true, you know. Or at least, it's not accurate. I have to confess your words have stung but today I sat in the garden having a cup of tea before I went to work and I really thought about what you have written. Setting the public humiliation aside, I can see how you have come to the conclusion that none of us care. But it's a false conclusion. Of course we care. It's just life – we're all busy, and you've done such a good job with the kids they don't need to be hanging off your apron strings all the time. And me? Well, you know me, I just pootle on, trying to keep a roof over our heads and the wolf from the door. Sorry for the clichés, I'm not a writer like you, but they are clichés for a reason. Keeping a family going is mostly just hard bloody work. There are no medals. No one pats you on the back and says "Well done on that house insur-ance application, thanks for cooking that lovely shepherd's

pie and top marks for the homework enforcement." You
just have to get on with it. But we can only get on with it if
there is someone at the centre holding us all together. So
rather than think of yourself as peripheral to us, think of
yourself as the sun around which we all orbit.

    Martin.'

So he can string a sentence together after all. I lean my head
back against the wall and think about all the times I have sat in
an empty kitchen while the rest of the family get on with their
lives. I have put my life on hold to be utterly available to them
without even realising it. I never book myself in for anything. I
don't plan trips out for myself because I feel I should be around
just in case they need me. Where would I go, anyway? Who
would I go with? Once the housework is done and the dinner is
prepared, there are only about three hours left before they all
come home again and I've never liked the idea of them coming
back to an empty house. I never had to when I was growing up.
Mum was always there with a Wagon Wheel and a cuddle. I've
always felt: what's the point of having a family if you're never
there? Might as well not have had kids if you enjoy life more
without them. Increasingly, though, I have felt ridiculous for
feeling like this. Like some sad woman who gets dolled up for
what was just a hint of a date, only to be left sitting at the bar,
watching the world fly past the window. 'The sun around which
we all orbit'? I don't know much about the solar system but I've
done enough science homework with the kids to know that the
gravity of the sun keeps the surrounding planets in a pattern of
motion. They only stay in their orbits because there is no other
force in the solar system which can stop them.

    It's not even a choice.

I don't know if I want to be the force that stops them spinning off into the atmosphere. Maybe I want to fly away into the clouds too.

Maybe that's what Mum wanted really. Was that what that was all about, the ashes off the top of the Empire State Building? It was always a bit 'out there' for a woman who considered foreign travel 'showing off'.

The assistant arrives back and pushes a bundle of flowery dresses through the curtain.

'Try these,' she says.

They are sweet. Sort of vintage. Trouble is, so am I. Vintage needs to be worn by the young. The old just look like they've stepped out of a war newsreel.

The sun. I remember Lorcan telling me that the sun, although four-and-a-half billion years old, is only 'middle-aged', and has roughly the same number of years left before its outer layers blow away, leaving its slowly diminishing core. I felt vaguely depressed when he told me that, like the sun was me. I couldn't work out if it was the idea of being only halfway through it all or the inevitable disappointing end to my existence that made my heart sink.

I try the dresses on with no enthusiasm. I feel dowdy. Eventually I throw them all in a pile and run from the changing room. I don't want to disappoint the nice young woman by rejecting all her choices so doing a runner feels best. On my way through the store I grab a white T-shirt, some navy chinos and a pair of slip-on shoes. $200. I might look like one of those adverts for chair lifts you see in the back of the Sunday supplements but at least I won't feel ridiculous. Or look like a sausage.

Chapter Thirty-three

It's 6 p.m. I've been here for twenty minutes already, hiding in the lobby. I don't want to look too keen. There are hoards of people milling about in Rockefeller Plaza, mostly tourists like myself. I can see why Gina has avoided the place – it's overwhelmingly horrible. I sit inside near the elevators watching the queue for Bar 65, the no doubt overpriced cocktail lounge on the 65th floor. I feel a pang of empathy for the lumpy women and freshly scrubbed men who have got dressed up in shirts and smart shoes for the privilege of paying $100 to ride to the top of a building. There's not even a drink thrown in – that's extra. I Google the history of the place. How ironic that its architects were appointed the day before the stock market crash of 1929. A philanthropic capitalist gesture in defiance of the great depression, mass unemployment and lengthening bread lines. I read about how the workers, grateful for the jobs and renewed purpose, showed their gratitude by erecting a small Christmas tree during the festive season of 1931, and decorated it with strings of paper, garlands of cranberries and tin cans. I let out an involuntary sob. I've always been a sucker for Christmas.

'Hey!'

Gina is smiling at me. I rub my eyes with the back of my hand and stand to greet her.

'Hi!' I say, relieved she has come. I wasn't even aware until now that I thought she wouldn't.

'Shall we?' she says, indicating the queue.

We slot in behind a Japanese couple.

'So how has your day been? Have you been packing to go home?'

'No. I went shopping.'

'Oh! I didn't have you down as the shopping kind. Where did you go?'

'Saks,' I smile, already apologising for my predictability.

'Bucket list?'

'Something like that.'

Gina smiles knowingly. I'm not sure *what* she knows but I have a vague sense that she knows things about me that I haven't told her. It's at once thrilling and alarming.

The queue moves quickly and soon we are leaving our stomachs behind as the elevator pulls us skywards. At the top we are spewed out into an elegant lounge. Glasses gleam, a pianist plays generic lounge jazz and small tables of tourists ignore their cocktails while they drink in the view. It's astonishing. The grid system of the city comes into its own up here. I rush to the glass walls outside and gasp when once again I see the long rectangular oasis of Central Park laid out like a velvet carpet on a stone floor.

'Ah – the office!' says Gina behind me.

'Isn't it incredible? I think this is the most beautiful thing I've ever seen.' The twinkling lights of the city at sunset, the vast pink sky, the sense of perspective and awe all at once.

'It's pretty cool, actually!' says Gina, laughing a little at her own pleasure.

We stand for a few minutes, silently taking it all in.

'Shall we get a drink?'

'Yes, let's,' I say, reluctant to leave the view.

We take a seat and order. I get a Manhattan – because, well, it would be rude not to – and Gina orders a Club Soda. I feel awkward now. Exposed.

We drink and Gina talks about her work, her small rent-controlled apartment in Brooklyn, her parrot called Colette, how she likes spoken word poetry and how AA meetings are a big part of her life. I sip my Manhattan self-consciously.

'Is this OK? I mean, are you OK with me drinking?' I ask. Am I being insensitive? I've never really known an alcoholic – at least not one that has admitted it.

'It's fine. Seriously, if I had a problem with people drinking around me I'd never go out. You do you. Or are you asking your-self if it's OK? 'She smiles.

I suppose I am – But I order another. My stomach turns a little at the sensory memory – the last time I tasted this it was coming up rather than going down. Emboldened by the alcohol and intoxicated by the view, I find myself staring at Gina. Why is she here? What does she want?

She smiles, sensing my questions.

'OK,' she says, 'go ahead.'

I blink.

'Go ahead with what?'

She laughs.

'You look like you have a question.'

I blush. How can I ask her why she has shown this much interest in me? Nobody shows this much interest in me. Why would a youngish, attractive lesbian park ranger from New York City want to spend time with a dusty old suburban housewife from an unfashionable London suburb? What could possibly be in it for her? Unless she belongs to a very niche lesbian commu-nity that fetishises comfy slacks and total libido bypass? I don't know how to ask her these questions without appearing to be a total, presumptuous idiot. I've been through this with Jodi and Shula. Am I going to be that heterosexual dick?

'Well . . . I suppose, if I'm honest, I'm not totally sure why you're here. I mean, I think I need to tell you that I'm married. To a man. Called Martin.'

It seems that I am.

Gina smiles.

'Thanks for the information.'

'God, I mean, not that you . . . you know . . . I'm not saying that you're trying to . . . but just in case you think I'm in the market for . . . or that I'm trying to, you know, get you to . . . God, I'm such a knob, I'm sorry.'

She laughs. 'A "knob"? Is that what I think it is?'

'That was so stupid. Sorry. I'm just not used to people . . .'

'. . . being nice to you?'

'Yes.'

'That's a bit sad. Well, what can I tell you? You want to know why I asked you to go to lunch? You don't understand why a stranger would accompany you on an evening out? You have no idea why anyone would want to give their time to you?'

I nod. There is a lump in my throat. It's hard to hear how low my self-esteem sounds. Gina smiles warmly.

'Are you a Scientologist?' I quip, unable to cope with the sudden intimacy.

'No. I'm not.'

'Then . . . why?'

'Because. Because I could see you were in distress. Because you looked down. Because you laugh a lot but your eyes are sad. Because I know what it's like to feel invisible. To have people walk by you on the street. Because I vowed to help any woman I saw struggling on her own. Because life is short and full of pain and if you can help someone in their hour of need then you haven't wasted your time on this planet. Because we're all struggling, and the fellowship is about reaching out and holding on to each other. Because I'm better when I'm helping you. Because I don't know you but I know you deserve this.'

I gulp. 'So you're not trying to get off with me, then?'

Gina laughs, and I join her even though my eyes are wet with tears. We talk for at least an hour. She tells me about what it was like to sleep rough, how her father beat her and her mother wouldn't accept her sexuality, how couch-surfing in various friends' houses was preferable to staying at home and how her ex-girlfriend, Audrey, ran off with their therapist Carolina. She talks about how much she loves being in the park, how the wildlife and the changing seasons and the crazy people she meets make her feel so present on the planet. She talks about how she's done with monogamy, but not with sex. I blush. A lot. She talks about AA, about how tough it is to know that your sobriety is an ongoing battle. She recites the serenity prayer at my request, and I find myself moved to tears again.

'God, grant me the serenity to accept the things I cannot change, courage to change the things I can, and the wisdom to know the difference.'

She asks me about the kids, Martin, my life back home. At first I toe the party line, telling her funny stories about them all: the cute things they said as toddlers; the time Paddy and Lorcan were cast as icicles in the school Nativity and they were so pleased, even though it was set in Israel and they were at the very least climatically incorrect; how Amelie was entranced by *The Wizard of Oz* as a child and to this day knows the entire script. As I start to mention Martin, I find it harder to dredge up the happy memories. With a jolt I realise that I don't have many recent ones. It's all a blur of domestic duty, dove-tailing each other neatly to make sure the house runs smoothly and there is food in the fridge. The bins go out on time. The bills get paid. The shirts are ironed.

Where is the joy?

'He sounds like a good guy,' says Gina generously. I can see she is reading my reticence.

'Yes, he is. And yet . . .'

I'm two Manhattans down and I feel looser now.

'And yet?' prompts Gina.

I sigh. 'I don't know. It's just, I mean, maybe I just need to try harder. He seems perfectly happy. I mean, I'm sure he'd like more sex – sorry to be blunt – and I think sometimes he looks tired, but generally he seems content, and I can't help feeling it must be me. There must be something wrong with me, right? I mean, I love him and everything, whatever that means, and I love my kids, but I can't help feeling like I'm re-reading the same book over and over, and sometimes I could scream with boredom.

'I don't know why I'm thinking of this now, but when I was a child I begged my mum for a tortoise and eventually she caved in and let me have one. I loved that tortoise. I called it Speedy Gonzales!! (It was a cartoon character, before your time, forget it.) But after a while it got a bit boring and I asked my mum how long they lived and she said, "A hundred years." I was devastated. A hundred years! How can you love something for a hundred years? I would be dead before it was! And I would have had no opportunity to have a different pet.'

Gina is smiling her amused smile again.

'What happened to Speedy?'

'He ran away. Well, walked away. I think he sensed my indifference.'

'But husbands aren't tortoises, right?'

'Apparently not.'

'So *you* ran away?' Gina seems determined to find out what really brought me here.

'I suppose you could put it like that.'

'How would *you* put it?'

I tell her about the blog, about my mum and the ashes, and the note, and the accidental public sharing, then the thrill of having followers. I tell her about the awful scene in the kitchen, my escape, The Hotspot Hotel, Topknot, and the fact that since I have been here I have felt a compulsion to 'live a little', whilst at the same time duty bound to return home.

Gina nods her head wisely through most of this but doesn't say anything.

'So here I am,' I finish. 'I was going to go home tonight. I've been meaning to go home for the past three nights.'

'And why haven't you?'

'Because I keep thinking of things I want to do first.'

'You make it sound like going back home is death – like living can only happen here.'

I think about this. How is it that I can talk so openly to her when I have never really admitted these things to myself? I'm almost surprised by what is coming out of my mouth. My life sounds like a living death. It certainly feels like it sometimes. Like the rest of the family are living their lives, and I'm just the screensaver, an inanimate backdrop. Is that why I've been so easily dissuaded from going home? Was it really about dispersing Mum's ashes, or seeing Central Park and coming to the Rockefeller?

'Maybe it does feel that way. But that's stupid, isn't it? Doesn't that make me ungrateful? Depressed? I don't know.'

'You know what I think?' Gina takes hold of my hand and stares at me sternly. 'I think it's time you had some fun.'

I blink hard at her. My hand feels clammy in hers.

'Fun? What is this "fun" you speak of?'

'You know – doing things because they feel good? Following your desires. Planning things you enjoy. Being silly. Laughing. Doing something new. Feeding yourself with art, literature, hot dogs – whatever!'

I consider how absurd this sounds to me. 'Fun' isn't a word I associate with myself very readily. I think I used to be fun, but I can't remember how. Now it feels like being asked to do something really hard and unattainable – like sudoku or cable knit.

'We can make a checklist. I love lists,' says Gina, taking out her phone.

'OK, so you wake up in the morning with a totally free day – no commitments, no chores—'

'I'm having fun already!'

'No, come on – we can do better than that. Take the bar higher.'

'Erm . . . OK . . .'

I wrack my brains for a single thing I can remember that is fun to do.

'I used to like popping bubble wrap . . .'

'COME ON!!!'

Worryingly, depressingly, my mind is a blank. Fun. All I can think of are activities the kids used to love that would depress the hell out of me. Water Parks. Crazy Golf. Paintballing. All expensive organised attempts at diverting you from the point-lessness of it all.

They say you should take up a new hobby if you're bored. Yoga. Or Knitting. Or learn to play a musical instrument. I can't think of anything worse.

Gina stares at me, her mouth open in disbelief. Her teeth are even and white. I take another sip of my drink and pretend to think harder.

'OK, OK, this is really sad. What did you enjoy doing when you were young?'

I raise my eyebrows.

'Sorry, younger.'

'I didn't really have hobbies. I had a few good friends. We laughed a lot. We used to sing. We had scooters. We drank in the park. We used to dare each other to do stupid things in the supermarket . . .'

It doesn't sound like much of a youth when I say it like that. I feel annoyed. I hate it when people press me to have fun. It makes me angry.

'Why is fun so important? And why when you are older? I thought being an adult was the serious bit. Growing up. And anyway, I hate the idea of going back to my youth. How sad. Isn't that what men do? Fast cars and ill-advised leather jackets, like wrinkly extras from *Grease*? I wouldn't want to be Sandra Dee. I don't want to be sixteen again. All that uncertainty and heartache. All that thinking about yourself all the time. I hate the idea that I'm heading towards the last third of my life and all I can think about is what the first third was like. Surely the middle bit must have meant something?'

Gina stares at me for a long beat.

'OK, let's come back to that. Think back to before you met Martin, to before the kids. What did you do on an average weekend? After work? I mean, did you work?'

'Yes, I did. I worked in a publisher's. For twelve years. I was an editor.'

'Cool!'

'Not really. It was a small publisher's. Mostly factual stuff.'

'That can be cool. What was the book you most enjoyed editing?'

It's so long ago I can hardly remember the details. Just the tube journey, the lunches, the drinks in the pub up the road. The work itself was OK, but not much about it connected with me. I think for a minute. I remember one book I worked on. It was mostly photographs. Motorbikes. I had to edit the copy and I didn't really know what I was doing because the language was quite specialised. There was one picture of a woman, quite an old woman, with flowing grey hair, no helmet, speeding along on a huge chrome monster of a bike, the handlebars set wide apart. I remember thinking she looked very happy. And faintly ridiculous. But happy. I remember thinking I could never be that impervious to judgement. She seemed so old to me then – though probably only about seventy – and she was very silly to be riding a motorbike with no helmet. If she crashed that would be it. And she was wearing shorts! Yes, denim cut-offs. Her legs were thin and wiry. Completely bare. If she'd come off that bike she'd have taken the skin off her entire leg.

It's dark outside now, and the tourists start to drift off.

I tell Gina about the photograph.

Her eyes twinkle in the candlelight.

'OK,' she says, picking up our jackets, 'I'll come and get you tomorrow morning. Be ready to have some fun. Wear whatever you like. Bring money. Bring your passport. Bring a change of clothes.'

I gulp. 'Why? Where are we going? Why do I need my passport?'

She laughs. 'Because who knows what the day might bring? We need to be ready for whatever might happen. Be ready for adventure. Take it as it comes. See where the mood takes us.'

This sounds horrendous.

'But what about my flight? What about going home?'

'You're not due back for another nine days, right?'

'Well, originally, yes but—'

'"Originally" is good. You can go home then.'

We head back down in the elevator and say goodbye on the street. It's cooler now the sun has set, and the passers-by move quickly along the sidewalk. Everyone is going somewhere.

'OK, I'll be outside your hotel at ten,' says Gina, giving me a brief hug.

'I feel like we've just planned a heist,' I say.

She pulls back, her hands on my shoulders. 'Maybe we have,' she laughs.

I take a taxi back to the hotel, my head spinning. Is it the Manhattans? The jet lag finally kicking in? Or is it more like . . . excitement? I feel a bit giddy, a bit frightened, but when I put my head on the pillow and close my eyes I am smiling. I drift into a deep sleep and dream of bubble wrap, Crazy Golf and a huge red bird.

Chapter Thirty-four

I wake early and pick up my phone. I have five messages from home.

Lorcan has finally got in touch.

'Mum can u get me sum Jolly Ranchers and sum Fluff and sum Reece's Pieses pleeeeeez?'

He's over the humiliation then. I can see that his second message was sent a few seconds later.

'Mum?? U kind of owe me! Altho I am kind of famous now lol'

Martin has messaged again.

'All quiet on the western front. *Very* quiet here. All good. Debbie brought a lasagne round last night. It was a bit odd. Not the lasagne – that was lovely – but I think she feels sorry for us. Take care love.'

Lasagne, eh? She'll be trying to get her maudlin slippers under the table, then. She always liked Martin. He can't stand her.

Amelie:

'We won our netball match and Rodney wants to get back together but I said no. He's not the right bus. Love you. xxx'

I smile. She did listen, then.

Paddy:

'Mum – you have really pissed me off. Where are my football socks? I had to wear the old ones today and I couldn't get them off after PE and I'm still wearing them and Dad is being really annoying and won't pull them off for me.'

Far from the walls crumbling down around their ears, the earth falling away beneath them and the sky caving in on top of their heads, my leaving them has meant that . . . everything is pretty much the same. I can even detect a hint of . . . fondness? They are possibly just starting to miss me a little. Martin seems to be coping. So I am going to have fun. Apparently.

BLOG 18 – Fun Times

Day five of my great escape. Today I am planning on having fun. The only problem is I can't really remember what that is.

I can't think of what else to write. Who is this blog for anyway? I plough on, hoping inspiration will strike. What would my followers do? Maybe that's the way in.

Can anyone here help me? If you were told that in an hour's time you were being taken out for the day with no responsibilities weighing you down at home, what would you do? Where would you go? How would you know when you were having fun?

I realise this makes me look like a right sad sack – but I'm genuinely curious. How do you drag yourself out of the domestic doldrums? Because guess what? – I may have temporarily exiled myself from my family but it turns out I brought myself with me. Turns out, maybe it's me that's the problem. I don't know how to relax and enjoy myself. Even typing 'enjoy myself' makes me cringe. The last time I had fun was 2004. Before the kids were born. I can't be sure but I think it involved large quantities of tequila and going topless on a rooftop in Edinburgh.

I'm here in New York City, one of the most exciting cities in the world, I have days stretching ahead of me and I can't think what to do. Or rather, I can't think of how to enjoy the days. I've forgotten. Any clues?

I shower and dress myself in the new chinos and an old, vaguely clean blouse. It's not really a great look and I find myself fretting about my hair, my make-up. I have my death-lips lipstick and in the bottom of my handbag I find a deceased mascara. I spit onto the brush and dab at my non-existent eyelashes. I have half an hour before I meet Gina. I feel an impending doom. She thinks she's rescuing an interesting English eccentric for a great day out, when in fact she'll be wasting a day of her life on someone who is about as much fun as anal polyps.

I check to see if anyone has responded to my latest blog.

I have four replies already.

'I have no idea. No, life is shit and I never have any fun. I would like to go for a walk or maybe to the theatre or the cinema. I'm not asking for the sun, the moon and the stars. Just a little bit of a life.'

Bloody hell. She sounds worse than me.

> 'My idea of fun is lying on the sofa under my blanket with cat
> and kindle. Sometimes a glass of wine, cheese and biscuits and a
> snooze are involved.'

Jesus. Dream big, people. I was hoping for a bit more excitement
than that.

> 'It's not about where you are but how you live! I watch funny cat
> videos and that gives me a laugh. I think you have to remember
> that those small, insignificant things count as fun as much as the
> big things do. Go for a walk and try to find the fun in every step.
> Skip if you have to! No one cares!'

Cat videos? Really?! I get what she's saying but I'm not skipping
for anyone or anything – I have to cross my legs when I sneeze
in case I wet myself.

The final comment is a bit more on the nose.

> 'Open your heart. Take yourself seriously. Be kind to yourself.
> Imagine you are taking a really lovely friend out for the day, some-
> one who has had a hard time lately. What would you do to make her
> enjoy her day? You'd consider her. You'd check in with her. You'd ask
> what she liked to eat, what sort of mood she was in, whether she'd
> like to be with people or be in nature. You'd want to make her
> happy. Now do that for yourself. And laugh! At anything. Everything.'

It's time to go. I head downstairs and pass Topknot at the desk.

'Good morning, Ms Woods,' he coos. He really is intrigued by
me. Every time I walk though the lobby he stops what he is

doing and I can feel his eyes on me. God knows why. Maybe he thinks I'm a low-rent call girl.

'Morning!' I chirp back. Outside, the loud roar of an engine makes us both jump.

'Ugh, masculine toxicity!' tuts Topknot as he follows me out onto the street, keen to berate the offending motorist. I look left and right, anxious to spot Gina before she spots me. A biker, astride a most glorious glistening easy-rider machine, sits revving his engine.

'Do you have to do that right outside the hotel? The carbon emissions are gross!' whines Topknot, hands on hips.

The biker removes his helmet. Shakes out his shoulder-length dark hair.

He is a she. Gina. It's Gina.

'Ready for some fun?' she says, holding out a spare helmet.

'Uh . . . erm . . . Jesus, when I said about the old woman on the bike I didn't mean, like, literally I'd like to go on a bike. I'm a bit old for all this!' I stutter.

It's a huge, beautiful beast of a Harley Davidson, all shining chrome pistons, black leather and low-slung handlebars. Topknot stares open-mouthed. I look from him to her and back again, and before I can think about it I am straddling the pillion seat and wrapping my arms around the leather-clad woman in front of me.

'Bye!' I wave as we roar off down 2nd Avenue. Topknot raises his arm in a slow, bemused salute and I am laughing.

I am laughing.

Chapter Thirty-five

It's too exciting to be scary. The wind catches in my mouth when I try to speak, so I cling on as Gina expertly weaves in and out of the mid-morning traffic. At every stop light the usually cool New Yorkers smile. We pull up at an intersection and wait for the lights to change. I lift the visor on my helmet and shout into Gina's ear.

'Don't tell me this is your bike!'

'No!' she shouts back over her shoulder. 'It's Sally's.'

'Oh Sally's!' I laugh, none the wiser. 'That explains everything. How come you ride it so well?'

'I'm a lesbian. It's in our DNA.'

'Why aren't you at work today?'

'I called in sick.'

'Naughty!'

'Aren't I? But everyone deserves a mental-health day once in a while.'

I ponder this as we buzz along the avenue. Why do I get the feeling it's not her mental health she's concerned about, but mine?

I don't really care. It feels good to be on the back of this machine. I used to love my old Vespa. 50cc of throbbing horse-power – about as nifty as a hairdryer going uphill and just as noisy. I've always resisted doing anything I did as a teen – it seems so desperate. So middle-aged. But I can't deny it now, I feel a real thrill.

'Where are we going?' I shout after twenty minutes of hair-raising zig-zagging in and out of the stationary taxis and cars.

'Somewhere FUN,' shouts Gina.

We're heading towards the Brooklyn Bridge. I can see its huge towers racing upwards, the wire cables fanning across the bright blue sky. I feel a lightness, a sense of possibility. Today I'm just going to let things happen. Go with the flow.

We sail across the bridge and I gasp at the structure. It's so bloody beautiful. The traffic is heavy and we crawl along as I crane my heavy helmeted head upwards to admire it.

'This is amazing! How old is it?' I shout.

'I don't know. Around one hundred and twenty I guess . . . It was built by a woman!'

'Really?!'

Gina laughs.

'Kind of. Although you won't find that in the guide books. Emily Warren Roebling. Her husband, Washington, was the engineer but he got sick and couldn't leave his bed, so his wife Emily directed the build while he watched through his telescope.'

'Wow!'

'Yeah – pretty cool.'

'Well, you know what they say – behind every great man is a great woman!'

'I wouldn't know,' says Gina, 'I've never stood behind a man.'

I grin. Touché.

We cross into Brooklyn and make our way through the streets. The view along Brooklyn Heights Promenade is breathtaking – the buildings rising like the Emerald City from the East River. Down towards Cobble Hill Gina takes a left away from the water.

'Hungry?' she says over her shoulder.

I haven't eaten since yesterday and it's almost eleven. I've not even thought about it.

'I suppose I must be!'

'OK.'

Three minutes later we pull up at what looks like an old-fashioned drug store. 'The Brooklyn Farmacy & Soda Fountain' is etched onto the glass, and while Gina parks the bike I stretch and peer in through the window. It's faux-frozen in time, with '20s vintage decor and a few young staff wearing T-shirts bearing the title 'Jerk'. It's the kind of place I would normally run a mile from. The kind of place my kids would die for. My heart sinks a little. Why has she brought me to a place like this? I was hoping for a little deli off the beaten track, a non-touristy gem serving fantastic coffee, sophisticated omelettes and fresh greens.

The menu on the front window here seems to be inordinately proud of the liquid heart attacks it sells – ice-cream floats, fudge milkshakes and candy-coated sundaes. It looks 'fun' – in a very predictable, highly marketed way.

'Cool, huh?' says Gina, resting her helmet on her leather-clad hip.

'Yes. yes. Very nice,' I say, following her in. We sit at the vintage bar on vintage stools and peruse the vintage menu. The first item on the menu is called SUNDAE of BROKEN DREAMS.

'I'll have that,' I say flatly. Apparently it's 'a salty-sweet combination of vanilla ice cream, warm caramel, broken pretzel rods & fresh whipped cream'. It's also 'so good you can cry over it!' Should suit me down to the ground.

'Broken dreams, huh?' smiles Gina.

'Can we get a Sundae of Broken Dreams for my dramatic friend here and I'll have Breakfast in Bed,' says Gina with a wink, as the young waitress blushes and scrabbles for her retro pencil.

'What's Breakfast in Bed, dare I ask?' I say, trying to get into the spirit of the place.

'"A warm buttermilk biscuit and coffee ice cream drizzled with pure maple syrup from Maine topped with fresh whipped cream and house-made candied bacon bits",' quotes Gina.

'Sounds revolting,' I say.

'Hey – don't knock it till you've tried it!' says Gina.

Is she flirting with me? I blush too.

I look around at the various families and tourists already lapping up these sickly treats before lunch. Everyone is smiling. The children's eyes are glistening with expectation. Even the staff look happy to be here.

'Not a fan of ice cream soda?' asks Gina. She looks a bit crest-fallen and I feel like I'm spoiling things. She is trying to be nice and I'm not biting.

'Erm . . . no, I don't know, I mean, the kids would absolutely die for this place, and Martin has a very sweet tooth so—'

'But how about you? What do you like?'

'Honestly this is fine! Thank you! It's really sweet here.'

'I thought you'd like it because it's old.'

'Thanks!' I say, mock offended.

'I don't mean that! It's kind of a sweet story. This place was an old drug store, turn of the last century, but it was about to be condemned – then a TV exec stopped by to ask for directions and fell in love with the place. She commissioned a programme about revamping old buildings and here it is!'

I look around with fresh eyes at the beautiful tiled floor and the shiny chrome counter.

'Is this a metaphor?' I say, looking back at Gina.

'Excuse me?' she says, confused.

'I'm the condemned building and you're the TV executive?'

Gina looks aghast. I smile. Gina bursts out laughing.

'It really is just an ice cream,' she says.

'Hmmm . . .'

Our order arrives. A slick, tall glass crammed with about five thousand calories and a long spoon, I dig in. It's absolutely delicious, the salty pretzel pieces offsetting the sweetness of the warm caramel to perfection.

'How are your Broken Dreams?' smiles Gina, crunching on a maple syrup bacon bit.

'Out of this world,' I say, 'but I can't eat all this. Help me!'

'Just leave what you don't want.'

'What??? You obviously weren't raised by an Irish mother!'

'I wasn't raised by any mother.'

'Oh yeah. Sorry.'

'No biggie.'

'My mum would kill me if I didn't finish everything on my plate.'

'And you don't have a major eating disorder?'

'No, just a major guilt disorder. She would show us a picture of starving children if we left so much as half a fish finger.'

'You have siblings?'

'A brother. Aidan. He lives here actually. Honolulu. Property.'

'You going to see him?'

I roll my eyes.

'No, he's always "super busy".'

'That sucks. What is it about people in your family that leave you to run around strange towns with dykes on bikes? Don't they realise the trouble you could get into?'

I blush again.

'What sort of trouble could I get into?' I ask, stirring my ice cream coquettishly. My God! What is happening to me? I'm clearly not used to any attention, male or female, and I've turned into a coy debutante.

Gina laughs. 'Come on, let's find somewhere more YOU,' she says, leaving forty bucks on the counter and scooping up our helmets in one smooth move. Her hair swings from side to side as she strides out through the door. Is it just my imagination or does the room stop and stare?

Maybe it's just me.

Outside, the sun is high in the sky and the bike seat feels hot. We pull off and head south along the East River. We pass alongside Greenwood park and down through Dyker Beach Golf Course.

'This is where all the lesbians come to play golf!' shouts Gina.

'Really?' I ask.

She laughs.

I see a sign for Coney Island. I've always wanted to come here. I don't know why. Something about the faded glory of the seaside in the '50s. I've heard it's beautiful. I can see the ocean, smell the salt. I love the sea. We drive under a huge sign 'Welcome to Coney Island – where the fun never ends!'

Gina parks up near the seafront, where the wooden boardwalk cuts between the beautiful sandy beach and the food shacks jostling for early-season custom. We climb off and stretch. The sun is warm on my skin and I feel my body relax. Yes. This is what I love. Being near the water.

'Better?' smiles Gina.

'Better. I love the water. To be near water. For someone from a small island I rarely get to do it.'

Gina peels off her leather jacket and slings it over her shoulder.

'How about a swim?' she says.

'Swim? I – I haven't got a swimming costume!'

'"Costume"? You don't need a costume to go swimming! Come on!' To my absolute horror Gina sits down on the sand and starts pulling off her boots, her leather trousers and her socks. She's athletic, tanned, her vest top and pants pristine white.

'I'm not doing that!' I laugh, trying to cover my mortification. How can I reveal my wobbly white blubber, the skin dry and sagging around my middle, the greying bra and baggy knickers no one ever gets to see? I haven't shaved in weeks. There could be all sorts of undergrowth poking out from places it shouldn't be poking out from.

'Come on!' laughs Gina, tugging me down beside her. 'You said you love the water!'

'No way!' I say, feeling anxious now.

'Yes way!' laughs Gina, yanking at the hem of my chinos. 'Come on, you know you want to, and if you want to have fun you have to stop being such a damn pussy!'

She's not wrong.

'Pussy? Who are you calling a pussy?' I say, pulling my blouse over my head. Before I can think about what I'm doing, about how awful I look, how silly I will feel, how on earth I will get my pants dry in time to get back on the bike, I am stripping off and running full pelt across the sand and into the ocean. I hear Gina screaming behind me – 'YES Ciara! Fucking YES!!!' – and my breath catches as the first freezing wave hits my thighs. I scream. It's fucking cold. The waves recede and I stand, flapping my arms as the goosebumps erupt all over my body. Gina splashes me from behind – she has followed me in and is slapping her hands in the water with abandon.

'Fuck! It's cold!' she squeals. She looks like a little girl in her vest and pants, her hair already hanging in limp wet strands.

'Don't splash me! Don't splash me!' I scream.

'How are you going to get used to it if you don't get wet?'

'Let me acclimatise first! It's so c-c-cold!'

My teeth are actually chattering.

'Don't wait to feel warmer – you won't! Just dive in!'

Gina plunges head first into the next wave while I stand shivering, hesitating. Fuck it. I dive in after her. Despite the intense shock of the cold all around me, my arms and legs start to thrash through the water, perfectly synchronised after years of teenage swimming. It's years since I've swum in the sea. I've always been too paranoid to go in when I'm on a beach with the kids. Once I left Martin in charge, went for a leisurely swim and when I came back he'd lost one of the boys and the other one was sunburnt. We got screamed at by the elderly French lady who found Lorcan, then spent the afternoon looking for sunburn cream.

I swim and swim, tilting my head expertly at every second stroke. My arms are tired but I keep going because the sensation of movement, of covering distance, is so liberating. Finally I stop and tread water for a while. I look back at the beach. Gina has given up and gone back. She stands at the water's edge and waves when she spots me, flinging her arms around in exaggerated support. I don't feel cold at all now. I feel totally exhilarated. I float on my back and look up at the sun in the sky, the same sun that shines down on my quiet tree-lined London street, that warms the daffodils in my weed-infested window boxes and renders the cat paralysed on the shed roof. How can this sun be the same and yet this moment be so utterly at odds with my normal life? How have I come to be treading water so literally across the Atlantic after years of treading water in my kitchen? How on earth did I make that jump?

I remember once reading an advice column where a woman was moaning about her relationship but saying she couldn't leave. The response was 'Well, if you can't leave it obviously hasn't got bad enough yet!' Is there a tipping point? Do you just have to sit it out until you can't sit it out any more? I think about Martin. The thing is, it's not *bad*. But I couldn't in all honesty say what's good about it. About us. I shudder, gather my strength and head back to shore.

'Wow! You were like a mermaid out there!' says Gina, throwing me a towel.

'You brought towels?' I say, grabbing it gratefully and covering my flabby middle in a well-rehearsed move.

'Of course. Be prepared for fun. Always.'

We dry ourselves, and I even manage to peel my underwear off under the towel without exposing myself. Finally winning at life! I barely recognise myself today – swimming in my undies then strolling commando along the boardwalk.

The sun is really warm now, and we sit on Brighton Beach drinking hot coffee in paper cups, watching the Russian men smoking at their roadside tables. I feel like I'm on holiday, but with none of the migraine-inducing stress from having to deter two teenage boys from killing each other and one teenage girl from killing herself.

Gina is quiet. I sense she knows I am relaxing and doesn't want to disturb my peace. How did this kind, funny and sweet woman find me? I already feel like we are friends and I've only known her two days. I realise in this moment how crushingly lonely I've been, how desperately, shockingly possible it is to live in a noisy, chaotic house full of people, to sleep alongside another human being every night for years and yet feel totally alone. I stare out to sea and watch two tankers far off on the horizon coming at each other from opposite directions. From where we are sitting it looks as though they are about to collide, but of course, it's just perspective and they glide past one another, probably miles apart.

'Is this more like it?' asks Gina, stretching out on the sand.

'Yes. Yes it is.'

We must have fallen asleep because when I open my eyes the sun has moved and there is a chill in the air.

Gina is sitting up rubbing her eyes.

'Ready to go, Sleeping Beauty?'

'Wow. I must have needed that.'

'All that swimming! Are you hungry?'

'I don't know. I don't know anything today.'

Gina smiles.

'Sounds good. Come,' she says, gathering our towels. We load our wet things onto the bike before she leads me on foot through some back streets. Every other shop is Russian, and most of the women standing waiting to serve eye us hopefully as we pass. At a place called Skovorodka Gina ducks in and pulls me with her. She orders *khachapuri*, *tanaka* and *pelmeni* – flatbread, fried chicken and lamb dumplings – as well as the most unlikely plate of pickled things I've ever seen. Pickled watermelon? I take a tentative bite – it's such an odd taste but it's not totally unpleasant. I feel my senses are being overloaded. I can't help but revel in the fact that I am not having to jolly anyone along on this extraordinary day full of weird and wonderful tastes, sights, smells and sensations. I'm not having to sell it to a group of mini

Tripadvisor trolls (aka my children) who decree everything apart from their phones 'boring' and every food apart from pizza 'disgusting' whenever we go anywhere. I laugh out loud at the giddy freedom of it all.

'You OK?' asks Gina.

'Yes. I am. I am, I believe, having fun, if fun means I don't want to strangle anyone and I don't have to do anything for anyone else.'

'Sounds like a low bar but hey, it's an improvement!'

We jump back on the bike and I ask where we are going next. It's early evening now, just about the time the kids will be having their school lunches. For a brief second I wonder how they are, then push them out of my mind. I want to enjoy today and not let guilt or irritation get in the way. They wouldn't give me a second thought if they were here so why should I? Maybe it's time to reject the bit in the Mum job description that says 'selfless'.

Gina doesn't answer but instead pulls off abruptly and I grab at her waist as we lurch backwards. A few minutes later we are back in Coney Island and parking up outside somewhere called the Freak Bar. Its frontage looks like an old circus tent, and it boasts freak 'sideshows by the seashore'. Gina pays the five bucks for us to go in and orders me a Mermaid beer. There are a few punters inside nursing early-evening cocktails, but they are currently being outnumbered by the 'freaks' that roam from table to table. As we sit down we are approached by a belly dancer who jiggles her hips at us in the hope of getting a couple of dollar bills. Gina obliges with no embarrassment whatsoever by slipping a five-dollar bill into the woman's tinkly bell belt. How does she do this? If I was on my own in here I'd get anxious and say something hilariously stiff like 'No thank you very much!' A man with a large and bored-looking snake wrapped around his neck wanders past but doesn't bother us – he can see we've just been done by the belly dancer. There is a poster stuck to the bar advertising a fire-eater later on tonight, and at the weekend there is a burlesque show. I wonder at the world, and how different our parallel lives can be – while I'm emptying the dishwasher and mopping the floor before bed in suburban London on a Friday night, there will be women here getting ready to pour themselves into basques and writhe around on rickety chairs.

Gina excuses herself and heads to the loo – or 'restroom' as the curiously coy Americans call it. I pull my phone out of my pocket. It's the first time I've looked at it since we left the hotel and a small shower of sand spills onto the floor. I have a message from Amelie. She probably wants to know if I bought her the entire make-up counter she asked for, if I've been to the Apple Store yet and if the clothes I bought are things that she would be seen dead in. I take a swig of my beer and settle down to read it. It's long. She must have written it before school.

'Mum.

I've been sitting on my bed crying this morning. Not because I'm sad. I'm really angry. I was shocked and upset last week when we first found out about your "blog", and then you left for your "holiday" from us, but now I've had time to think about it all, I am actually really fucking angry. How dare you? How actually DARE you? You used us, you used our lives and our mistakes and our problems to get yourself some followers. We are only children, Mum, and we are going to be stupid and make mistakes sometimes, but we should be able to do that without the whole world laughing at us. Now everyone at school knows about our family. People keep asking me if I'm all right and yesterday my form teacher told me she was always available if I "need to chat"! Do you even know what you've done? It just makes me think you hate us, and that you don't care how we feel. And what about Dad? I know he can be annoying but he is really trying hard now. He took us all for pizza last night and he had three beers and looked really sad. What are you doing to this family? If you are so unhappy you should do something about it, not take it out on us. And when are you coming home? You know I've got my Year 10 mocks in a couple of weeks. Are you planning on being around for those, or should I tell my teachers I need extra time in the exams because of family problems? Am I THAT girl now?

A.'

I feel winded. She's right. How dare I? A few minutes ago I was sitting here charmed by the shabby sideshow and the themed beer. Now I feel ridiculous. And cruel. And intolerant of what is basically normal teenage behaviour, everyday marriage ennui. Of course they are upset. Of course it's me. It's all me.

I burst into tears of shock and self-loathing. What kind of woman am I? I'm in the Freak Bar and it turns out I'm the biggest freak here.

Gina returns with no idea of the tsunami that just hit this shore.

'Ciara? Are you OK?' she asks, her face a mask of concern. She pulls her chair close to mine and puts her hand on my back. I sob. Gut wrenching, loud sobs. She doesn't say anything. She strokes my back and waits for the storm to subside. After a few minutes I am spent. My body shudders involuntarily and I let out a deep sigh.

'Do you want to tell me what's wrong?' she asks. 'Is the snake man bothering you?'

I laugh a sad little laugh. Can I share this with Gina? How could she, a childless, single lesbian, even begin to understand the complex, painful tugging to and fro of a mum-and-daughter relationship?

'I got a message from my daughter.'

'OK,' says Gina, rubbing my back. I feel awkward and shy but it's nice to feel a consoling hand.

'She hates me. And I don't blame her. She says if I'm unhappy then that's my fault and I shouldn't be dumping it on them. She says I've humiliated them all and they don't deserve it because they are only children and Martin is trying his best.'

Gina considers this for a while like a barrister listening to the prosecution.

'OK. She sounds pretty together for a teenager. But here's the thing.'

I look up at Gina now. I really want to hear the thing.

'You're just a person too. And you're doing your best. You were Ciara before you had kids and you'll be Ciara long after they fly the nest. Don't forget to do you.'

'Yes, yes,' I say impatiently, 'but all that "look after yourself, look after number one" stuff is a bit redundant when you have kids. You can't just give birth and then say "not my problem" – that's part of the deal; they ARE your problem. Forever.'

'Well, not in my case, I had to take care of myself and look at me! It's not like I became a homeless lesbian alcoholic – oh, wait a minute . . .'

I smile.

'Seriously, Ciara.' My name in her New York accent sounds soothingly Irish. 'OK, you did something that upset them. You showed them a mirror and they didn't like the reflection. So what? They'll get over it. You probably said some pretty mean stuff to your mom, right? And you adored her.'

Instantly I remember the time I wasn't speaking to Mum because she wouldn't let me go out on a Sunday night. I only wanted to hang around the park with my mates but she said it wasn't a respectable thing to do aged thirteen. I called her a 'fucking bitch' and got sent to bed at 8 p.m. The next day my friends blanked me outside my house. We always walked to school in a gang and I was nervous to walk past a certain alley-way on my own. I went back home and knocked on the door warily. Mum answered, her hands wet from the washing-up. I could see she thought I'd come to apologise. She raised her eyebrows expectantly.

'Mum, I hate you but will you walk to school with me?'

Her face froze for a second then she burst out laughing. She didn't answer me. She just put her coat on and we walked silently for the ten minutes it took to get to school. She never mentioned it again.

'I did say some terrible things to her. But she didn't tell everyone. She just let me grow out of it. Now there isn't a day goes by that I don't regret how I was.'

'And your kids will be the same. You just have to ride it out.'

'It might be too late.'

'Bullshit. They'll welcome you back with open arms.'

'I mean, for me. It might be too late for me.'

Gina stares at me. I look around at the people laughing and drinking, the belly dancer with her cheap nylon veil, the sticky rings that our glasses have left on the small table-top and it all suddenly feels extremely tawdry.

'Come on. Let's get you out of here,' says Gina, picking up our helmets.

Back on the bike we are silent. It's dark, and crossing the bridge from Brooklyn into Manhattan would be a magical experience in a different mood – the lights are strung in ropes from tower to tower, and the Manhattan skyline buzzes with electricity and life. Gina pulls up outside the hotel and stares up at it.

'How much does this place cost?'

'Don't ask. Mum left me a thousand pounds. That's gone right about now. But I'm OK.'

'Do you like it?'

'Like it?' I hadn't really considered the question.

'No. Not really. It's right up its own arse.'

'Excuse me?' asks Gina, laughing.

'It's pretentious. Expensive. Self-consciously hip.'

'Then why the hell are you staying here?'

'I panicked. I thought it would be nice. I thought I'd get in trouble if I moved.'

'Story of your life, huh?' I smile despite my low mood. Story of my life indeed. 'Look. I have to go back to work tomorrow but why don't you come stay at my place? It's clean, it's nice, you can relax and be yourself. This place ain't for you. Last thing you need is to feel fake. Come on – pay your check, get your things and we'll hit the road. I have to get the bike back by ten.'

I consider this extraordinary offer.

'I should go home. I've made enough mistakes already.'

'Bullshit. You haven't made enough. They'll be fine. Let Amelie be angry. Let the boys learn how to use the laundromat.

Let Martin notice that you aren't around. Give it a week and then go back.'

She looks at me earnestly, with just the slightest hint of need. She's right, of course. What good would running back do now? I have nothing reassuring to say – 'Don't worry, everyone, I'm back in my box now and everything will return to exactly how it was before! Kids! Walk all over me! Martin – ignore me for weeks then expect full-on passionate sex! Everyone carry on with your lives just like before – discard what you don't need and let me pick it all up for you because I literally have *nothing better to do*!'

'OK,' I hear myself say. 'Give me five minutes.'

Chapter Thirty-six

I throw my things into my bag and take one last look at the view from the bathroom window. Now that I'm leaving I realise it's the only good thing about this place. Downstairs Topknot is knocking off for the night so it's him I get to check out with.

'You're leaving us early, Ms Woods . . . how so?'

'Family emergency,' I mumble. His eyes slide towards the window. Gina is clearly visible talking on her mobile.

'OK, well, that's fine, that will be one thousand two hundred and forty-nine dollars, please.'

I gulp. Jesus. I grope around in my bag for the stash of cash I changed at the airport. I've had to dig into a bit to buy things and endlessly tip people so I'm a bit short.

'Can I pay two hundred on my card and the rest in cash?'

Topknot sighs but says, 'No problem.' He hands me my receipt with a smile. 'I haven't charged you for tonight . . . seeing as it's a family emergency,' he says. I swear he almost winks as he nods towards the window.

'Thank you. That's very sweet of you,' I manage before stumbling over my bag and crashing out through the doors.

Gina props my small case up on the saddle between us.

'Jump on,' she says. 'Lesbians TO THE RESCUE!'

Gina's apartment is back over the bridge. I feel lighter returning. Brooklyn is obviously my kind of New York – forget the fancy avenues and swanky hotels of Manhattan. I have no idea why I am doing this but I'm sick of second guessing everything. And anyhow, surely the *only* way to escape your humdrum-nuclear-family-domestic-live-burial is to be rescued by a lesbian on a motorbike?

'Come in, come in!' says Gina, throwing my bag down in the cluttered hallway. The apartment is tiny. Tucked away on the fourth floor of a building that houses a fried-chicken shop at ground level. A large sofa dominates the living space, and a small kitchen with two tiny hobs and a massive fridge is tucked into one corner. There are plants and books everywhere but it's clean and tidy. In the far corner of the room stands an ornate parrot cage.

'This is Colette!' says Gina, unlocking the cage. 'She's an African Grey, and she is a piece of work!'

A beautiful grey parrot with a red tail eyes me from its perch.

'Colette wants a peanut!' says the parrot in a spookily accurate copy of Gina's voice. Gina laughs and pops a peanut into Colette's beak.

'She's a little suspicious of women – every time I bring someone home she gets jealous – but she'll get used to you in a couple of days.'

Every time? I think, wondering about the notches on Gina's bed post.

There is a small bedroom and an even smaller bathroom leading off the lounge.

'You can have my bed. I'll sleep on the couch,' says Gina, noticing me clocking the only bedroom.

'No, no don't be silly, I'll sleep on the couch.'

Gina ignores me and puts the kettle on one of the hobs. She bangs it a few times until the light comes on and there's something so beautifully domestic about this small action that I start to cry again.

'Hey, what's up?' she says.

'Oh God, ignore me. I'm so sorry. I just feel like I miss home but I don't know where home is any more.'

'Makes sense,' she says. 'But here is home right now, so just try to relax. I'll run you a bath.'

She throws me a box of tissues and heads to the bathroom. I hear the taps squeal as she wrenches them on and soon the steam is seeping out of the door along with the sweet smell of lavender. The kettle boils and Gina makes us both herbal tea – camomile and lemon, or something equally revolting. I cup the large, friendly mug with both hands and sip it nonetheless.

'Your bath is ready, madam,' she says, appearing with a large fluffy towel over one arm. 'You take a bath while I get the bike back to Sally. I'll be half an hour. I've left some clean sweats for you.'

There are candles. The bath is low, the sides barely two feet above the floor level, but it sinks deeper as you get in. I ease myself into the water, which is just the right side of scalding, and spend twenty blissful minutes thinking of nothing but the joy of being still. I feel instantly at home here. The candles flicker along the edge of the tub and the steam creates a pleasing haze. Could I live here? In another universe where Martin, Paddy, Lorcan and Amelie never existed? Could I make a life here? Perhaps it would've been better if I had been a lesbian. I've never met a lesbian in a dull, unhappy marriage. You don't hear about shit gay marriages much. Maybe there are some, now that gay marriage is legal. I make a note to ask Gina about it. I could have been a lesbian, or at least tried to be. I had the opportunity, if only on paper. There were so many GaySocs at my university it was kind of rude not to be. I don't really have any form – never kissed a girl unless you count Sarah Goggins when we were seven and no one chased us during Kiss Chase. I drag myself out of the bath and dress myself in Gina's comfy grey jogging pants and hoodie.

Colette squawks and flaps her wings.

'What should I do, Colette?' I ask. She blinks, hops from side to side, says nothing.

'Thank you so much, you've been dreadfully helpful,' I say in my best Mary Poppins voice. I hear Gina coming back and arrange myself in what I hope is a relaxed pose on the sofa. I want her to know I appreciate this, but now she is back I feel shy. Am I attracted to her? I mean, any normal person would be, male or female. She's gorgeous – in a very natural way. I can see that. Even me, who doesn't want to be touched, kissed or penetrated by anyone or anything ever again thank you very much.

'Hey. Feeling better?' she says, plopping down on the sofa beside me. I draw my knees up around my chest.

'Much. Thank you. I don't really know what else to say. You've been so kind to me. Kinder than anyone I can remember recently. I don't know how to repay you.'

'You are repaying me. You're here. I like hanging out with you. It helps me too, you know?'

'Really? Hanging around with a depressive menopausal middle-aged straight woman helps you? Jesus, you must be in a bad way.'

'Yeah, you remind me how far I've come!' she says, but her eyes are smiling. Maybe that IS it? Maybe she really is a co-dependent addict who needs to help others in order to feel better about herself?

'Feeling better about home?' she asks.

I let out a totally non-satisfying sigh.

'I don't know. My head tells me I ought to go back, but the idea makes me feel physically sick. That's not great, is it?'

'I was thinking while I was out . . . you know, it wouldn't hurt for you to stay here for a while longer. It would be fun. I'll be at work most days so you can do what you want. Plenty of time to think.'

That's the last thing I need. It's thinking that got me into this mess. Thinking and blogging and daring to have a life beyond the kitchen. Daring to assert that the way my kids speak to me is not nice. But however heavy the guilt weighs on my tired heart I can't quite find it in myself to feel sorry for them all, abandoned back at home. The only thing I really miss is the dog, and even she ignores me if I don't have bacon. My phone pings. A message from Martin.

'Just to say all is well here. Had a chat with Amelie. She's OK. She'll be fine, you know how she is. Boys both got merit points for cookery today – came home with delicious bread (of course, then had a fight about whose was best) but we are all fine. Have a break. We know you deserve it.'

His niceness makes me feel worse. I hate it when he unexpectedly plays the New Man card, the 'I understand' face. He probably thinks I'm having a nervous breakdown. Maybe I am. If that's a 'get out of jail free' card I'll take it.

'Fuck it,' I say, 'I'll stay.' Gina grins and pulls a sleeping bag out from under the couch.

'Slumber party!'

At fifty? Really?

'Thank you so much, you've been dreadfully helpful!' says Colette in a crystal-cut English accent.

Chapter Thirty-seven

And that's what I do. I spend the next week at Gina's apartment. Colette mimics almost everything I say. She hates me. Her favourite thing is to sigh very loudly – it's a bad habit I've developed and she has picked up on it. Gina laughs indulgently.

'Parrots have the same intellectual capacity as three-year-old humans, you know,' says Gina.

'Yes, I bet they do, but I've run away from all that! I don't need to be taken down by a feathered toddler!'

Apart from Colette, we fall into an easy, relaxing routine. Gina gets up, makes coffee, curses at the hob a few times. She makes oatmeal or I go out for bagels, she does her morning yoga, goes to work and I swan around New York watching obscure foreign language films, visiting galleries, drinking beer.

The best film I see is German. It's about a woman who goes for a weekend break in a log cabin in the mountains but wakes up to find her hosts gone. When she explores the country lanes to try and find them she hits an invisible wall and can't get out. She spends the next two years living alone behind the wall, learning how to hunt for food, writing her diary on any paper she can find. Eventually it runs out and she dies. It's not exactly a romcom. I love it. I'm giddy with recognition as I come out of the fleapit cinema into the broad daylight. I hit my wall long ago, but I feel as though I've just smashed through it.

That night Gina takes me to a spoken word event. It's full of women with interesting haircuts free associating. Not really my thing – I don't exactly associate out loud, let alone freely. But I love the energy of the place, the women all clapping or clicking their fingers in support. It's a world away from the hunkered down 'grin and bear it' brigade I associate with. One woman tells us she is recently separated from her husband and she riffs on the theme of his pants for about twenty minutes.

'Pants like cow pats lying on the floor
Well not any more, not any more!'

The audience whoop. I wonder if any of them have children? How do they navigate the horror of it? They look too carefree to have kids. And anyway, it's a school night. They must be child-less, or they wouldn't be out on a school night.

It's at the spoken word event that something pivotal happens. I'm sitting quietly nursing a beer. Gina has gone to the restroom. The MC – a young black woman with cropped hair and a winning smile – asks if there are any mums in the audience. I raise my hand tentatively. I'm not alone. There are about twenty of us! None of them look like mums – whatever that means – apart from me, and it's me the MC singles out.

'How old are your kids, Mama?' she asks, her voice low and intense over the mic.

'Erm . . . er, they are . . . erm . . .' I falter.

'She can't remember!' shouts a heckler, and the crowd laughs. I get a round of applause.

'Where you from?' asks the MC, quick to spot my non-native accent.

'London,' I answer, blushing furiously.

'Cool! What you doin' here in Brooklyn? Your kids back home in London?'

'Yes,' I say, and the crowd whoops again.

'I like your style!' says the MC. 'How did you manage that?'

'Quite easy really, I just picked up my bag and left!' I laugh, and the crowd laughs warmly.

'You got a little something you want to say to us all, London Mama?' she says, offering me the mic. 'Because tonight is open mic night and we'd love to hear from you, how you got away from those pesky kids!'

'No, I don't . . . I mean, I am not a poet, I don't write poetry, sorry!' I say.

'Sure you are! We're all poets, right?' she asks the crowd.

'Hell yeah!' shouts a woman roughly my age.

'You see, we have an open mic spot every week, it's kind of like improv poetry slam flow kind of a vibe, and we have kind of a theme, and this week the theme is "I love you but . . ." – now I'm sure you got something to say about that!'

The crowd whoops and cheers, urging me to get up. I spot Gina coming back from the restroom and something in me clicks. I feel the wind change. Plates shift. I get up and make my way through the crowd to the small stage. The MC hands me the mic and the crowd goes quiet. She whispers in my ear 'I love you but . . .?'

I stare out into the dark room and feel all eyes on me. Shit. I have to say something, but what? How do you 'flow' when you've been blocked for so long?

'I love you but . . . I don't like you much,' I start. A few women shout 'Yeah!'

> *'I love you but stop leaving your dishes in the sink*
> *There's a dishwasher just inches away, and who do you think*
> *Has to fill it up when you're done?*
> *I'm loading dishes when I should be having fun!'*

Loud cheers at this. I'm starting to like it. It's hardly ground-breaking but it's mine.

> *'I love you but I can't lie on the floor*
> *And let you all treat me like I'm not here any more*
> *Or tell me I'm stupid, or tell me I'm fat*
> *Or tell me my cooking isn't all that*
> *I love you but I hate it when you laugh at my clothes*
> *When I show you my love and you turn up your nose*
> *When you forget that I gave up my life for you*
> *But you can't put down the seat or even flush the loo*
> *I love you but this ain't a life I'm living –*
> *You all like to take but you're not about giving.*
> *I love you but I can't keep on faking*
> *Motherhood – the gift that keeps on taking!'*

I can't really hear what happens next because the room goes into a sort of slow motion. I know that all the people in the room stand up and cheer, because Gina tells me later. She says that the MC takes the mic and drops it for me, that I am asked to come back the following week, and that people want to know my social media details so that they can follow me. I have no idea how I managed to come out with all that stuff. None of it hasn't been said before but I managed to make some of it rhyme! Some of it was witty. Some of it was sad. I enjoyed it. I want to do more. If I can do this off-the-cuff what could I be capable of with a little more consideration?

' "Not a poet"?' Gina says when we're back in the apartment brushing our teeth for bed, 'Yeah, and I'm not a lesbian park ranger!'

*

As the days pass, Gina and I find our own easy rhythm. If I'm home when she finishes work I get us some dinner – I don't cook, of course, but there are loads of amazing takeaways. If I'm out I'll text her and she'll come and meet me. We laugh a lot. She really enjoys 'roasting' me – mostly my accent, my fear of cockroaches (they are everywhere) and my capacity to worry over silly little things. But her teasing is fond. I think she really likes me. And I'm starting to feel ... not love, exactly, but a deep appreciation for this park-ranging, outdoorsy lesbian Mother Teresa. I feel like I've been saved – mostly from myself. I haven't felt so happy, so *seen* in years. Decades. I'm giddy with it.

I tease Gina about her clothes – mostly utilitarian boilersuits from thrift stores which she, of course, looks fantastic in. I don't sleep much – we talk late into the night every night, and Gina is up at seven each day, but I find I'm not tired. I wake with butterflies of excitement to just be around her. The kids and Martin send me the odd message, but with less frequency now. Things seem to be running very smoothly without me, and Martin even makes a point of letting me know the kids seem calmer. He is working from home a lot, and has rediscovered his love of cooking. He tells me the kids have asked him if I can stay away for another two weeks. Nice to know you're missed.

The days fly by. We talk. A lot. The biggest conversation happens two nights before I'm due to fly back. Gina has been quiet all day as we walk the High Line through Chelsea, looking at the graffiti and the expensive apartments whose windows dare you to peep in.

'What will you say to Martin when you go back?'

I stiffen at the mention of his name.

'What do you mean?' I ask, trying to mask the panic I feel.

'Does he know about me?'

'Ha ha it's not like we're having an affair!' I redden at the word.

'Aren't we?!' She looks mock-afflicted. 'I just mean, does he know you're staying with me?'

I haven't told him. As far as he is aware I'm still blowing my inheritance at The Hotspot Hotel. To be honest he's so money-conscious he'd probably prefer me to have a torrid lesbian affair than spend seven grand on a hotel room.

'No, he doesn't know, and I think I'll keep it that way. There's no need to tell him all the details.'

Gina looks at me for a long beat. 'Are you ashamed?'

'Ashamed? Why would I be ashamed?'

'Ashamed you shacked up with a strange lesbian? You're not worried he'll be jealous?'

A dry, hollow laugh escapes my mouth. 'Jealous? Martin? The only time he's ever been jealous is when I won first prize in the golf club meat raffle.'

I ignore her bemused look.

'I feel kind of insulted!' says Gina. 'Guys like that need to wake up. If I had a dollar for every lonely housewife who's upped sticks and shacked up with their local friendly dyke I wouldn't be working in the park no more, let me tell yer.'

This comes as a bit of a shock. Although she does a neat line in winks and slow grins, Gina has never made any reference to our 'relationship', whatever it is.

'Don't be insulted. All I can say is that if I was looking for an escape route to the island of Lesbos you'd be the first dinghy I'd jump in.'

Gina can't help but laugh. 'Seriously though – what are you going to do?'

'I don't know!' I snap. I don't want to talk about this any more.

We walk in silence for a while, then in the distance I see a man with his arms outstretched. He is almost naked apart from a pair of white pants.

'Jesus!' I blurt.

'Relax. It's a statue. The Sleepwalker.'

As we draw closer I can see that the incredibly lifelike man is indeed not real. His eyes are closed, and his arms reach out in front of him. His skin is pale, his head bald and his body slackening around the middle. Various tourists take it in turns to pose for pictures. Some hug him, others stand grinning alongside him, and one woman wraps herself around him in a mock embrace. It's curiously unsettling. His arms seem to be groping, pleading for something. I want to run a mile from his needy nakedness.

I turn away, and instead focus on two women – a couple, walking towards us arm in arm. One of them is smiling. The other is not. The smiling woman has flowing blonde curls and wears utilitarian chic clothes. Her eyes sparkle, and her wide mouth reveals a row of perfect white teeth. She looks young and full of life.

'Hey!' says the smiling woman to somewhere just beyond me.

Gina turns from the naked man and her face freezes.

'Audrey!' she says. She looks stricken. Audrey. Her ex-girlfriend. The woman beside Audrey rests a proprietorial hand on her shoulder. She's a bit older – my age, maybe, but cool, dressed in jeans and a T-shirt, her dark hair cropped close to her head and large silver earrings dangling from her ears. Carolina. Their ex-therapist.

'How are you, Gina?' asks Carolina.

'I'm good. Thanks.'

They both turn and stare at me expectantly. Audrey looks from me to Gina a few times, her eyebrows raised in the hope of an introduction.

Out of nowhere Gina grabs at my hand. I grasp it firmly in response.

'Oh this is Ciara,' says Gina, feigning a casualness I know she is not feeling. Her cheeks are flushed pink and her hand feels clammy in mine.

'Ciara! Hi!' says Audrey, attempting an awkward hug. I don't let go of Gina's hand.

They exchange a few pleasantries about the walk, the weather, some mutual friends but I can't take much in because I am watching Gina, willing her on. I know this is the first time she has seen Audrey since the bad break-up two years ago and this is big for her. And there is another seismic event taking place. I am holding her hand. And it feels nice to have her strong, caring hand in mine. Like she's got my back and I've got hers. It feels good. Finally the dreaded first encounter is over, and by some unspoken signal we all know it's time to say goodbye.

'Take care of her,' says Audrey pointedly to me.

'Oh I will,' I say. 'She's precious.'

As we walk off I cling on to Gina's hand and she whispers, 'Thanks' – but I can see that she is crying.

We walk in silence again. Suddenly Gina bursts out laughing.

'Why are you laughing?!' I splutter, relieved that the tension is broken.

'"She's precious"?!!' Gina has tears in her eyes but this time it's not pain.

'I did my best to make them think I'm your lesbian lover and this is how you repay me?!' But I'm smiling too. Gina looks down at our intertwined hands and smiles. I let go. The mood is broken now, the moment has passed and I suddenly feel foolish. I'm fifty and here I am holding hands with a woman I just met. I can't deny I felt . . . something.

We slip off the High Line and find a cafe. We order coffee. And that's when we have The Conversation.

'So how did it feel – being a lesbian for five minutes?'

I blush. 'Nice.'

'Wow, talk about damning with faint praise!'

'What do you want me to say?'

'I want you to say that it was a life-changing moment when your closet door was finally ripped off its hinges and you emerged smiling into the lesbian light.'

'Do you?' I ask, not able to look up from my coffee cup. I can feel my cheeks, my neck, my whole torso flushing with embarrassment.

My future flashes before me. I'm here, in NYC. I'm divorced, and remarried. To Gina. We live in her little apartment in Brooklyn and I work . . . I work in a deli somewhere . . . no, I am writing a blog about being an expat ex-heterosexual . . . it's called something like *Same Sex in the City* and it's hugely popular. We have a wide circle of really interesting friends and we go out all the time. We love each other on a spiritual level but we also have an incredible physical connection and a very healthy sex life.

I have to stop there, mid-fantasy because I've never done it with a woman and I can't imagine ever wanting to. It's not a homophobic thing – I am physically shut down. My libido is so low you'd need a hydrophone system to detect it. I am, as Martin so casually once remarked, 'cut off from the neck down'.

'Hey,' says Gina. I look up and she is smiling at me. 'I'm kidding. It's OK.'

'I don't think I want to be with anyone any more,' I say. 'Man, woman or goat. I think if anything happens to me and Martin I'll live on my own forever.'

Gina looks at me sideways. 'How come you put everything into this marriage?'

'What do you mean?' I feel defensive already.

'I mean, maybe it's not you that's broken. Maybe it's the system. Who says you have to find The One, then love them through thick and thin forever? Sounds like a shitty deal to me.'

'I know, but there are compensations ...' I say, trying to remember what they are.

'Like what? Companionship? Doesn't sound like you have much of that.'

'Well ... not much, no, but ... you know, someone to grow old with ... who knows you, has known you well even if you have drifted apart over the years ... someone to take care of you if you are sick ...'

'... someone to change your diapers when you're incontinent? Sounds like you're describing a carer not a partner. I used to think me and Audrey would be like that. I thought we'd be together forever. I was torn apart when she ran off with Carolina. In pieces. I thought I'd never get over it. But seeing her just now made me realise a lot of things. She was kind of boring. It was great at first but we just kind of ran out of love.'

'Ran out of love? Don't you mean "fell out of love"?'

'No. There was no falling. It just kind of reached an end. We should have quit two years before Carolina came on the scene. We went to Carolina for help. Well, she *helped*, I guess. I am better on my own. My life is bigger. And I'm going to make sure I stay that way. I'm never going to be with someone who makes my life smaller again. Maybe some things just end. And maybe that's OK.'

I feel panicked by what Gina is saying. 'It's easy to say that when there's just the two of you. Much harder when you have kids.'

'Why? Just because you're parents it doesn't mean you stop being people, you know, with hearts and souls.'

'I know, but you have these people you have made together and you can't help but feel that splitting up would be . . . well, rude.'

Gina roars with laughter at this.

'You're so fucking British! It's rude to split up with the father of your children?!'

'It's like being on a seesaw – you both get on it at the same time, and if one of you decides to jump off the other one is dumped on the ground. It doesn't seem very fair.'

'It isn't fair. Nothing is perfect. Nothing is for ever. We're all going to die. Get over it.'

'Jesus, are you trying to cheer me up or encourage me to top myself?'

'Neither. Nothing matters. It's all good.'

I stare her down. The encounter with Audrey has set her free. 'Why have you gone all euphoric and existential on me? You're scaring me!'

'It's the truth, Ciara! You think the whole world is interested in your life? You think you have a unique insight? They want to read your blog so that they feel better about their *own* shitty lives! So quit whining about it and do something different with what time you have left! Isn't life a series of episodes? Maybe this episode of your life is over, and maybe that's OK!'

'Yes, well, you're refusing to accept there is the small factor of, you know, *my children!!!*' To my horror I find I am furious. 'Easy for you, a childless single lesbian in a big metropolis, to bang on about The System. You didn't buy into it. Good for you. But I did. And I built my life around my kids. And now I feel like a cuckoo in my own fucking nest and you're telling me to just, to just, *turn the page* as if they were never born? It's one thing sticking it to the Man, Gina, but there are three other people's lives at stake here too. What kind of woman leaves her children, for fuck's sake?!'

Gina squares up to me in her chair. 'A very unhappy one. A very frustrated one. A very drained and disappointed one.'

How is it that near-strangers can not only see your truth but also don't mind telling it to you? I stare at her, confused and fuming and somehow calm at the same time. It feels like lancing a boil – painful, necessary.

'Is this our first fight? Wow, this is moving fast – you'll be bringing your pot plants in next,' says Gina, trying to lighten the atmosphere.

'Come on, let's go. You need a drink.' And we head off to the nearest bar.

Chapter Thirty-eight

And I get so drunk. Again. So gloriously rat-arsed that Gina has to pull me into the taxi and apologise to the driver while I sing Carpenters songs at the top of my voice.

'Hey, is it me or you that has the problem with alcohol?' she asks, 'You might want to take a look at that.'

I'm so riotously pissed that when we get back to her flat I sit on the stoop asking passers-by for a cigarette. Finally Gina drags me inside and makes me eat some crackers – it's all she has in the cupboard and I need to eat. We sit on the couch while she shoves the dry biscuits into my mouth.

'My flight back is on Sunday. I can't believe it. I'm going back to Blighty. In less than two days. I've been here two weeks. I've been in this apartment for most of that. I love it here. I love you!' I say, flinging my arms around Gina's waist as I slide down on the couch.

'I love you!' screeches Colette from her perch. She sounds ridiculous, which means I sound ridiculous.

'Oh fuck off, Colette!' I say.

Gina is silent. I close my eyes and feel comfort. I could sleep for a hundred years like this. I'm drifting off when she suddenly speaks.

'You don't have to go,' she says quietly.

I sit up. She's looking straight at me and there is something in her eyes – need? Loneliness? Love?

'What should I do, Gina – you're clever, what should I do?'

'You could stay here a while longer. You get ninety days on your visa.'

'Ninety days? That's, like, *three months*! That's a long holiday. I can't do that. No way. The family. They'd kill me. Not that they haven't killed me already. No, I can't stay.'

Gina looks sad then. I focus on her lips and wonder what it would be like to kiss them. They're soft and full.

'I guess you're right,' she says returning my gaze. We stare at each other for a long beat. Her face keeps coming in and out of focus. I find myself leaning forwards, tilting my face to one side. Does she lean in too? Our faces are inches apart. She stops and I lean again. Our lips meet. The softest, gentlest brush of lips against lips. Then her hands come up and cup my face. Our lips open and our tongues are pushing into each other's mouths. I find my hands are in her hair, pulling her closer to me. I'm so drunk I start to feel dizzy, but I love the feeling. I'm giddy. I feel that dull ache in my groin – a long-forgotten kindling of desire. Is this going to happen? Like this, now? I can't think. I don't want to. I just want to feel this. Abandon. No fucks left to give. Something just for me.

Gina pulls away abruptly and stands up.

'What's wrong?' I say.

'I can't do this. We can't do this. It's not good.'

'It feels good!' I say, grabbing for her hand. I miss, and lurch forwards.

'You're drunk' she says, not unkindly.

'That's true. But I feel good. Come here,' I beckon.

Gina says nothing. She takes my hand, pulls me up and guides me towards the bedroom. This is really happening. I try to remember if I'm wearing decent knickers. Probably not. Well, fuck it. I'll just take them off quickly.

Gina pulls at my T-shirt, throws it on the floor. I laugh. She makes me sit on the bed and tugs at my trousers until they are off too. I try to remember how to do a 'come to bed' face but I feel like I've had a stroke and when I catch sight of myself in the mirror I see a leering old woman in grey pants.

'Go to sleep,' says Gina gently, pulling the covers over my body.

I try to protest but she is gone and within moments the world is black.

I wake to the smell of fresh coffee. The radio is on. My unconscious has kept me busy all night with dreams about horses – their soft mouths, their sad eyes, the way they nuzzle you in the neck. Like a creeping fog the events of yesterday come oozing in. Oh God. I drank so much. The cigarettes. The singing. Oh God – we kissed. Gina kissed me. My stomach lurches. Am I going to be sick? Is this a hangover? The morning after the night before? I feel nervous. What does this all mean? Why did I do that? I haven't so much as touched another person in an intimate way since I met Martin, and there I was ramming my tongue into another woman's mouth without so much as a by your leave. I must be finally losing it. What on earth am I going to say to her? What is she expecting now? I don't remember what happened after we kissed. I check my body for signs of action but I'm still in my underwear and I'm sure I slept alone. Gina has been on the couch all week, refusing to let me swap places with her. I feel a terrible sense of guilt. I've not so much given her the wrong signals as waved a massive green flag and said 'Climb on board!' This is such a mess. She was already heartbroken and now she's found someone else but that someone else is me – fucked up, uptight, MARRIED HETEROSEXUAL ME!

I pull the duvet over my head and hide. She's going to work today – Saturday. If I just stay here for an hour she'll be gone. Maybe I can run away while she's at work? Would that be really cowardly? I can hear her singing along to some song on the radio. It's The Carpenters – 'Top of the World'. How weird. Oh God. She sounds really happy. I've been scooped up by a caring and kind woman who is fixing her own broken heart and now I've gone and stomped all over it with my newly found confidence, taking advantage of her kindness to experiment with my mid-life crisis egotism. I groan out loud.

'Morning!' says Gina, placing a tray with coffee, juice and croissants on the floor by the door. 'Hope you're not feeling too rough. I'm heading out to work now but I thought I could maybe swing by the Korean place you like and pick up dinner on my way home?'

I peer up from the bed pretending I've just woken up, that everything's normal and nothing absolutely life-shattering passed between us last night.

'Sounds nice,' I say, rubbing my eyes in a pantomime of nonchalance.

'Great – see you later,' she says.

I hear the door slam behind her and I sit up, trying to work out my next move. I could just go. I'd leave a note, of course. I start to concoct it in my head.

'Dear Gina – Sorry to have gone without saying goodbye! One of the kids is sick and I had to rush home. Thanks for everything! Keep in touch!'

No, too blasé.

'Gina – I am sorry about last night. I was drunk and got carried away and wanted to feel something, but it was unfair of me and I shouldn't have done it. I really hope you find someone to love soon, but it won't be me. Honestly, if I was in the market for someone new I can't imagine it being anyone nicer.'

Too dismissive. Oh God. What am I going to do?

I get up, shower, start to pack my bag. I can't just leave. We have had an amazing time these past ten days. I want to at least honour that. I decide to message her. Maybe we can have lunch and I can explain before I go. I send her a text.

> 'Meet me at the cafe Central Park 1 p.m.? Disgusting
> pastrami sandwiches are on me!'

She replies straight away with a thumbs up and a smiley face. She is keen. I dress carefully – nothing that she has said she likes, no perfume. I don't want to look like I'm trying to look attractive. I don't know who I've become these past two weeks. I used to be decent, I didn't lure lonely lesbians into my own little well of loneliness – I just sat there on my own looking up at the sky.

*

I arrive first and buy lunch for us both. She's late. I check my phone. Nothing. I pick at the bread and throw crumbs to the birds. A Northern Cardinal hops out onto the path. It's warm, and the park is full of people smiling. I scan the perimeter of the lake but I can't see her. A family strolls past – a young couple with a baby in a pram and a toddler on a scooter. They look happy. A hand lands on my shoulder.

'Boo!' says Gina, landing heavily beside me.

'You scared the life out of me!' I say, jumping. I am so nervous I feel jittery.

'Sorry. Did you get lunch? I'm super hungry!'

I hand her the sandwich and she tears into it.

'You not eating?' she says, noticing me picking at crumbs.

'Not hungry.'

'Hangover from hell? You were pretty drunk last night. I don't miss that.'

'Yes, I know I was pretty drunk. I'm sorry.'

'Don't sweat it. It's cool.'

She carries on eating. She looks calm, confident, happy. I'm going to have to break it to her.

'Look, about last night . . .' I begin. She stops mid-chew and turns to me. She is grinning. I can see the meat hanging out of her mouth.

'I was very drunk, as you know, and I . . . erm, well . . . I . . .' I can't think of what I want to say. I am terrified and shocked at myself. I have never given anyone the brush-off before. I've never been close enough to anyone to have to brush them off.

'Ciara,' says Gina, putting her sandwich down and taking both my hands, 'it's cool. You were drunk. I got lonely. We kissed. It's no biggie. I know you're not into me like that, and I don't want you to be. I mean, don't get me wrong you're kinda cute but straight women are not my thing, and I'm not into being anyone's lesbian saviour. I am not a lesbian lifeboat.'

I'm stunned. She's fine with it. It's OK. It's all OK. I let out a huge sigh of relief and she laughs. I laugh. Then I notice something else wriggling around in my unconscious. I feel . . . hurt.

'Good to know I'm that forgettable!' I say, only half-joking.

'Hey, what is it they say? "It's not you, it's me"? I'm not looking to get into any kind of relationship like that again. It doesn't interest me. I want to be a free agent, don't want to get into that whole lesbian cliché.'

'What lesbian cliché is that?' I ask, trying to keep up.

'You know – "What does a lesbian bring on her second date? Her furniture." All that coupling up for the sake of it, for the security, like other people can be your blanket. I know so many people who do that. So many lesbian couples in matching fleeces, getting fat and sitting around with their cats. No thank you, ma'am, not for me. I didn't fight my way out of the closet, get kicked out of home and live on the streets just so that I could end up bored to death like all you heteros!'

'Thanks.'

'No offence . . . I mean, you're adorable. And I'm not saying if you offered yourself on a plate I'd turn you away, because I think you know that I wouldn't. But it wouldn't help you. Not really. You can't jump ship straight onto another. There's got to be some time in the water.'

We sit in silence then. Gina holds on to my hand. I was going to run away so why does it feel like I've been dumped? Even cool Gina, living life on her terms, not reliant on anyone or anything, even she needs some comfort, surely? What's so wrong with wanting a blanket, a fat arse and a cat?

'I was going to go home today. I was going to change my flight. Leave you a note.'

'Wow. You're such a . . . knob?'

'I know. I'm sorry.'

'I finish at six. Let's go get dinner. Your last night.'

'Okay. Meet me at the secret burger place.'

'Really? Your last night?!'

'The kids will kill me if I don't go there – Amelie has read all about it.'

Gina goes back to work and I spend the afternoon shopping. I buy far too much make-up from offensively loud shops and spend a fortune on teeth-rotting 'candy'. I haven't got anything for Martin. I can't think of anything he'd like. Maybe I'll grab a bottle of whisky at the airport tomorrow.

At six I make my way to Le Parker Meridien hotel. It's a swanky, glittering monument to marble and hushed poshness, but tucked behind a grand red curtain there is a grotty, graffiti-covered burger joint. It's been on Amelie's To-Do list for three years. I take a booth and get my phone out. There's free wi-fi so I decide to FaceTime her. She'll either be so thrilled to see what it's like that she forgets she hates me, or she'll be even more furious because I'm there without her. Either way, I want to see her face, remind myself of why I need to go home. She answers quickly.

'Hi, Mum,' she says lightly, checking herself out on the screen.

'Hello!' I say, waving manically like she's either deaf or on a distant shore. 'Guess where I am!'

'New York,' she says, refusing to play ball.

'Yes, New York but *where* in New York?'

'I don't know, Mum, why don't you just tell me.' OK, so she's in one of those moods. I swear if I had a basket of kittens right now she'd drown them.

'The Burger Joint! The Secret Burger Joint! It's really cool! Look!' I pan around the room and show her the queue of diners waiting to order from the cardboard handwritten signs, the walls covered in the scrawled names of past visitors.

'That's cute. What time are you back tomorrow? Did you get my make-up? Lorcan says he wants white chocolate Reese's Pieces and Paddy wants Tootsie Rolls.'

And there it is. Slam-dunked back into the role of unwilling servant, dispatcher of sugary snacks and teenage fickle need.

'I'll be home late evening. And yes, I've got a lot of the stuff.'

She goes back to inspecting herself on camera and the connection freezes on her face pouting experimentally.

'Hello? Hello?' I say. 'You've frozen. Are you still there? Hello?'

The call drops. So does my mood. It's been so good not to feel like anyone's maid these past two weeks, and although I am looking forward to seeing them all I have the sinking feeling that nothing will have changed. My grand gesture of walking out on them is being perceived as just that – a gesture, a tantrum, a temporary blip. Normal service will be resumed shortly. The self-serving teenage zombie army marches on, trampling anyone that falls in its wake. I need a beer. My phone pings. A text from Martin.

'What time flight arrive can pick up?'

I don't want him to pick me up. I reply.

'No I'll get tube or uber don't worry. Home around 8'

'OK. X'

Gina arrives and squeezes into the booth next to me. The place is heaving now. Not such a well-kept secret, then. I order Gina The Works and myself a beer. I don't feel hungry any more.

'Not eating?' she says.

'No. I feel sick. I'm going home. Tomorrow. I'm going home.'

'It will be OK. It will. And if it's not – change it.'

And for her it's that simple.

Maybe it is.

Chapter Thirty-nine

The cab crawls along the North Circular. It's raining – not that fine, late-spring drizzle which soothes, and waters dry window boxes, but that 'Fuck You and Serves You Right for Not Wearing a Coat' downpour that London skies enjoy inflicting so much. It's relentless, and the windscreen wipers work maniacally to keep our view clear. Not that there's much to see. The houses look small and grey. The sky is too low. There's some sort of sporting event on near west London, so the capital is doing its best to welcome me back looking its very worst.

I can scarcely believe I was in New York this morning. It's late evening here. Back in Brooklyn Gina will be thinking about lunch. She was so good to me. I wonder if she'll ever know the impact she has had on me. How can she? I'm not the first woman to take refuge in her home for a while. I said that to her last night and she was annoyed. 'Just because I don't hang on to them all like they're the last lifeboat on the freakin' *Titanic* doesn't mean I don't love them all *at the time!*' I laughed when she said that. It's so fantastically scurrilous to hear a woman talk like that.

And now I'm on my way home. It feels like I've been gone an age. Two weeks on the calendar but two decades back in time in my head, to a time before kids, before Martin, before I disappeared. Gina said I must follow my heart. If only I knew where it wanted to go.

Right now we're going nowhere fast, but far from being anxious to get home I find myself willing the traffic to go slower. I have no idea what will happen when I get back. If I walk in and they all dive for the presents then go upstairs to their rooms, leaving me and Martin to stare awkwardly at each other, I think I'll scream. I've been away and I feel different. I don't want to feel the same, the same as I was before. I don't want to feel the blanket of domesticity being lowered over my head, a hand pressing down on me like I'm a criminal in a police drama. I don't want to be arrested by *normal.* There's been too much normal. Can we shake things up? Is it worth a try? I feel tired. Work. It's all work and no play. Do we just need date nights? Two-for-one curry evenings at the local Wetherspoons and nothing to say. I close my eyes and try to think of the bars, Central Park, Mum's ashes flying off into the sky, but my mind keeps interrupting with flashes of The Sleepwalker, his arms reaching out to ensnare me. I fall asleep, and only wake when the taxi turns suddenly. I look up. My street. Our street. We're here. We double park and the cab driver goes to the boot to get my suitcase. In the thirty seconds it takes him to do this a crocodile of cars appears behind us and they all start hooting impatiently for us to get out of their way. Welcome home. I pay the cabbie and mouth apologies to the first driver waiting. She winds her window down.

It's Debbie Downer. Of course it is.

'Oh hi, Debbie – I couldn't see who it was ha ha ha!'

Debbie smiles thinly.

'Welcome home. I have to say, they've all done very well. Martin's been a star. The kids are actually doing really well too. Amelie is smiling and Meredith says the boys are more mature.'

Fuck Debbie Downer. Fuck Meredith.

'Listen, Debbie, I'm really sorry if I offended you, it was just a bit of fun, the blogging—'

The cars behind Debbie toot in irritation.

'Can't stop now. Let's have coffee – tomorrow after school drop-off?' she smiles, clearly enjoying her view from the moral high ground.

'Great!' I say, forcing a smile back.

'You can tell me all about your . . . little holiday.'

Instantly an image of my hands in Gina's hair while we snogged passionately flashes across my mind. I push it away.

She pulls off and the cars scurry up the street. I turn and face the gate to my house. Inside, the family are knocking about, idly watching the clock, lazily anticipating my return. I wonder if Martin is nervous? I could vomit. The front garden is neat – Martin has had the mower out for the first time this year, and even the edges are trimmed. He must have had the strimmer out too. Martin loves a strimmer. I pull my suitcase quietly up the garden path and search for my key. Just as I go to put it in the door I freeze. There's shouting going on inside. Amelie and the boys. Apparently someone has been using her moisturiser and the boy who is guilty is accusing the other boy of being the thief, who in turn counters with doubts about the first boy's sexual preference and therefore keener interest in beauty products. Martin is shouting now too.

'For God's sake! Do you think your mother wants to come back to this nonsense?'

They carry on arguing. Feet thunder up the stairs, oblivious to my frozen figure's shadow through the stained glass. A slap.

'Owww! GET OFF ME!'

I close my eyes. Take a deep breath. This is home.

Part Three

Chapter Forty

The water is warm for this time of year, but still I shiver as I towel myself dry and hurry into my clothes. I've got half an hour to get back to the flat, shower and get ready. It's going to be a hectic weekend. It's the first meet-and-greet I've done. I'm nervous, and the swim hasn't done its usual job of calming me down, showing me perspective. The kids arrive later tonight. I've got their favourite cereal in and there are pizzas in the freezer. They love it here. It was always a dream of mine to live by the sea, and it's only an hour from London. Martin came with me to find it.

Martin. He's been amazing. He is so happy – a different man. At first it was difficult – the kids were in shock, Martin was devastated, I was numb. I couldn't carry on. I had nothing left. It didn't feel like a choice – it had to happen. Couldn't do it any more. There were tears, fights, disbelief, recrimination and terrible sadness. It was like a death. Grief swept through the house like a chill wind. I felt powerless, even though it was me calling the shots finally. I wanted to go. I had to go. People raised their eyebrows when it all came out, that I was leaving my husband and kids in the family home and moving away. It's dads that move out, isn't it? Dads are the bad guys.

Well, not in my family. It made much more sense for Martin to stay. He wanted to stay. He's better at all the practical stuff than me now anyway, and the kids have their own lives. They didn't want to move, and I don't blame them. I go back there every other weekend and in between times they come here on the train. They have stopped fighting quite so much. I think they have pulled together more, now that they can't take everything for granted.

I'm not saying it's been a good thing for them – I know I'd get shot down in flames for suggesting that – but it was unavoidable and within the chaos there have been some unexpected gains. Amelie is nicer. She talks to me now. She listens to me. She asks how I am, and sometimes she even texts me to say she loves me. She is growing up. Maybe she would have anyway. Daughters have a habit of doing that. Despite the upheaval and emotional turmoil she did really well in her GCSEs – better than expected. I think if I'd been hovering over her every minute, nagging her about her revision, she would have failed just to spite me. We're not as vital to our kids' success as we think.

The boys are still the boys – I think they will fight each other to the grave – but they are more thoughtful. Kinder. Not to each other, of course, but generally. So it's been an unexpectedly positive move for them too. I am astonished and chastened by the changes I have seen in them. I try not to let myself think they would have been better off without me all along. I know that's not true, but there is something here about letting them get on with it. How can anyone grow and mature with helicopters flying low overhead all the time? Why are we so focused on our kids? I remember when our family dog, Bennett, had puppies when I was young, and Mum sold them all. We begged her to keep one but she refused. When the day came for them all to go I was so upset because I thought Bennett would be sad. She didn't bat a whisker. She looked bloody pleased to be able to resume her normal business of barking at shadows and sleeping. We should all be more dog.

That was the title of my first Insta hit. It's grown from there, and I couldn't have done it if I'd stayed at home. I had to move out. With Mum's inheritance I was able to buy this flat by the sea. Mum would love it, although I'm sure she'd be mortified at what we've done, but it's at least partially her fault. 'Live!' she said. So I will. I am. Every day. It's hard sometimes, but I am alive. I feel alive. That's what she wanted for me, that's what she saw in me, but she couldn't tell me while she was alive. Couldn't betray the Mammy Brigade.

And anyway, Martin couldn't be happier. Turns out he's not the saggy Y-fronted buffoon sleepwalking his way through life I had him down as any more – my leaving has given him the kick up the backside he needed. Within six months of me leaving he was merrily shagging his way through every childfree weekend with Penny, a youngish widow from work. He wears nice jeans, irons his shirts and I can't remember the last time I saw any nasal hair. I was a bit taken aback – there I was thinking he was blanketed up and stabled for the rest of his life before the knacker's yard, when all the time he was under starter's orders. Penny is lovely – we had lunch last week. It was weird but I felt happy for them. Why not have another go on the merry-go-round before we shuffle off? I tried to enlist Penny in teasing Martin about his fastidiousness, his stinginess and his various annoying habits but rather sweetly she wasn't having any of it. She was quietly protective. She is seeing him with fresh eyes. It takes a couple of decades for that shit to irritate you, I guess.

It's pragmatism really, to move on and start the irritation continuum again – why let it all build over two more decades until you actively loathe each other when you could cancel, reset and start afresh with someone new and a clean annoyances slate? Makes sense. Like painting over old wallpaper or rubbing out the wrong answer in a test. I wish it was as simple for me, but Gina is right – my answer is different. I don't want to shack up with anyone new. Not interested.

For now.

Gina is coming tonight too. It will be her second visit. She came just after Christmas with a woman she was seeing for a while – a monosyllabic painter with green hair and a pierced neck. It didn't last long, but that's Gina: 'Not every story is a saga – some stories are short, some are long, but they all end eventually.' I love having her as a friend. I have other friends too now. There's Saffron, who is twenty-five and so kind, Georgia, a woman my age I met at the local theatre, and Belle, the woman who owns the tea rooms down the road on the seafront. She's divorced too, a bit older than me, and her kids are away at college. We go to concerts together, and sometimes we drink wine on the beach at night. She's funny. Clever. She gives me books to read. I'm in a book club. I know, you can take the woman out of suburbia . . . but this book club is cool. We only read books by women. There are young women in the group who teach us oldies about intersectionality, about being 'woke', about non-binary gender fluidity, about feminists who are 'sex positive'. It's interesting and liberating in a way that women's groups in my day were often not. We tell them about our lives as mums and wives and they shake their heads like we have been modern slaves, and they listen like we are telling them the most exotic tales of lives lived in another continent. Maybe we are.

In many ways I'm the same, I haven't succumbed to the worst clichés of middle-aged liberation – I don't have any tattoos, I haven't got a young lover and I don't do competitive yoga – but I feel so different. I feel like I am myself, not just a reflection of what everyone else needs me to be. Which is why my Instagram account has been the massive success it has.

It was Saffron who first got me on to it. I told her about my blog one night at the book group, and she read it. The next week she came in, hugged me, said it was brilliant but that I was wasted in that format. She told me that blogging is 'dead', and that 'no one reads any more', and that if I really want to create an audience for my 'content' I should become an 'influencer'. Apparently all you need is a pithy tag, and to know how to make hashtags your friend. HashtagLive! has become huge. She helped me, and now my 'brand' has over seventy thousand followers. She makes sure that TheMumThatGotAway stays true to my 'brand aesthetic' by monitoring my filters, and she keeps me 'open to different platforms'. I'm still not entirely sure what that is but it's got nothing to do with trains. She's been amazing.

I write the content and she chooses the images. I'm taking a photography evening class because she says I 'have an eye' and I should develop it for my work. I get money from advertisers and I earn a modest living from what I write. My content is mostly stuff about being a divorced mum living away from my kids, which you would have thought was quite niche, the web equivalent of a quiet little corner in a tatty pub where a few women cry softly into their large gins, but it's a niche which has quickly become quite crowded and raucous. It turns out there are thousands of us, and thousands more who want to join us, or at least bask in some vicarious joy. There is a splinter group who call themselves The Coven after being trolled for being 'witches' – apparently only evil and cruel women could leave their children with the other parent in the family home and seek a life for themselves again.

Tonight is my first foray into 'taking it offline' – meeting some of my followers. Saffron says there has been a huge response to the event but we won't know how many until we get there. It's a casual meet-up at a local seafront bar – trendy, breezy, on the beach. We named it 'Live!', of course. Thanks, Mum.

'You've got to show yourself living your best life!' says Saffron. 'Show them what they're missing!'

'I'm not saying everyone should run away, Saff!' I say. 'I don't want to be the poster girl for divorce and child abandonment. It's not for everyone!'

'I know that, but you're selling an idea – a radical idea, that motherhood is not the end of life! So we need to market that. I want wine, cool music, important conversation, networking, laughter, seriousness, beautiful things everywhere . . .'

So that's what we are doing. Only now that it's less than an hour away I am shit scared no one will turn up and it will just be me, Belle, Saffron and Gina, with the kids glaring at me like I've wasted their precious weekend.

I rush home on my vintage bike. On the doorstep of my building sits a huge bouquet of stunning antique pink roses. Surely not for me? I peer at the card poking up.

Ciara

On the reverse it says

Go get 'em, Sis! Love Aidan & Kelly xxx

Sweet. My brother may be a selfish, rich, middle-aged cliché but he has great taste in flowers. I leave the bike in the hall and carry my bouquet up the stairs. I let myself in and not for the first time I allow myself a smug little smile at my neat, bright flat, where everything stays where I left it and no one else's pants are on the floor. Sadie comes rushing to greet me, wagging her stumpy tail furiously. Even she is nicer now we are here. I had to bring her because Martin said he wouldn't keep both the cat and the dog – so of course I chose the dog, because cats are . . . you know . . . *cats.* They are essentially haughty bastards – and I'm done with being ignored. I shower and put on my outfit – a pastel-pink jumpsuit and white Converse, for heaven's sake, but I LOVE it. I'm just putting on my make-up when the buzzer goes. It's the kids. And Gina. They have arrived at the same time. This is interesting. I let them in and wait at the door as they clatter up the stairs chatting loudly. I can hear Gina holding court already – 'Yeah, I just got here! You're Amelie, right? I love your jacket – cute!'

The boys arrive first – so tall, so gangly. They smile shyly, delighted to see me. Amelie next, swinging her enormous 'weekend' bag in front of her, then Gina.

'I see you've met already!' I say, ushering them in.

'Mum – what are you wearing?!' says Amelie. Here we go.

Gina laughs. I roll my eyes.

'No, no, I mean – it's GREAT! Is it Urban Outfitters? I want that! Can I borrow it?' says Amelie.

'No,' I say. 'You can't. It's MINE!'

But we smile because we both know she will be wearing it by the end of the weekend.

I'm too nervous to eat but the kids tuck into pizza and I book a cab.

'Come on! We need to go, kids!' I say, checking my phone for the umpteenth time today.

'You OK?' asks Gina, appearing from the kitchen.

'Yes. No. Actually I'm shitting bricks. What if no one comes? What if they DO come? What if they hate me? What am I going to say to them?'

'Just be yourself,' says Gina. 'That's what this has all been about.'

We're squashed into a cab, crawling along the seafront. There are cars everywhere. I'm sweaty. Hot. I feel sick with nerves. I'm about to be humiliated in front of my kids, the kids I left behind for this new 'influencer' life, the kids who have been the unwilling subjects of my online musings, the kids who have been so good about it since, and who have even said they are a tiny bit proud of me. How will they feel when no one turns up and their mum is a failure, and it will have all been a flash-in-the-pan bit of nonsense?

Then I see them. Hordes. Crowds. Hundreds. Women. Women in twos and threes, women on their own, women with small babies, women in wheelchairs, women with grey hair, pink hair, blue hair, women smiling and laughing, talking to each other. Waiting. Waiting for me. Waiting for the bar to open. There is a buzz. The local paper is there with a photographer.

'Mum!' says Lorcan. 'It's like Fortnite! You've got a clan!'

Amelie is busy taking selfies with the crowd in the background. She's not pouting. She's smiling.

'Look!' says Paddy, pointing to a woman in an anorak at the front of the queue. She looks a bit like Debbie Downer but she's wearing a bright yellow dress and her hair is vibrant red. She turns. It *is* Debbie Downer. And I'm delighted to see her.

'Debbie!' I shout, and she turns, thrilled to have been singled out. I run to her and give her a hug.

'You've coloured your hair!' I say, not sure how to appraise the slightly Ronald McDonald ensemble she's put together.

'You inspired me!' she gushes. Her eyes glow. I'm moved to tears that even timid worrywart Debbie has been ignited by my Mumfluence. Someone asks for a selfie and word quickly gets around that I've arrived. There is a surge forwards. I lose Debbie as the security guard pushes me, Gina and the kids through the door and closes it behind us.

We turn back and stare at the eager faces waiting to get in.

'Look what you did!' says Saffron, appearing from behind the desk she has set up.

'And look who's here!' says Belle as she hugs me hello. I turn and see Jude – my best friend, my oldest friend – emerge from behind a curtain.

'Ta-dah!' she cries, throwing her arms around me. I burst into tears. They're all here – all the people that matter.

'Selfie! We've got to get a selfie up now, Mum!' says Amelie. She gathers us all together and we pose in front of the glass door, the crowd shouting and waving behind us.

We squeeze together, holding on to each other, laughing with relief, and the screen snatches at this moment – Amelie laughing, Paddy and Lorcan smiling, flanking Gina who has her arms around them, Belle and Saffron punching the air. Jude grinning so hard she could burst.

And me in the middle.

Me.